# connections: ragged & precious

by
# William Brakes

Versions of three of the stories in this collection, *Moving On*, *The Peridor* and *The Murmuring and Tumbling of Waves*, have been previously published in the collection 'An Eclectic Mix, Volume Six', edited by Lindsay Fairgrieve, published by ArcadiaAudio.

## Author's note

The game of Go features in several of these stories. It is (in this author's opinion) the best game in the world; it is almost certainly the oldest. It is not widely played, or even widely known, in the West, but it is played by millions in China, Japan and Korea. It is a strategy game for two players, chess being a natural comparison. However, until 2016 no computer had come close to defeating the best Go players in the world, whereas chess-playing computers have been dominant for some twenty years. This alone makes Go a game whose interest extends beyond the world of games-players. In the short piece 'Where do we go from here?' (the final story in this collection), the ramifications for the development of Artificial Intelligence following the recent computer success are scrutinised to a speculative but plausible extreme.

Some specialist terms from the game of Go are occasionally used in these stories where appropriate, but it is not necessary to understand the game in any detail (and anyway most of these tales do not involve go-playing at all). However, if the reader would like to know more about Go, the website of the British Go Association, http://www.britgo.org/, provides information about (among other things) the rules of the game, UK Go clubs and where Go can be played online. The present author will also try to answer any query you have: bill140347@btinternet.com.

The concept of 'connectedness' is a crucial one in Go and so provides a link to the title of this set of stories. Also important are the 'eyes' within a group of stones, separate spaces: a group attains the status of life through such spaces …

# Spaces

See the space between
the sky and the road,
between
after and before,
this way and this way.
Here is where we live.

See the space between
desire and the law,
imagination and reality,
the lip and the cup.
Here creation occurs.

See the space between
receiving and giving,
ignorance and bliss,
temptation and the fall.
Here bewilderment begins.

There is a space between
one empty trapeze and the next,
as they sway out of sync.
Here is where the gasps emerge.

There are spaces between words,
Within which meaning flourishes.

There is a space between
my meaning and yours.
On      that      we      can      agree.

There is a space between
those who see the spaces
and those who do not even look.

See the space
beside us.
Here is where we may yet grow.

# Contents

# My Mother's Maiden Name (and Other Passwords)

I am not a bad person. In fact, I'd say I was quite a good person. Not saintly, not Mother-Theresa-good. Not putting the world to rights by my selfless caring for others. No, not that good. Only, you know, well-behaved. Proper and decent. Law-abiding. 'Do as you would be done by': my mother used to say that. I try to be honest, caring, kind. Not to those who don't deserve it, of course; I'm not religious and all that 'love thy enemies' nonsense is too extreme. What I'm saying is that I'm basically a good person. Always have been.

So what am I doing in prison?

There is another mystery here: I do not have a name, or rather I do not remember my name. I do not know who I am, only that I am good. How can I be so certain of my goodness? Well, you know, don't you? You just know. Anyway, I believe it to be so, and believing is all I have. I do not believe I am a criminal.

**eyes watch - mouths whisper - brows wrinkle**

**monitors flicker - cursors beep - data accumulates**

**calculations are made**

The basic building block of living organisms is the cell. Every life-form consists of an accumulation of cells. Each cell contains the chemicals to constitute life: genetic material, molecules, proteins. I remember all that from biology lessons, a life-time ago. And there's a nucleus, there's always a nucleus. The nucleus is at the centre of the cell, and that's where I am. I feel like I'm a nucleus. This is my cell, the space wherein I live. It's just a room, but you can't call it a room because the word 'room' isn't right. The word 'room' is too warm, too soft, too human. This room-that-is-a-cell is not warm, not soft, not human. It is clinical and unnatural, callous and critical. Judgmental. It comprises soft curves, where there should be angles. It is small. It contains cold, functional components: a chair, a table, a bed. These words too are incorrect. They speak of comfort, familiarity and security. The furniture of this cell is not like the furniture of a home, of a room. It is moulded; it is secure and static; it is utilitarian. A prison cell is an alien world. Where is the protein? Where is the material content, the life-giving elements? This cell tolerates the nucleus but never embraces it. This cell may be preparing to eject me. I would willingly be ejected. Is that not so? I believe that to be correct. I do not feel at home here.

It is usually light in here, stark and bright, although at other times it is dark, as if the cell were slowly breathing, inhaling light and exhaling light, living a little and dying a little. Organic. When it is dark it is totally black, an empty blackness, and I presume I sleep at those times but I do not dream. During the dark times, food and water arrives. I do not know what mechanism delivers each meal and removes the remains of the previous one, but it happens when it is dark. That is another mystery.

**eyes watch - graphs are traced**

**lights flash - keyboards are fingered**

**protocols are formulated and considered**

Why am I here? What crime have I committed? I presume I am being punished. But if this is all there is to my punishment then it is not too severe. Removal of identity, restriction of choice, inhibition of activities: apparently these are considered to be punishment enough. So not a very serious crime. But am I capable even of that? I do not believe it to be so.

Occasionally my prison vibrates. The tremors are slight and temporary, so when they first occurred I thought I was mistaken. But now they have happened often enough for me to know they are genuine oscillations. Perhaps there is a road nearby where heavy traffic rumbles past. Or could this prison be perched on a cliff that is buffeted by tumultuous storms, hurricane winds and torrential rains? But then again, perhaps I am riding on a train that rattles along on occasionally uneven rails. I can imagine anything, believe anything. There are no windows in my prison. Neither are there doors.

I used to know nothing. But gradually I am gaining information. You might call it learning. I now know about Mother Theresa, about rooms with furniture, about roads and trains, a little about religion and biology. Crime and punishment. I have always known about my mother. At least, I knew I had one. I do not remember what she used to call me.

It is not cold in here, but neither is it hot. I am wearing a pale blue overall with long legs and long sleeves and a shirt-type collar. It feels tailored, soft like cotton, but probably it is not cotton; more likely I am clothed in some synthetic material. I have no shoes and there are no pockets in my overalls. Which reminds me: possessions, I used to have possessions I regarded as precious. Where is my wallet? My keys? My phone? I believe I once had a watch on my wrist, a ring on my finger. Is that so? More information, more knowledge. These feel like memories but perhaps they are new thoughts, newly received. How can I tell?

**eyes watch - ears listen - minds ponder**

**diagnoses are discussed and determined**

**judgments are agreed**

So here is the greatest mystery of all: where does the information come from? And is someone deciding what I should know? Who is that? I used to know nothing. But now I know a little. I still do not know my name. I still do not know why I am in prison. I know I do not need possessions. I have air to breathe: that is enough. Sometimes I sit on the chair and sometimes I lie on the bed: these are perfectly practical items of furniture. I can stand up if I wish and even walk a little, although there is not much space for strolling. I have food and water. I have a bathroom for ablutions. The bathroom is my name for the corner over there, where the facilities are located. Of course, 'bathroom' is not correct, no more than 'room' or 'bed', because it suggests chrome fittings, pastel tiles, a patterned shower curtain. This 'bathroom' consists of a sink in which tepid water arrives unbidden then seeps away too soon and a toilet that flushes unpredictably, all with a grey metal appearance like stainless steel and yet feeling warmer than that; it incorporates no sharp edges. I must have learned about bathrooms. I do not know how or when. Or why.

I am alive. That is the positive perspective I can place on my position and my mother told me I should always look for the positive in every situation. I remember my mother. Or is she, and the certainty that I have always known her, part of the information I have been given? Anyway, I do not remember, do not know, what she used to call me, what my name is. Or was. I am not young and I am not old. I have all I need but nothing extra, nothing that is superfluous or redundant. There is balance here. It is not displeasing and I will not allow myself to feel displeasure. I have no companion but I have no enemy. I have no fulfilment yet I have no distraction. I have no love but I have no hate. Some might call it Hell. Some might call it Heaven. I don't call it anything. It is a sort of life and it is also a sort of death. It is mainly a matter of attitude. It depends upon your point of view. I have that option, to decide the shape of my opinion; there is no-one to contradict me. I have my imagination and my logic. My body is imprisoned but my mind is not.

**eyes watch**

**inputs and outputs are measured and plotted**

# conclusions are drawn

A life without context is a problem without a solution. I cannot recall the beginning so I cannot envisage the ending. Because there are mysteries, the certainties become more certain, of increasingly crucial importance. I have oxygen and sustenance and health. I am alive. I do not need company or discourse. I have a mind and I have thoughts. It feels like I have a memory full of facts, but I am beginning to believe this to be new information, not old memories. (Where does this belief come from?) I know songs by the Beatles, by Abba, by Leonard Cohen. I know the names of Booker Prize winners, such as D.B.C. Pierre, Penelope Lively, Margaret Atwood. I know the chemical elements in the periodic table: hydrogen, helium, lithium, beryllium, boron. I know the dates of battles, the formula for solving quadratic equations, some Petrarchan sonnets, how to play Go, the names of capital cities, Hooke's law, the plots of television dramas, facts about planets, moons and stars, diseases and cures, the names of politicians and their parties, Olympic medallists, Oscar-winning films, the first twenty-five digits of л, football managers, card games, telephone numbers. I know my mother's maiden name and other passwords. I do not know my name or who I am. I am here. In this cell. That is all I know about my identity. Why do I need to know anything at all?

I do not need aesthetic niceties or beauty; I do not need art or literature, challenge or entertainment. Is this my opinion or have I been taught it? How can I tell? Should I be happy? Should I be sad? Should I know the difference?

**the orbit of the projectile is tracked**

**the trajectory is predicted**

**the velocity is automatically adjusted**

I need a story. I need to tell myself a story. I need to create a narrative, a route, a pathway; it is called a road-map. I must have the prospect of progression. I should devise a plan. Not a plan of escape. It would be foolish to consider that escape might be possible. This prison is secure. I have to work within the parameters of my situation. I have to be realistic, as my mother always used to say. I must not waste effort on dreams and fantasies. My plan should be practical and attainable.

**all is well**

**he is on track and will soon be there**

**he is alive**

I am alive and I have acquired a plan. I have been given a road-map. Already events are unfolding. My road-map is acquiring legitimacy. My route is upwards and outwards and then away. The ceiling-that-is-not-a-ceiling has a seam and it divides down the middle, the two blue oval sections slide apart. The floor-that-is-not-a-floor rises like an elevator, carrying me out between the two halves of the ceiling. The cell is ejecting me. Now I am outside. The sky is a strange shade of aquamarine. The sun appears to cast a yellowish light across the land. The grass is green. There is no redness. There is insufficient blueness. This is an alien world. I slide down, like a child in a playground, and walk towards what I believe to be trees. They are tall. They have brown stems and green leaves. So much strangeness. I am going to live here, but I have little notion of what that means. I will live amongst the aliens. I believe it to be so: I have been told that is how it will be. I have been assigned tasks. To introduce myself I now have a name. I am called Gabriel. My mother gave me that name. I believe it means 'good'. That is appropriate.

# Moving On

Dave and Lindsey both kissed me twice, once on each cheek. Jason, Lindsey's brother, shook my hand and waved as he turned towards his car.

'Take care of yourself,' called Jason over his shoulder.

'You've got our number,' said Lindsey opening the passenger door of the second car. 'Call any time.'

'Don't stand any nonsense from the locals,' said Dave, climbing into the driver's seat. 'And don't forget to let us know how you're getting on.'

The two cars drove off, with farewell beeps of their horns and I waved until they rounded the bend, heading for the hills. I sighed and gazed up at the wide blue sky, savouring the late autumn sunshine. I allowed myself a swift self-hug of sheer pleasure. I'd made it. I headed inside, to my future.

I don't believe in ghosts. 'Just as well or you'd go mad in this place.' That's what one of my friends said, those friends who helped me move down here and had just driven off. I'm lucky to have such good friends. Not so lucky with husbands, but all that's behind me now. I'm not sure which one of them said it, about me going mad, but I know what they meant. It's an isolated cottage, on the edge of the village but not really part of it, surrounded on three sides by a heavily wooded area – oaks and beeches and sycamores – and beyond that open fields. The building itself is old and lop-sided, unconventional, quirky, and you could say it has an air of mystery about it, spookiness, if you were that way inclined. Which I'm not. It's the peace and isolation that drew me to this particular location. A chance for a fresh start in a totally new environment, away from painful memories. I pictured myself enjoying hours of solitary leisure here, relaxing in the garden, or heading off to explore paths through the wood, my fragile legs permitting. Truth to tell, the interior is rather sombre and gloomy, a place of dark corners and eccentric spaces where an over-active imagination could weave exotic scenarios. But I've got more sense, I'm glad to say.

Having said that, even the most un-superstitious of us can sometimes succumb to the effect of strange moods and unfamiliar atmospheres and that's what I put it down to, what happened to me on the first night in my new home. In the evening, after the cars had gone, I began to unpack. I hadn't brought much with me and anyway there was no rush. The furniture came with the house because the previous owner died and her family had no further use for house or contents. Presumably her next of kin and other beneficiaries had scoured the place and ferreted away anything valuable, but everything else was included in the sale, even things like crockery and cutlery. There had been no point in me bringing my clutter down here, replacing one load of worn out furnishings with another, when what was here was perfectly adequate and suited its setting. So the only things I'd brought with me were clothes, books and a few knick-knacks that carried echoes of better memories. The first thing I did when I entered the cottage was to put *Gabriel*, my lucky mascot, on the mantelpiece. He's only an old cloth teddy-bear but he survived the accident, so deserves a place of honour. I can hear my daughter's scornful snorting, but this is my house, my choices. So there. My books are my most precious possessions. Unfortunately I had to leave quite a few behind and even so once we'd fitted all those boxes into the cars it was quite a squeeze getting the people in. It had not been the most comfortable of journeys.

In the main living room of the cottage, tucked into recesses to either side of the fireplace, stood two tall, invitingly empty sets of book-shelves which I was looking forward to filling with my precious tomes, carefully arranged. I don't own anything valuable but it's a wide-ranging collection. Some classics – Dickens, Jane Austen, *Mill on the Floss*, that sort of thing – up to modern authors like Ian McEwan and Hilary Mantel. I made a start, emptying the first two boxes, but it had been a long day and there was no need to overdo it. My knees were telling me they hadn't enjoyed the journey. So I settled down to a Dionne Warwick CD, some Italian red wine I'd brought with me and some simple thoughts. Everything was going to be fine. I'd had a few misgivings and some of my 'friends' had advised me against leaving the city and heading out into the back of beyond (as they termed it) but now the deed was done. I was here and I was going to stay here and I was going to be happy here. Content. Away from those wagging tongues.

It was when I went to bed that a nervous mood began to filter into my mind, darkening the brightness I'd carried with me throughout the day. It surprised me. I'm not the nervous type. Perhaps the wine was to blame or the journey or simply the excitement of the removal. I expected to flake out cold for a good eight hours – sleep comes easy for me, now I've recovered from the crash – but that was not the case. I lay in my bed, lights out and eyes closed and nothing happened. I opened my eyes and closed them again and still nothing happened: I remained resolutely awake.

After what seemed an age but was probably no more than half an hour, I sat up in bed. I didn't switch on the light, vaguely hoping I was sleepier than I realised and it would be better not to rouse myself still further. I felt cold. I was wearing one of my usual nightgowns, substantial enough, but perhaps it had been a mistake to turn off the heating. I always turned off the boiler at night in my London house and there I'd never felt cold. Presumably this cottage lacks modern insulation and so the heat dissipates more quickly. I wrapped my arms around myself and tried to analyse why I was not sleeping.

It was very dark. 'Pitch black' didn't seem a strong enough description: it was an empty sort of blackness. This was to be expected as I have no near neighbours and the only street lights are down in the village, and then there are only two or three as I recalled. I pictured them as rather dim. So where would light come from? Clouds had bubbled up as night fell, so the moon and stars would now be invisible. I had no experience of such total darkness. It was deep and hollow, in a sense bottomless, capable of swallowing anything whether living or dead. I moved my head from side to side to try to detect the substantial furnishings of the room, the corners and angles, the cupboards, the chest under the window. Nothing materialised. It was all hidden behind an impenetrable black curtain.

Also there was the silence, another feature alien to me. In the city I had become used to sleeping to an incessant rumble, of traffic, distant trains and occasional aircraft, neighbours' music and TV, people walking home along the street, shouting and laughing through to the early hours. Now, here, there was nothing. Silence as deep as the blackness. Not even a ticking clock, no rustling tree, no wind rattling the windows. I was tempted to say it was as quiet as the grave, but I'm not a fanciful woman. Still, deadly quiet it certainly was.

Within this total silence and blackness, my senses of vision and hearing had nothing to feed on, and, as if to compensate, my sense of smell seemed to gain in scope. I had noticed earlier a musty air around the place. No surprise there as it had been shut up for several months awaiting a vendor. Now, in the dark and the silence, that mustiness became more pronounced to my sensitive nose, containing within it a rottenness, a mouldering, the odour of decay. Putrid flesh I'd say, festering corpses I might add, but I steered my thoughts away from such macabre directions. Nevertheless, nasty and noxious were the descriptions that came to mind.

This analysis wasn't a sensible way of helping me get to sleep and I knew I should give in, get up and find some book to read. But I refused to be beaten by my new environment. I settled back down under the covers, made sure I was well tucked in to exclude drafts, closed my eyes and tried to think happy thoughts. But all I could think about was how the deep, deep, darkness enshrouded me, bore down upon me, cloaked me, accompanied by the strangely deafening silence and that stale and deathly smell.

I woke up with my mind full of fearfulness and dread, horror and alarm, my nightdress cold and damp with sweat. I was shaking. A shaft of sunlight arrowed through a crack in the curtains. It was morning. I must have eventually slept and my terrors were due to a nightmare. I was exhausted and drained and still in a state of torment, although the details of the dream were lost. It took a while for my thoughts to return to any sort of coherence. I recalled a long period of wakefulness after I had settled down for the second time, my mind circling round and feeding on nothing, but then I must have fallen asleep. It had been the most un-refreshing sleep imaginable, even worse than when I'd suffered the nightmares following the car crash.

A steaming shower, some strong coffee, a strolling exploration of the garden, and gradually I began to get myself back onto an even keel. Then I busied myself with plans for the day, encouraging my mind to forget about that dreadful night. It was nothing more than a restless episode accompanied by some bad dreams, to be expected when sleeping in a new bed. No need to dwell on it.

Breakfast consisted of two slices of toast, using the half-loaf I'd brought with me, and a small glass of apple juice. After that, determined to make the most of the autumnal sunshine, I decided to make my first excursion into the village. I don't yet have the confidence to show my face to the world. I wonder if I ever shall. I put on a pair of sunglasses, wrapped a scarf around my face to cover the worst of the blemishes and pulled the hood of my jacket up over the top. It was a shame to keep the sun from my face, but so it had to be: I was not willing for my damage to be subject to public scrutiny. Grateful for my stick, I shuffled down the hill.

I'd spotted the shop when we drove through the previous day, and as I suspected it was an all-purpose convenience store, not offering much choice but catering for 'every need'. I collected some basic provisions and a newspaper and I was introduced to some village ways by the young shop assistant. She told me about the mini-library she ran, the times of the church services and pointed out the directions to local landmarks, such as they are. Two elderly men were browsing through the magazines and one of them struck up a conversation with me. He already knew I'd moved in to the cottage and asked how long we would be staying. He seemed to think there were two of us. I told him he was mistaken. Not sure if he understood as my speech can sometimes be indistinct. He told me that Mrs Galloway, the previous owner, had been a nice old lady but kept to herself. I got the impression that not joining in with community life had counted against her. I hoped they did not expect me to contribute much. His friend joined in the conversation to tell me about the forthcoming flower show, the monthly dances organised in conjunction with the neighbouring village and various church activities; I nodded and smiled in what I hoped were all the right places without committing myself to anything. No doubt my weird appearance would soon be the talk of the village.

There is no escaping the fact that old buildings can carry within them a certain aura, a psychic ambience if you will, even viewed through sceptical eyes such as mine. As I stepped back into the cottage, breathing a little heavily from the climb, I had a pronounced sensation of not being alone. It felt as though someone has been there, indeed that they were still there. Not burglars, no sense of threat, but a presence, somewhat ethereal, perhaps spiritual, and yet also human. I expect it was that man in the village talking about me as though I were a couple. Or the general brain-fuzziness to which I'm sometimes prone. I was not concerned; I didn't take it seriously. I limped through the cottage, checking each room to be sure there had been no disturbance but, as expected, I found nothing untoward. Old buildings encourage thoughts of the supernatural but I easily discarded such influences, however much my unconscious might have continued to dwell upon them.

I lunched on the fresh rolls and cheese I had bought from the shop and then resumed unpacking, but I felt strangely restless. It was an odd sensation that I can only describe as displacement, a feeling of not being quite with it. Nothing to do with all that 'atmosphere' nonsense I'd felt when I came in. It was simply that the enthusiasm of yesterday had waned. I tried to rekindle it by attacking the books. After less than an hour, with several changes of direction as I re-thought how the shelves should best be arranged and a few pauses as I dipped into some of my favourite volumes, I abandoned the exercise, made myself a cup of tea and settled down to some serious reading. *Wuthering Heights* is one of my favourite Victorian novels, although I hadn't read it for a long time. I laughed anew at Lockwood mistaking a pile of dead rabbits for live cats.

After a simple dinner, a slice of steak pie with potatoes and broccoli (the only vegetable the shop could provide, something to do with it being a Tuesday, apparently), I contemplated switching on the television. I am not an enthusiast, but occasionally it can be a pleasant enough way to pass the time. But no, I thought of

Lockwood's first awkward encounter with Heathcliff and

returned to the novel. The evening progressed, darkness

seeped through and I put on some lamps; I lit the gas fire

in the lounge to supplement the rather paltry central

heating and read my way carefully through the early

chapters of Emily Bronte's dark novel and all the while the

approaching night grew in significance. This was not like

me, this sense of foreboding. I am not given to fanciful

notions. I tried to rationalise it. I was not frightened by the

thought of the silence or the darkness: that would be

absurd. But I was increasingly nervous at the prospect of a

recurrence of the terrors from the previous night. That they

lacked focus seemed to make their potential re-appearance

all the more unsettling. What was it I was frightened of?

Nothing, of course, because there was nothing to fear. I

kept talking my way out of it, reading some more of the

novel and taking generous sips of the rather pleasant

*Chianti*. I rubbed my knees: they were paying me back for

that walk into the village. I had a stab at the crossword in the paper but made little progress. I was running out of things to distract me and put off the time when I'd have to retire again for the night. It was ridiculous. How old was I? Old enough to know better.

The second night was almost a repeat of the first. Only worse. Again I tried to settle down, having meticulously followed my standard routine for unwinding and preparing for sleep and I felt suitably relaxed, but again sleep failed to come. I had placed a bed-jacket by the side of the bed, so when I sat up at about half past midnight I could wrap it around my shoulders and with it ward off the worst of the coldness: I hadn't been able to bring myself to leave the heating on. The jacket was ineffective against the cold; it was even less effective against the darkness, the silence and the sour fetid odour. This time I did put on the light and read a few more pages of the novel, trying to absorb myself in the details of Nellie Dean's narrative. But any relief could only be temporary. I glanced around into the shadows and corners of the bedroom. Solid and safe. They would remain precisely the same once the light was off. That was what I told myself. But it wasn't the furnishings I feared, nor what they might hide. I didn't know what it was I feared. The unknown, I suppose, the unknowable.

When sleep eventually came, the deep darkness and the silence and the stench chased me down into a second torrid night, where nameless invisible abstractions tormented and tortured me. I'd rather they had been monsters or fiends, ogres or demons, the figure of Catherine clawing at the window, objects I could name and so tame. I'd even have preferred more endless reruns of the sequence of events leading to the accident, that agony I had endured for so many months. But whatever was the source of my anguish remained unseen, invisible and therefore so much more abominable. How can you flee from fear if that fear will not reveal itself? I felt as though I'd lived through life-changing – indeed life-threatening – trauma, but I could recall none of the details.

When I woke up I felt even more fatigued than on the previous morning. Thank goodness the night was over;

I had got through it, even though the anxiety lingered and refused to be shrugged off. I have always been a positive person, an optimist, a 'half-full' sort of woman. I was not prepared to succumb. I would not assume the role of victim. I would rise to the challenge these night terrors presented. It was not easy. Prolonged and bewildering dread persisted through the morning despite the fact that I was now fully awake. For nightmares to make you feel powerless is to be expected, but this waking anguish magnified my impotence: I should have been able to take control of the situation in the light of the day, but I could not. Instead, this situation - the disturbances, the agony and the torture - had control of me.

It took longer than the previous morning, but eventually I did surface, I did emerge from the churning waters: my heartbeat calmed, I began to breathe normally, my thoughts gained some measure of coherence. It was time to actively resist, to fight back. I would not dwell on the fear, I would work my way through it, around it if necessary. The one thing I could do something about was the smell, that odorous mustiness. I resolved to use the rest of the day to subject the cottage to a thorough cleansing.

My first step was to throw all the windows as wide open as they would go. A brisk north-easterly blew through the cottage and this fact alone raised my spirits: the demons would soon be blown away. Under the kitchen sink I found various cleaners and disinfectants, cloths and scrubbing brushes. It wasn't that the place was unclean. It had been given a meticulous soak and shine after the death of Mrs Galloway, the evidence for which was apparent, but I felt I was adding an additional layer of freshness and lightness, expelling the tired, rancid remains that had somehow lingered in the cracks and crevices. The kitchen surfaces soon had a sparkle that spoke of hope and promise and wholesomeness.

For a proper spring-clean I knew I should have taken down the sombre yet sumptuous curtains from the living room and attacked them in the garden, but I couldn't manage that, so as a compromise I applied a carpet-beater *in situ*. Then I hoovered up the resultant clouds of dust, generously sprayed polish onto all the surfaces I could find and buffed them up with vigour. I paid particular attention to the grandfather clock in the corner, removing a layer of accumulated grime, although I couldn't persuade it to come back to life. I was distracted for a while when I discovered the lid of the piano stool was hiding a lovely cache of old music, mostly light classical pieces together with some well-known show tunes: I imagined a future evening when I might rekindle my rather limited keyboard skills and tackle these musical entertainments. It would be another weapon to combat the disorder persisting still on the edges of my mind, threatening to envelop me even as I did my utmost to ignore it.

The staircase proved tricky, with its steep and narrow steps and a sharp corner half-way up. I had to re-plug the vacuum cleaner into a bedroom socket to complete the task. I didn't bother too much with the spare room, which was dark and sparsely furnished, a bare light bulb hanging in the middle of the ceiling, an unmade bed in the centre of the room and a ragged mat underneath it covering uneven floorboards. That room could wait for another day. I closed the door on it. But I did a scrupulous job on the main bedroom, working into all the nooks and recesses, the cupboards over the wardrobe, wiping clean the crucifix and dark paintings on the walls, spraying light polish on the Ottoman under the window and the panelling behind the lavish armchair. Finally I flushed through the bathroom, pouring cleanser down the various outlets, scouring the porcelain and polishing the old-fashioned taps. Once I'd finished, a light lavender scent lingered in the air throughout the cottage. I still thought something more positive was called for. I wondered if the village shop would run to some potpourri. Probably not. Perhaps I could bring some flowers in from the garden. I am not a fan of cut flowers, but something sweet-smelling might be what was needed to complete the job.

As I lay down to sleep on the third night in my new home, worn out from my labours, my knees burning from the unusual demands I had inflicted upon them, I wondered why I had bothered: that sour, musty, putrid smell was soon filling my nostrils once again. Perhaps it was the spare bedroom that was the source of the odour. Or perhaps the smell so pervaded the very structure of the building, was so embedded in its essence, that no amount of disinfectant or lavender spray would remove it. Then I wondered if the stench had its source in my imagination, that it was fictitious or in some way metaphysical; perhaps I had brought the smell with me, carried it in on my body, within my books. None of these is the sort of conclusion I am naturally drawn to: I rejected them as soon as they occurred to me. But it didn't matter. The origin of the smell, its cause or reason, carried no importance. Its role was as a precursor, a harbinger of another night of terror, a first sign that I was heading down that same pathway, a course with no side-turns, a journey into drowning darkness filled with nameless fears.

There were differences from the previous two nights that impinged on my senses but did not make the experience any less unpleasant. My perception of both the darkness and the silence was altered, neither being as absolute as on the previous two occasions. In the middle of the night, I sat upright in bed as before, shivering in spite of the bed-jacket, and stared into the unfathomable blackness only to find I could perceive variation within it, shades and texture within the darkness. I saw a chain of lights, faint and distant, moving slowly from left to right, then looping up into a full circle, before shrinking and fading, eventually dissolving. Isolated diamond pinpoints, like stars, glinted: now here, now there, to left, to right, to vertically above me. Alongside these sights, these visions, came a similar modulation to the silence, no longer that numbing nothingness. I discerned a faint rumbling, like the deep-throated growling of some animal, but coming from far, far away. That was joined by the silver tinkling of tiny bells, first steady and rhythmical, then fragmented and aperiodic, syncopated. Almost a tune, an echo of a memory. And after that came the whispering. It started faintly, virtually subsonic, and gradually grew, so when I became aware of it I already knew it had not just begun. I tilted my head to left and right, trying to focus on the source of the sound, but the whispers were mobile, shifting and indistinct. They sounded almost human and then altered into an ominously alien timbre, before becoming blurred and distorted, voices but not from any living throats. The mere act of trying to pinpoint the source, to bring it into focus, caused the whispers to slip to the side and to fade, like the lights, like the growling, like the bells. And still the invidious smell rolled across my inward breaths in waves. What was I seeing? What was I hearing? What was I smelling? What phantoms were hounding me down into the long, long night? Whoever, whatever, they were, they brought with them elements of mystery, of ambiguity, of complexity that disconnected my mind, set it flying. A night of tortuous sensations awaited me. I knew it would be so. I was not wrong.

I remembered those preliminaries, but I was thankful I did not remember the nightmare or nightmares that followed that night. I awoke in the morning to the now familiar sense of having survived some horrendous, harrowing experience. Barely survived, if that made any sense. I felt ravaged, torn, wrecked. Exhausted as though chased for a lifetime through hot deserts, mighty oceans, dense forests; thoughts tumbled and swirled without focus; and I felt so, so weary, deprived as I'd been of the replenishment of proper sleep for the third consecutive night.

As the day stirred I was soon aware that something had changed. The dazed aftermath of the night stayed with me, the sense of being insubstantial, semi-transparent and disconnected did not relent. Not at first and then not at all. I remained in a state of partial life, somewhere between sleep and wakefulness, throughout the day. I carried out inconsequential activities, the energy that had driven me through unpacking and cleaning on previous days having dissipated, no longer dwelling within me. I felt empty. I felt numb. I had no focus. By mid-afternoon, the spectre of another night was already beginning to invade my senses, but it did not bring the accompanying fear, or even trepidation that I had begun to anticipate. This time I looked forward to the end of the day. I had no idea why this should be the case, but rational thought no longer appeared appropriate. For whatever reason, I welcomed the night.

And the night welcomed me. In place of darkness there was light; in place of silence there was melody; and even the sour smell was tinged with sweetness. I fell asleep rapidly, slept long and awoke slowly the following morning. I was at peace and as the night faded I emerged at ease, comfortable, no longer involved in a mortal battle. Sense did not return, not even to the extent it had the previous day. This was not the same as any of the other mornings. I was no longer the same. I was still confused but not alarmed by the confusion. I could relax, relish and float through this misty sensation and there was no longer any reason to resist. For long minutes that eventually stretched into hours I inhabited a half-state, hazy and fragmented, free from the dreams but still deep within the luxuries of the dream-world.

I lay on my bed, outside the covers, staring at the beams that criss-crossed the ceiling. I did not move. I scarcely thought. I expected at any moment to return to my previous state, but it did not concern me that I did not. I was content. I was correctly situated. I was prepared. The images from the night, incoherent and chaotic, flickered around on the edges of my perception, haunting me, but I was not in distress. I was changing. Or I had already changed. Reverted was a word that came into my mind, unbidden. I felt light, as though I were floating some millimetres above the bed rather than lying upon it. I felt flimsy, insubstantial, shadowy. I was no longer grounded in the world. I was adrift, free. The upper reaches of my mind lay flat and tranquil. But deeper down, for the first time in months, thoughts of the accident tumbled around. The moments before. Flashes from a film. Part memory, part the invention of a tortured brain. The argument. The last argument. I did not think these thoughts as much as experience them. I did not want to but I had no choice. I was not in control.

\* \* \* \* \*

The man drives fast and the woman in the passenger seat looks nervous.

'Slow down, there's no need to drive like a madman.'

'We're late.'

'And whose fault is that?'

'Well, it's not mine, that's for sure.'

The woman sighs and looks out of the side window. Her face carries a resigned look. The man continues to manoeuvre the Volvo at speed down the country lanes, making no allowance for the gathering gloom. He switches the headlights to full beam.

'It doesn't matter if we're a bit late,' says the woman, 'it's only Dave and Lindsey. And they said eight – *ish*.' She emphasises the final syllable. 'I don't suppose the others will be there on time. Not all of them, anyway. Certainly not Jason and his friend, what's his name? Kevin. Keith. Something like that. They're always late.'

'I don't care about that pair of queers. They're hardly role models. If I'm due at a place at a certain time I like to arrive there at that time. It's polite.' He emphasises the key words with thumps on the steering wheel. 'It's how I was brought up. If more people paid regard to proper manners the world would be a better place.'

'Don't I know it,' says the woman, quietly. She's only speaking to herself but it's loud enough for the man to hear.

Headlights flash past on the other side of the road. The man slows a little. He puts on the windscreen wipers.

'Is it raining?' asks the woman.

'Well, no, of course it isn't. I just thought I'd put the wipers on to see if they're working.'

'They said it wouldn't rain till tomorrow.'

'Seems they got it wrong. Surpise, surprise. *They.* That's the BBC for you.'

The woman does not reply. She narrows her lips. She seems to be expecting what comes next.

'That idiot who does the forecast. Too young to know anything. Wonder who she slept with to get that job.'

The woman sighs.

'Don't get me started on the BBC. Crawling with corruption from top to bottom.'

'Oh no,' says the woman, speaking quietly again. 'Not again.'

'Full of long-haired commies. Can't move for political correctness. Newsreaders have to be black or female. Preferably both. Whatever was wrong with Kenneth Kendall and his crowd? Proper voices, they had. If you're spastic you've got it made. Like that woman with one arm on kid's TV and the guy in the wheelchair. Never mind if they're any good at the job. And given half a chance it's sex, sex, sex, rammed down your throat, morning, noon and night.'

'But that's life, isn't it?'

'What is?'

'Sex.'

'Well not for some of us, it isn't.'

'Not for you and me, that's for sure.'

'Don't start.' The man shakes his head vigorously.

Steel enters the woman's eyes. A sternness comes to her lips and the set of her jaw. A limit has been reached.

'You're all right, though, aren't you?'

No answer.

'You get yours elsewhere. Poor Jane isn't it? The latest? Married with two kids, but that doesn't bother you.'

'What are you on about? You know nothing. Always wittering on. Get off my back, will you?'

The car lurches forward under renewed acceleration. The wipers scrape the windscreen ineffectively. The man leans forward, eyes flaring. The woman leans back. She opens the glove compartment and takes out a small cloth teddy-bear, She holds it on her lap, grasping it with both hands like it's a comfort.

'I've had enough,' she whispers. 'Enough.'

The first impact is slight, little more than a click. An oncoming van has strayed towards the middle of the narrow road and clips the car's wing mirror on the driver's side as it passes.

'What was that?' The man looks right and jerks his head. His right hand pulls on the steering wheel. The car veers towards the oncoming traffic. The man grabs the wheel firmly with his other hand and wrenches it to the left. He has over-compensated. The car heads towards the nearside bushes. The man brakes hard. The car skids.

The car hit the hedge at speed. The front nearside wheel impacted on a low horizontal branch. The car reared up and cartwheeled. It ploughed through the bushes and plunged down the bank, turning over and over. It bounced and then rolled again. It stopped lodged against a tree trunk. There was a pause. Then the car burst into flames.

Some time later a team of paramedics brought the mangled and charred remains of two people into the trauma centre of the Princess Alice Hospital. There were procedures that had to be followed but none of the medical staff involved expected either person to survive. The injuries were severe, the signs of life meagre and the prospects, as relayed to the waiting children and their spouses, were poor. But in the event, only one person died; the other survived. The survivor endured a long and painful recovery, through multiple operations for repair and reconstruction. Eventually the survivor resumed some sort of normal life.

* * * * *

Night returns. It is welcome. It is welcoming. The darkness returns and so does the silence and the all-pervading stench. All return as though they had never gone. I no longer fear these phenomena. Now I feel an affinity for them. I feel part of them, they are a part of me. This is my place, my state, my night. This is my environment. I am soft and still and light and this is how it should be and I am ready.

A little after midnight I rise from my bed. I drift out of the bedroom, relishing the darkness, inhabiting the silence, wallowing in the bitter odour. I stand by the full-length mirror on the landing. I avoid mirrors these days, used to avoid mirrors, have avoided mirrors ever since the accident. But now I stare at the luminous image, and study it carefully. The slashing scar begins at the right temple, crosses the cheek and curls around the mouth to the cleft of the chin. This sinuous gash gapes as crimson red and fleshly raw as on the night it was created. The skull has no hair, no eyebrows, all burned away as are the layers of skin from forehead, nose and cheeks. One ear is missing; of the other only a gnarled fragment remains. And the eyes, oh the eyes. Large and unblinking, bulbously protruding, ivory white and reptilian; unrooted orbs, inhuman, unhuman. This is the face of the body that could not be saved.

I return to the bedroom and settle myself in the plush armchair at the foot of the bed and wait. I wait for the whispering. I do not have to wait long. First there is the creaking of the mattress, scraping signs of unsettled slumber. The scuffling of bedclothes. A pause filled with a silence alive with potential. Then the whispering begins. In a gradual crescendo it grows into mumbling and breathless groans. I recognise the familiar cursing as the voice grows louder, the sounds of panic, the signs of terror. It is time. I rise up and hold myself beside the bed and summon the lights from within me to shine forth in all their glory, the music chimes and the odour from my body fills the room. The man, the keeper of the body that could be saved, screams the most fearful scream, scrambles from the bed and stumbles through me and out onto the landing. There he is confronted by the full view of the mirror, his naked body alight, my radiant image behind him, above him, around him. His second scream is louder and longer than the first and is indicative of a greater horror. In his panic to escape he slips on the top stair and tumbles down and down, his head strikes the corner and down the second flight the body goes, down and down and lands in the hallway. It does not move. It will not move again.

# Special Occasion

'Get that down you,' says Vince. 'Put hairs on your chest.'

The hunched youth at the table takes the open bottle and slouches back in his seat, hood up.

'And take that hood off.'

Keith rolls his eyes and tosses off his hood. Two thin wires are dangling from his ears.

'Earphones.'

Keith says something under his breath and snatches the nubs from his ears.

Vince turns and speaks louder: 'Here's yours, Dad.'

The other hunched figure at the table, an old man with several days of grey stubble on his wrinkled face, peers through thick lenses and reaches out to clasp the tankard of dark beer.

Vince leans the tray against a leg of the table and sits down, a pint of pale liquid in his hand. He raises his glass: 'Cheers.'

His two companions grunt in unison and take sips from their drinks. Silence settles over them like a glacier.

'Wel, this is nice, isn't it?' says Vince. 'Just the three of us.' He takes another sip of beer and wipes his lips with the back of his hand. 'Lads together.'

We're in a corner of The Black Horse. There's Vince, there's his father George, there's his son Keith. The male line. This pub doesn't do food, so Sunday noon is not a busy time. A few regulars are leaning on the bar, a smattering of couples and groups are sitting round stained tables.

'Didn't you get no crisps?' asks Keith.

'*Any* crisps,' says his father, automatically. 'Don't want to spoil your lunch. Mum's cooking special.'

Keith rolls his eyes.

Old George fusses with his hand in his jacket pocket, takes out a crumpled packet of cigarettes.

'You can't smoke in here, Dad. It's the law.'

His father places a cigarette between his lips. 'I'm not going to light it, am I? I might be old but I'm not stupid.'

Vince takes a long gulp of his beer. 'Didn't Keith do well, Dad?'

'Eh?' He's holding the cigarette between his teeth.

Vince repeats his words, only louder.

'No need to shout, I'm not deaf. What's the blighter done now?'

'I told you. GCSEs. Passed them all. And got two A stars.'

The old man takes the cigarette out of his mouth and snorts. 'Oh aye. A – flaming - stars. What a load of cobblers. Exams these days. Nothing to 'em. So long as you can spell your own name.'

Keith sits up. 'That's so not fair. Tell him Dad. I had to work like shit to get them grades.'

'Language Keith.'

'Oh that's right. You have a go too.' He leans back, lowers his eyes and mutters: 'Fucking hell.' His left fist is round the bottle, on the edge of the table. His right hand is below the level of the table, thumbing his phone.

'What's that you said?'

'Nothing Dad.'

The bottle of Bud, the glass of Guinness and the pint of lager are each raised to their respective pairs of lips. Vince wipes his mouth with the back of his hand and looks around the bar. Young Keith stares back at his phone. Old George sucks on his cigarette and closes his eyes.

'Well, this is nice,' says Vince again, folding a beer mat. 'We should do this more often.'

George opens his eyes. Points at Keith with his cigarette. ' 'As 'e got a girlfriend yet?' The other two look at him.

'No,' says Vince, then looks at Keith.

Keith rolls his eyes.

'See them girls over there,' says the old man.

Vince looks. Four girls (short skirts, emphatic make-up) are giggling as they flick peanuts at each other and scroll through each other's phones.

'When I was a lad I'd 'ave been over there, giving 'em the old rabbit. An' betcha I'd 'ave left with one on each arm. Get in there, Keefy.' He gestures with a bent elbow.

Keith glances over his shoulder. 'They're year nines Grandad.'

'What?' says Vince, looking round. 'How'd they get served? They're drinking spirits. Don't the staff in here check ages?'

'Doh,' says Keith. 'Get real, Dad. There is such a thing as fake ID, you know.'

Vince's mouth hangs loose. 'What do you know about false identity?'

Keith ignores him.

Vince tears the beer mat in half and folds the halves.

'Is 'e queer, then?' asks George.

'Shush,' says Vince, placing his finger to his lips and looking over his shoulder. 'You mustn't use words like that. Not these days. They'll have you.'

'Well actually,' says Keith. 'You can. It's called respect. All about reclaiming the … you know. Whatsit.' He's still thumbing his phone under the table. 'It's the same with black kids. It's perfectly okay to call them …'

'No,' shouts Vince, to drown out his son's next word. He smiles around at the various faces that have turned in their direction. He whispers to Keith. 'Behave yourself. Or else.'

'Anyway, no Grandad. Since you ask, I am not of the homosexual persuasion.'

The drinks are getting low. Vince looks at his watch. 'Time for another.'

His father is gazing at his empty glass.

His son's eyes are in his lap.

'Same again, then.'

He comes back with three more drinks and two bags of crisps.

'Not cheese and onion,' says Keith, ripping open one of the bags and taking a handful. 'I hate cheese and onion.' He stuffs the crisps into his mouth and makes a grimace.

The three men take gulps from their fresh drinks.

Vince tears the bits of beer mat into crumbs. 'You coming to ours at Christmas, Dad?'

'Do I 'ave any choice?'

'Course you do. But you'll enjoy it, you always do. Turkey and all the trimmings. A nice game of Monopoly in the afternoon. *Eastenders* special, then a film.'

'Not *The Great Escape* again.'

'We tried a James Bond the other year.'

'Load a crap that was.'

'You choose then.'

George paused, considering. 'I don't like that there cranberry sauce.'

'We know that. We always scrape it off your plate.'

'I'm just saying. And that Deidre better not be there.'

'Don't start, Dad. We have to invite her. She's Linda's Mum. She'd be on her own if we didn't. She's not that bad.'

'She's a pain in the arse. The way she goes on. 'Er and 'er dog and 'er cakes and God knows what else. Yak, yak, yak. And she wouldn't sell me the fourth station. Stupid cow.'

'Harsh,' says Keith, looking up. 'But fair.'

'Watch yourself,' says Vince.

'Oh, you don't mind him saying all sorts, then I just say one thing ...'

'Too right. He's older than you. Entitled.'

'That's so not fair.'

Eventually the glasses and bottle are empty.

Vince scrapes together the remains of the beer mat. Looks for an ash tray.

Old George seems to be asleep.

Keith is texting: 'OMG. I'm soooo bored [sad face]. Get me outta here [screaming face]. Pleeease [winking face]' He adjusts the setting on his phone and it rings: a tinny version of the *Birdie Song*. 'Gotta go,' he says, leaping out of his seat.

'Hey, where you off to? Breaking up the party.'

'It's Joe. Won't be long.'

Vince looks at his watch and calls after him. 'Half an hour. No later.'

'I'd better be off too,' says George. 'People to see. Places to go.'

* * * * *

Outside the pub, the old man hobbles off to the left, leaning heavily on his stick and muttering under his breath about the rain. He throws his cigarette into a puddle in the gutter. Once he's round the corner his back straightens and his stride lengthens. He's still mumbling to himself but his face brightens as he climbs the hill and lets himself into a ground floor flat. He's greeted by a smiling, buxom, white-haired woman. 'Hello George. Get those wet things off. I thought you'd deserted me.'

They embrace warmly.

'Am I pleased to see you, Deirdre.'

* * * * *

Keith comes out of the pub ignoring the drizzle, slouches to the right, leans against the wall, taps his phone and holds it to his ear. 'Kirsty? I'm out. Thank God that's over.'

'Are you coming up?'

'I haven't got long. Mum's doing lunch.'

'Please.'

'Tempting. I need some sanity. Families are so shitty. Remind me, next time.'

'Come up then. I've got something I need to tell you. Funny, you saying about families. I'll explain when I see you.'

* * * * *

Vince goes up to the bar and orders another drink. He'll wait for the rain to stop. 'Special occasion?' asks the bartender.

'Well yes,' says Vince. 'Since you ask. It's my birthday. Not as you'd notice.'

'Many happy returns.'

'Thanks.'

# The Peridor

I have come down onto the sand again this morning, to savour once more this breadth and this flatness, to breathe the openness, to dwell for a while on this borderline. The tide is low. The tentative light from the sun is filtering through the mist and touching the crests of the sandbanks, those low humps lounging like sleeping Gullivers, exposed at the retreating of the sea. My fork is leaning against my shoulder like a sloping rifle, with a yellow bucket swinging behind. I feel conspicuous, a matchstick silhouette against the leaden seascape, with black boots and a grey woollen hat. But I am not the only one. There are others here who look like me and are digging like me. We keep our distance as we always do. There is no need for territorial battles here: the beach is wide enough to accommodate us all. I do not know what the others are digging for, but I presume it to be worms. There must be money to be had by selling bait to the cluttered shop in town that caters for local anglers. I do not know because I do not ask; I do not ask because I do not care; I never talk to the others and they do not talk to me. I have not come to the beach for conversation and neither have I come for reward. I am not digging for worms. I am digging for something different. I am looking for a heart-shaped crystal shell, a peridor.

This is not such a foolish endeavour as you might imagine. This is not an idle fancy. Because there was a time when I found a peridor, right here on this beach. To be accurate, it was Sally who found it, but I was here when it happened. It was many years ago, when I was young.

\* \* \* \* \*

The first week of that holiday was entirely ordinary, nothing special. I was content enough, as my expectations were not great at that age and I was not a rebellious child, not given to angry self-assertiveness or to bouts of sulking. I was ten years old and an only child, serious and obedient and content almost all the time. This resort was our regular holiday destination so we had an established routine. My parents took me on excursions that were familiar, to places we knew; there were no surprises but I was not disappointed as I was not a lover of surprises. It was the same as every other year and that was fine by me. So, to begin with, that holiday was entirely ordinary.

Sally was staying with her parents in the caravan next to ours. When they arrived, towards the end of our first week, the adults had introduced themselves to each other and Sally and I had been made to shake hands and say 'Hi'. We were fodder for their thoughtless ridicule, as they joked about how we could be playmates, being of a similar age and without siblings or friends. But I didn't like playing with girls. I didn't even much like playing with boys. I enjoyed spending time on my own, reading mostly, or bird-watching like my dad or just walking and admiring the scenery. I was content to tag along with my parents to the places they wanted to go, looking at things they told me to look at, re-assuring them (should they choose to ask) that I was enjoying the holiday.

Although this is a seaside resort, we did not often go to the beach. If we did our project would be to make a sandcastle. My father would design it and tell me where to build the walls, how wide the moat should be and what sort of turrets it needed. I would do what he told me. We had done this on one occasion during that first week. I believe he enjoyed it more than I did, but I didn't mind, I was content that it was an activity we could participate in together and that it gave him pleasure.

But the second week of this holiday was different. It started with a very hot day and so my father decided it was 'beach weather', and in a break from tradition we went to the rock pools below the cliffs. By coincidence, Sally was also there and the two sets of parents were soon engaged in adult conversation. Sally and I both had nets and buckets and spades and began to trawl through the rock pools together. To start with we were not really together, simply doing things side-by-side, playing in parallel, each immersed in his or her own, private world.

Neither of us was particularly good at rock-pooling. We didn't find any crabs, apart from two dead ones I uncovered and pointed out to her. Mostly, we dragged our nets through the water and poked the sand with our spades, turning the clear pools into brown slushy puddles. And then Sally started telling stories. Probably she was only talking to herself, but I listened and gradually became part of the stories as they became part of me. Each new pool we came to, each pile of rocks we clambered over, each patch of seaweed, shells or shingle we scrambled across, for Sally it became the location of a fantasy realm.

Her stories were populated by a mixture of characters, some of whom I had previously heard of and some that were probably made up. There were kings like Neptune, Triton and Poseidon, there was a Yellow

Submarine, there were porpoises and turtles, Ariel the mermaid, lobsters that danced, snails, seahorses, sea-goats, Salacia and Vernilia, an octopus tending its garden, fishes and crabs and ... oh, there were loads, so many creatures, most with exotic names I can no longer remember. The creatures may not have been original, but the tales she told about them were new, at least to me. Some of them were funny, some were violent, some were romantic and others were sad. I wondered where this had all come from. What world did Sally live in? It was certainly a different world from mine.

Jumping off one of the rocks, I stumbled against her, she gave me a shove and so a game of tag began. We dropped our nets and buckets and ran all across the beach, sometimes dodging the rocks, sometimes climbing over them, slipping on the seaweed, scrunching through the shingle. At one point I swerved too violently and ended up sitting down in one of the pools. My shorts were saturated and I felt very soggy and embarrassed as only a ten-year-old can be. Sally laughed outrageously. That made me feel even more sorry for myself so I was close to tears, and then, at the look of sheer delight on Sally's face, I saw the funny side and joined in her laughter.

The tide was still going out and beyond the rock pools a stretch of sand was revealed and we had races there. Although Sally was a year older than me I was faster than her and beat her every time. I was pleased and she didn't seem to mind too much.

As the afternoon slipped towards evening, Sally said we should collect some treasure. She meant shells and fancy-patterned stones and other curious pieces that the eager-eyed can find on any beach. I had never noticed them before. We competed with each other to find the biggest or most striking object: 'Look at this, Joey'; 'Sally here, quick ...'; 'Wow, look at this one sparkle!'

By the time we had been summoned to return, we both had half-full buckets which we rattled in triumph. Back at the caravans, we washed our treasure in soapy water, admiring again the colours as they glittered and gleamed, and laid them out to dry in the rays of the dying sun. Even as we were still admiring them, the colours began to fade, the rosiness turning to dull brown, the gold to beige, the silver to dirty grey. Once dry, the treasure retained none of its earlier allure.

Apart, that is, from one shell, shaped like a heart and almost as big as my hand. It continued to glitter and glisten, if anything gaining in luminescence as it dried. Sally picked it up.

'Aren't we the lucky ones?'

'What do you mean?'

'Look what we've found.'

I looked. It was a shell. It had a crystal sparkle to it, very pretty and all that, but just a shell. 'It's just a shell,' I said.

'Oh no. That's where you're wrong. You don't know anything, Joey.' My parents and teachers called me Joseph. Sally called me Joey.

'So what is it? If you're so clever.'

'It's a type of fairy, a crystal fairy. It's called a peridor.'

I couldn't think of anything to say to that. I had never heard of a peridor. But Sally clearly had. She seemed to know everything about everything. I stared at the peridor, seeking answers. 'Can I hold it?'

'Careful now.'

I held it. It was very pretty and it shone with a delicate light that seemed to come from within. And it felt warm on my fingers. Then, to my astonishment, it started to vibrate. I dropped it. 'Ouch,' I said, although it hadn't hurt.

'I said be careful.' Sally picked it up. 'It's precious. Sensitive and delicate. And it'll grant our wishes if we're kind to it. But first, we need to name it. We shall call it *Gabriel*.'

\* \* \* \* \*

It is a favourable circumstance when the low tide coincides with the dawn: the temporal world and the physical world are aligned and synchronised, in pleasing agreement. On the threshold of a fresh beginning, full of harmonious ease, I anticipate the ascent to come, starting from the zero that is here and now; all is before me, everything is potential, optimism permeates my heart and my soul. Slowly, the tide will lift with the sun and the day will evolve through a naturally rising curve. This will be a good day. Today, perhaps, I shall find a peridor.

I dig and I rake and I sift. Piles of dark sand accumulate like mole hills around me and delineate my meandering path. I have found nothing of interest. So far. It is an easy task; it has its comfortable rhythm: dig and rake and sift and dig again, rake again, sift again, bend and stretch, bend and stretch, bend and stretch. The tide is flowing now and the weak sun is gaining ground. There is still an autumnal chill to the air, and it will be so for a while. It is not like that other time, when it was high summer and it was hot and Sally had found the peridor and we rode through the desert.

* * * * *

We began slowly, side by side, traversing the sand in leisurely fashion. The heads of the ponies were hanging low as though they were exhausted by their labour, burdened by expectation, reluctantly fulfilling their duty under the weight of the sun's rays. Perhaps they were merely bored by the lack of variety, by the routine, by the tedious repetition. Their handlers urged them on with patience but persistence, and in response the steeds maintained a shuffling, strolling cadence. I looked towards Sally who was riding the pony on my right. She smiled and raised her hand in the air. I saw she was holding a heart-shaped stone. It was *Gabriel*, the peridor.

It was then that we mounted the camels. They also walked sedately, but their stride was longer, the rhythm of their gait less even. We bounced on the saddles, rising and falling, pitching forward and bending back and it made us giggle and then we laughed and laughed. Sally was wearing a white robe with a hood that looped over her blonde hair. Looking down I saw I too was dressed in Arabian costume, a cotton kaftan-like garment with high collar and stiff sleeves and a red chequered scarf around my head. Sally kicked her mount and it began to run. She was soon thirty metres or so ahead of me. I dug my heels into my camel's sides and chased after her.

With the lengthened strides, the ride became smoother and we raced each other effortlessly across the endless desert, our enthusiasm as boundless as the surrounding landscape. The sand stretched across the wide panorama in all directions, contours gently shifting as the breeze lifted the top layer of sand, producing intricate patterns of swirls and eddies. Behind us the clouds of sand kicked up by the animals' hooves soared like masses of clustering locusts, tracing our journey, shading the coppery vista and veiling the sun. Sally spotted an oasis away to our right and called for me to follow her as she veered in that direction.

We were soon settled in the shade of the palm trees, sipping milk from coconuts and allowing our camels to drink from the cooling lagoon. All was calm, all was peaceful. We felt relaxed and serene. We hardly spoke, because there was nothing that needed saying. We simply savoured the stillness and succumbed to the drowsiness that enveloped us.

When the bandits came, we were taken by surprise. By the time we were on our feet, one of the villains had already used his cutlass to slice through the rein of the taller of the camels and set it loose; the beast seized its opportunity for freedom and bounded friskily into the distance. We scrambled onto the remaining animal. I sat at the front of the saddle and Sally held her arms tightly around my waist. We galloped away as fast as we could, heads ducked low as the rattle of gunfire rang all round us, permeating our ears, filling our thoughts. Gradually the sound of shooting grew fainter and we rode a little less wildly, breathed a little easier and shared a look of mutual congratulation. We had escaped; we were safe.

Back at our caravans and back in our normal clothes, we ate our tea with relish and relived the day. Our words tumbled over each other as we shared the emotions we'd experienced, how excited we'd been, how scared, how exhilarated, how evil the bandits had looked with their moustaches and their shouting and their weapons and their bullet-belts. Sally said they were called bandoliers. That night we slept contentedly despite the violence of our dreams.

\* \* \* \* \*

The sand underfoot becomes spongy, then softly yielding and then turns perceptively wetter. It feels as though the sea is seeping through from beneath, oozing through the layers of earth, up to the surface. It happens slowly, imperceptibly, but look away for a moment and it has gained ground faster than you could have imagined. Before long, the waves will be rippling around the ankles of my boots. I pick up the empty bucket with my fork, place it across my left shoulder and plod with a heavy tread up the beach to the edge of the shingle. I am not as disconsolate as I appear: there are other places I can search. I stand still and turn, looking across the blurred greyness of the sea that has already covered the sand. The sun has failed to penetrate the mist, the haze persists. There is a windsurfer catching the breeze, sliding across the deepening water, his sail providing a crisp red flash against the monotonous pencil-shading of sea and sky. I think of Sally. I think of her smile as an antidote to my frowns, her sparkle compared to my apathy, her red upon my grey. I think of the gold of her hair, the silver of her eyes, the crooked turn of her upper lip when she laughed. I remember Sally.

* * * * *

The next day was even hotter and sunnier and we were back below the cliffs. Sally said that *Gabriel* was taking us on a treasure trail and that I should follow her. I was happy to do so. I would have followed her anywhere. She marched ahead with her arms outstretched in front of her, holding the peridor between her palms. She shouted instructions back to me: 'Ten paces forwards'; 'Pass round the flat rock'; 'Turn right and head towards the overhanging branch'. I followed her as we wound our way along the beach, across the slimy green boulders, around the dark pools, grateful for the occasional sections of firm, even sand. After a while we passed the remains of a shipwreck. It was *The Argo,* Sally said, and it was a sign we were nearly there. It had been carrying gold bullion and other treasure, and had encountered a violent storm which was why it ended up stranded on this beach. All that was left of the ship was a partial skeleton, a few curved wooden struts sticking up, like the remaining ribs of the carcase of a whale, pecked clean by generations of predators.

The final segment of our path led us directly towards the cliff. It looked like a dead-end, but as Sally halted and I came alongside her, she pointed to the left where part of the cliff-face stood out from the rest. There was just room to squeeze behind it and we found ourselves in a passage, narrow and low. We had to crouch down but could still manage to walk through. It was gloomy and getting gloomier as we left the sunlight behind and headed deeper under the cliff, but the peridor emitted a soft glow, shedding an eerie light for a few metres in each direction, enough illumination for us to see our way. The air grew chilly and the passage smelt musty, as though it were not used to company. By the light from the peridor we could

see the water running down the craggy walls to either side.
The floor was uneven and slippery and I nearly fell once or
twice, grasping Sally's arm to save myself. I was a little
scared but did not tell Sally.

'Is it far?' I asked, whispering because it seemed the
right thing to do.

'Round the next bend. *Gabriel* says.'

And then we emerged into a large cavern. Sunlight
must have been seeping through from somewhere,
because the cave was far brighter than the passage
through which we had come. The walls and the floor of the
cave and its domed roof all had the same glistening wet
appearance. There was a green ghostly aura that flooded
the space, a sense of other-worldliness, suggestive of
magic and mystery. The atmosphere was cold and damp.
But the main thing was the treasure.

In the centre of the cave was a large wooden trunk
with shiny metal straps and clasps. Its lid was open wide
and pouring from this mouth was a glistening fountain, a
waterfall of jewellery. There were bracelets and necklaces,

rings and brooches and all manner of gems, ruby red, emerald green, sapphire blue, intermingled with bright, shimmering, burnished gold. We each dug both hands deep into the treasure trove, as though we were delving into a liquid pool, grabbing handfuls of jewels, then letting them slide through our fingers. Again and again we dived in, laughing at the sparkling depth, at the bright rippling, at the wonder of it all.

'We're rich,' I said.

Sally stopped and took a pace backwards. 'Oh no,' she said. 'No. We can't take any of this. It's not ours.'

I wanted to protest, to argue. But her face told me the decision had already been made. I picked up a few more trinkets and then threw them back into the trunk. 'Whose is it, then?'

'It belongs to the cliff. To the sea and the shore. *Gabriel* says. It must stay here for all eternity. Its magic offers protection. It keeps everyone safe. Safe forever from the forces of evil.'

Before we left, I slipped a diamond ring into my pocket, but I must have dropped it on the way because when we arrived back at the caravans it had gone.

* * * * *

I walk where the hem of the shore is repeatedly oversewn by rolls of foaming seawater, waves that splash and suck, invade and draw back, always the same but always different, every tongue of the sea familiar and yet unique and fresh and original, assertive and yet apologetic, and I look through the water when it is clear and shallow and momentarily still, seeking the radiance of the heart, of the crystal, of the fairy. The radiance of childhood. The radiance of a memory. The memory that was Sally.

* * * * *

Because this was a week in summer at an English seaside resort, we had to endure the obligatory rainy day. That is what my father would have said. Something like that. Both families stayed in their own caravan and listened to the rain. In our caravan we all read books. Then we played a game of scrabble. My father won. Then we read some more. I listened to the rain. It was the type of day I would normally have enjoyed, with time to myself, time to think and time to read, but on this occasion it was not the same. I did not enjoy this day. I could not give my full attention to the story I was reading. I thought about Sally and wondered what she was doing. I thought about *Gabriel*, the peridor.

Our neighbours joined us for tea. Sally showed me the painting she had been working on throughout the day, an intricate design of serpents and snakes and dragons in orange and yellow and red. It was wild and exotic and beautiful. As our neighbours were about to leave, Sally slipped *Gabriel* into my hand. She said I could look after him for one night. I felt so proud.

In bed that night, I held *Gabriel* close to my ear. He wanted to know my secrets. I said I had no secrets. I asked him if Sally had told him any secrets. He said she had told him one. I asked him what it was.

'Sally says she thinks she might love you.'

I realised that now I had a secret to tell him. 'I love Sally,' I said. 'Tell her.'

\* \* \* \* \*

Along the line of the high tide, much debris accumulates along with the seaweed. I walk along, nudging at the stones with the toe of my boot, disturbing the shingle, looking and nudging, searching, searching. There are many shells here. Some of them display flamboyant patterns of colouration, others are intricately shaped; and then there are those that respond to touch, revealing subtle textures. But none of these is a crystal fairy, none of these is a peridor. This is all dead detritus, inert material that may have once had its origin in the teeming life that lurks under the waves, but which has long since had that life squeezed from it; it has been dehydrated, desiccated, sucked dry and then been abandoned in death, marooned here on the beach. There is nothing with any life here, nothing with any power. There is no object with the power to lift me into flight. Not like the peridor.

\* \* \* \* \*

The day after the rain was the day that *Gabriel* took us flying. We were on the cliff-top, Sally and me. It was fine and sunny but also wild and blustery. Seagulls were leaning into the wind, wings spread wide, feathers smoothed back. We played our normal games, chasing and racing and pretending, but the wind kept catching our hair and taking our breath and making us laugh. We stopped for a while to pick daisies. It was Sally's idea. We made daisy chains and Sally told me stories about pixies and magic rings and angels. She made the biggest chain in the world and held it up to the sun, looped around her wrist, and the breeze lifted it and we watched as the daisies danced. She was holding *Gabriel*, the peridor, in her other hand and that's when she told me that *Gabriel* would take us flying if we wanted. She looked at me as if it were my choice. I nodded as emphatically as I could.

We ran down from the lighthouse, hand in hand, and when our feet left the grass we felt the uplift carrying us clear of the ground and we were flying. We veered out over the edge of the cliff, looking across the water towards the wind turbines whose blades were spinning fast and glinting in the sunshine. We gained height as the updraft caught us and then spiralled yet higher, looking down on the seagulls as they continued their normal day without regard to us, then looking up at the blue, blue sky. The more we flew the more adept we became, steering to the left, steering to the right, banking and diving. We kept our inner hands clasped. Probably we could have separated and flown independently, but neither of us wanted that: we were better as a pair. We were soon back over the lighthouse and we circled that tower several times, still holding hands, with our free arms stretched wide. I felt as though this is where I belonged, here in the sky where, full of the sheer thrill of being alive, I was free to follow the wind, with Sally by my side. At times it was more like floating than flying, as we drifted, coasted, rode the wind. Our flight took us out across the houses and we looked down onto the patchwork of gardens. We spotted some children playing in a paddling pool, a man with a bald head mowing a lawn, two old ladies drinking tea and a young man without a shirt chopping down a tree. Then we laughed as we caught sight of a woman in her back garden pegging out her clothes. I was thinking of the rhyme about the sixpence and the blackbird and I know Sally was thinking the same.

I did not want the flight to end, but Sally said it was time. We flew a few more circles but the passion had gone, the shadow of the ending had engulfed us. We flew back and landed in the space between our caravans and we were sad that our feet were back on the ground.

* * * * *

The tide is rising. The beach is growing narrower. The sun has still not penetrated the mist. It will not do so now, it is too late. The air has grown chilly. The wind is strengthening. My time on the beach is nearly over.

* * * * *

'It's our last day,' she said.

'Yes.'

We paddled some more on the edge of the sea, not talking, feeling the sand seep between our toes, feeling the sun on our backs and the gentle breeze on our faces. We moved a little deeper. The waves were not high enough to make jumping them much of a game, but we jumped them anyway and squealed. Then it was deep enough to swim and we swam a little. Neither of us was a strong swimmer, expending a lot of labour simply to stay afloat, splashing too much. Sally was better at it than me but even she soon grew tired of the effort. We stood side by side for a while, the water nearly up to our waists and looked out at the rows of dunes, humps of sand revealed at low tide like sleeping Gullivers waiting for the Lilliputians to arrive.

'What does *Gabriel* suggest we do?' I asked.

Sally looked at me, as though she had never heard of him. Then: 'Oh.' She looked away, waiting. 'The peridor says we should go to The Island.'

'Which island?'

'Just "The Island". It's also known as Paradise. When Adam and Eve lived there it was called the Garden of Eden. It is a place of perfection, an island of dreams and music.

'Where is it?'

'Out there. See. The last hump, the small one.'

'How do we get there?'

A pause. 'We walk. Through the waves. Then we paddle. We wade a little, swim if we have to.'

So that is what we did. On our last day.

* * * * *

I sit on the edge of the promenade and watch the tide coming in. The waves are higher now, whiter, more sure of themselves, assertively claiming the dominance that is their due. There is scarcely any beach left. The diggers have all gone. The windsurfer has been joined by two others. From the south, a cloud of knot swirl around, a collection of individuals, each bird taking its turn to soar and then dive. The flock coalesces and then fragments into tendrils of arcing, curving, sweeping fingers, that quickly circle back, as though the more impetuous birds had tasted the vacant sky, glimpsed its openness and sought instead the sanctity of the closed community. Organised chaos, orderly wildness, pattern in flux: always changing, yet always the same. It depends how you look at it; it all depends upon your point of view. You can choose what you wish to see.

I did not find a peridor today. I will return on another day and I may have better luck. But it has not been a wasted day. This space at the junction of the sea and the sky and the shore has brought me comfort and pleasure. It always does. It has also brought me pain.

'I think I might love him.' That is what Sally said. According to the peridor. 'I think I might love him.' That declaration provoked such rapture within me, such elation and delight, and these emotions have persisted down the years. I feel them still. But mixed with this pleasure has been the pain. I am glad that Sally said those words, so glad. But why could she not have been more certain? I wish she had been more certain. If only Sally had been more certain in proclaiming her love for me.

# For the Love of Go

The final round begins. The shades have been pulled across the windows to keep out the distracting sunlight. A low buzz comes from one of the neon strips. Clocks tick. Maxwell focuses on the empty board between him and his opponent. He takes a black stone from his bowl. He recalls previous games with this opponent: she plays aggressively, enjoys attacking weak groups but can leave herself vulnerable. Maxwell breathes deeply, once, twice, and clears his mind. He reaches across the board and places the stone on the far right 3-3 point.

Judith sits at the breakfast table. She carefully cuts the card with the kitchen scissors. She is determined not to cry. It's not only today, she tells herself. Anyone can forget a date. It's all the other things. For instance, the slovenliness: the ring around the bath, the books and go stones cluttering the table, discarded clothes piled on the floor. He needs a mother, not a wife.

Maxwell plays cautiously, conservatively, securing territory, keeping his groups safe. His opponent builds thickness and a white *moyo* is materialising. It is not yet a cause for concern. The game is going well. So far.

And he never gets around to doing things. Anything. Those shelves are still not up. The grass at the back is knee-high and rising. The dripping of the bathroom tap gets worse. Sometimes she could scream. He's never here, and when he's here he's on the computer. Playing Go. She'd rather it was pornography. Judith wields the scissors with venom.

Maxwell estimates the score. It's not good. He's behind, a long way behind. But that's assuming all the centre becomes secure white territory. He imagines some reducing moves. That probe would be *sente*, and then he could play there and he'd have some good follow up moves. He counts again. He'd still be losing. Reduction isn't going to be enough. He needs to invade. Now, before it's too late.

Snip, snip. Last Friday really took the biscuit. He knew Mum and Dad were coming. Nine o'clock before he showed up. Some excuse about a game going on longer than it should have, his opponent wouldn't resign. She's heard it all before. They had to start. His was in the oven, dried out. Served him right. Not that he noticed. World of his own. And how long is it since they made love? Properly, that is.

Maxwell invades too deeply. His opponent licks her lips and raps her next stone onto the board, occupying a key point. He can't live in there, he needs to escape. Play lightly, don't try to save everything. There's a route out, but she would attack from that direction and then she'd have a springboard into the side territory. He'd be torn to shreds. Maxwell over-stretches with his escape move. His opponent cuts. He knew she would.

Judith carefully cuts the card into smaller and smaller pieces. 'Happy' and 'Anniversary' are separated. So are: 'To Max', 'love' and 'Jude'. She places the pieces in a neat pile on the mantelpiece next to the clock. Instead of a note. She looks around the room, feels a shiver slide down her back and a pricking in her eyes. This is not the time for tears. Nor second thoughts. Hold it together.

The group cannot be saved; it must be sacrificed. Maxwell plays forcing moves on the outside. His territory becomes more secure as his opponent's territory shrinks. She'll have to play extra moves there and there: the capture is not worth so much. Now take some large end-game moves.

Judith picks up her small suitcase and leaves the house. She posts the keys through the letterbox. The taxi is waiting.

The game of Go is over. They count. Maxwell has won by three points. The players shake hands and re-play the crucial moments of the game, revisit their decisions.

* * * * *

Maxwell arrives home. The house is cold. He picks up the scraps of paper from the mantelpiece and drops them into the waste bin. He goes into the kitchen and opens a bottle of wine. He sends a text on his phone: 'All clear. She's gone. Come over. Mx.'

# Natural Justice

Only later did Baxter realise it was not a coincidence. At the time it merely seemed a particularly eventful day. It was the day Stella ran away. And it was the day the trees began to sing.

Stella always accompanied Baxter on his walks along the lanes and footpaths of the Northamptonshire countryside. She was seven years old, full of energy and curiosity. She was much given to careering off unexpectedly through undergrowth or cultivated field, in search of the perfect trail that would lead to the perfect prey. But always she returned promptly to Baxter in answer to his whistle. He was the focus of her life. As she was his.

It was the great oak tree on top of Finedon Hill that first sang. Whether its song was directed at Baxter or to the world in general was never clear. Either way, it didn't sing in words, not at first. It was more a sonorous sigh, soft and steady and suggestive of a mighty weariness, of a burden undertaken long ago that had persisted well beyond its anticipated duration. It was as if the tap had been loosened on a bottle of compressed gas, and, finally free of constraint, the breath could be expelled, whispered to the open sky. Gradually the sigh died away in a stretched diminuendo, only to rise again. This sigh, this groan, this whisper, this prolonged expiration, was repeated again, again, again. Then the repeats grew lighter and quieter and eventually ceased. The hill top, surmounted by the tortuously complex multi-limbed tree, returned to its normal state of peace and calm.

Baxter had been standing a few feet away, gazing across the valley when he first heard the sound, and had turned to stare at the tree as the groaning began. That first time, he didn't want to think of it as the tree singing. It was later he recognised this moment as the beginning of it all. He assumed at first – and who wouldn't? – that the wind was rustling the leaves or swaying the branches to produce the sounds. Except it was a quiet, warm June afternoon and the air was as still as an unspoken secret. There was no wind. In which case, he reasoned, some other quirk of nature must be the cause. Some animal in nearby scrubland, scurrying and foraging. Stella herself, perhaps. Then again, the sound wasn't like that; it was more, well, human, strange to say. So if not that, if not the natural world as source, perhaps it was some trick of the contours of the landscape that allowed a far away cause to yield a nearby effect. A loving couple's whispered conversation, a meandering tractor, a droning high-flying aircraft – some trigger that echoed across the undulations, the peaks and hollows of the countryside, losing its form and context as it did so, ending up as this whine, this stertorous moaning. But really, Baxter knew: the tree was singing.

He waited a while but the ancient oak remained silent. He walked around it, scuffing half-heartedly with his sandaled foot at tuffs of grass and small bushes, feigning to seek out the origin of these strange sounds. And then, when he had stopped expecting it, the singing began again, this time with the clarity of white moonlight. It was as if the earlier sounds had been preparatory throat-clearing. Now came a plain and clean refrain, growing in quality with the tree's increased confidence, gaining tunefulness and musicality. Baxter relished the tonal richness. In contrast to the heavy, laboured atmosphere the earlier groaning had engendered, this song had an authority that demanded attention. It was also a delight, a delight Baxter did not wish to end. For once, for Baxter, hearing was a pleasure.

He would experience that wonder again, and more besides, but not on that day.

The song faded away, the hill grew silent once more and it was time to head home. Baxter whistled quietly for Stella in his usual fashion as he set off on the path back down the hillside. A few strides further on he realised Stella hadn't joined him. He turned to look back up the hill. The oak tree continued to dominate the view, a solemn, majestic silhouette astride the skyline, its very silence now laden with potential. There was no sign of Stella. Baxter gave his special whistle again. When that produced no response, he whistled audibly, and called her name. He'd not done that for years, not since she'd been a puppy. He looked in all directions. A few small bushes and hedgerows grew in clusters. Was she hiding there? Where was she?

It was an hour later that Baxter, trudging with reluctance and full of sorrow, neared his home. He had scoured the hill and surrounding area meticulously, circling ever wider, whistling and calling repeatedly. But eventually he'd admitted defeat: Stella had vanished. Then, as he turned the corner of the stairs to his first-floor flat, he saw her. She was lying by his front door. She was shaking. She looked at Baxter with fear in her eyes. He bent down and stroked her head, tickled behind her ears. She lowered her head and whined pitifully. She had never run off before. When frightened, it was always the safety of Baxter's heel she sought. Something had changed. Stella had changed. Even now, although stroked and comforted, she looked at Baxter as though he were her enemy rather than her rescuer. Part of the problem rather than the solution.

Once the door was open, Stella slunk swiftly into her bed and curled up, her sad eyes raised towards Baxter. Baxter could feel her fear. She was still shaking. He sat cross-legged on the floor beside her basket. He caressed her and reassured her, partly out loud, but mostly through his thoughts. He tucked her favourite toy – Gabby, the cloth teddy bear – into the basket beside her: Stella hardly noticed. Baxter always kept some of Stella's favourite biscuits in reserve for special occasions. Now seemed the right time. Stella ate cautiously, with none of her usual enthusiasm. Later Baxter took her onto his lap in his easy chair and soothed her to sleep, like you would a child.

Baxter's hearing disability had been diagnosed when he was ten. No, diagnosed was not the word: the doctors never determined a cause or found a name for Baxter's affliction. They merely identified it as an aural problem. He'd been a sickly child, always suffering from indeterminate pain that could not be explained, a malady whose source could not be traced. He'd been slow to speak and his speech never became fluent or fully coherent. A hearing problem could have been suspected even had it not been for the times teachers or parents found him sitting in a corner with his hands covering his ears. The verdict, after much prolonged investigation and frequent consultations, was that Baxter's ears picked up sound frequencies that normal human ears did not. Through his teenage years Baxter continued to be subjected to an endless sequence of tests and investigations as specialists pronounced and proclaimed and disagreed and, in all meaningful senses, failed. There was (they said) no cure. The only remedy was to block the excess sound waves: earplugs were recommended.

The earplugs did not prevent Baxter hearing what he heard. Once he was old enough to make his own decisions he discarded the ear protectors. He learned to manage the pain. It wasn't pain, it was discomfort. It wasn't even discomfort, it was merely difference. Difference could be tolerated and difference could be managed. Baxter tolerated it and lived with it. Some in Baxter's position might have become angry, aroused and eager to rail against their fate. But that was not Baxter's way. He withdrew into his own private world. He sought escape from the oppressive effect of his plight, his 'difference'. When people talked close to him, they inadvertently contributed to his discomfort. Crowds were worse. Confined spaces didn't help. He spent as much time as he could away from people, away from traffic, streets and houses. He secured employment as a gardener. In the open air the pain was less. In the open air he could cope. In the open air he could be alone. And he sought the company of dogs.

Stella was his third pet, his third black miniature poodle, after Bella and Tina. With each of them he had established a connection, but in Stella he had found his perfect companion, his soulmate.

Now he settled her down for the night. Told her everything would be all right. Told her he'd look after her, protect her from harm. Always.

The next morning, Baxter found some old cord that he looped around Stella's neck so he could take her for a walk. He never used a lead, had never needed one before. But he dared not risk Stella running away again. The dog was confused but trotted obediently at Baxter's side as they walked to the corner, past The Black Horse, into Long Lane.

Dog and master were alone there. As usual. Long Lane was a road that led a long way to nowhere, so it attracted little traffic and few walkers. Stella kept to Baxter's side but the simple truths in her life had been overturned. She lifted her nose and was drawn towards her usual expeditions amongst the potent hedgerow and the tempting fields beyond. But she was nervous of what she might encounter in that undergrowth. In any case, the constraint around her neck prevented any deviation. Her confusion extended to her perception of the man walking beside her, her instinct pulling her towards her familiar protector, but at the same time being repelled by the way he had changed. Baxter reassured her: I have not changed, he said, in that way they communicated. It's not me, it's you, they each said. But both of them knew they had changed. Then the trees on either side of the lane started to sing.

Stella jerked to left and right, to the limits the cord permitted. She yapped furiously. She circled Baxter's legs, she strained, she somersaulted, her ears flapped, the cord tightened around her neck. Baxter sat down on the verge, grabbed her with both hands and held her close. The dog pulled away from him, scraped her paws on the unyielding tarmac, tried to get away. Baxter whispered in her ear, strived for a tone to sooth her, held her tighter. Stella calmed a little, but still shook and whimpered and hid her tail between her back legs, still strained to get away from her master's clutches, driven by the overpowering need to escape from the trees.

The singing was not the same as that of the oak tree. The great oak, after its husky start, had been authoritative and commanding, a rich lead tenor dominating and domineering. By contrast, the voice of the hawthorn from the side of the road was softer, subtler, less garish, a mellow baritone. The hazel joined in, its voice blending and harmonising with the hawthorn, producing music like the chatter of small children or the splashing of waves on rocks. To Baxter's ears there was another change. Now joined by blackthorn, holly and elder, the notes from this chorus of voices moulded into vowel sounds: 'oo, ee, aye, ow,' each syllable lasting several seconds before merging into the next. Then the whole sequence was repeated, with subtle variation: 'oo, ee, aye, ow'. These sustained tones broke into a rhythmic cadence, with counterpoint and syncopation, but the theme held strong. Crescendo and modulation provided shape to the voices as the trees and bushes combined their declarations and then greater clarity emerged: Baxter heard the vowels turn into words. 'Soon. We. Time. Now.' He listened more carefully. He was sure: there was no mistake. The foliage making up the hedges to either side of Long Lane wasn't just singing. It was talking. 'Soon. We. Time. Now.'

Baxter wanted to stay, to savour more of the music from the trees, hear more of their message, but he felt Stella's pain. The more the singing continued, the more fascinated Baxter became, but the consequence was more pain for Stella. Clutching her under his right arm, he reluctantly left the singing, talking trees behind and headed home, stroking and comforting his quivering pet, consoling her as best he could.

The next day was a Sunday and on Sundays Baxter went to Mrs Pritchard's to do her back garden. He never took Stella there. Mrs Pritchard had three cats and didn't want them upset. The garden was long and narrow and was laid mostly to lawn. The day was bright. Baxter mowed the grass, tidied the flower beds around the edges and listened to the trees. Mrs Pritchard's cats were nowhere to be seen. At the bottom of the garden was a row of tall leylandii, forming a thick, dark green barrier. Baxter was not surprised when they began a steady chanting to a percussive marching beat. It was a simple melody, a wordless refrain that, after a while, transmuted into lyrical shape and began to exhibit recognisable word forms. Baxter could hear the song: 'See us, Hear us, Feel us, Fear us.' It had an ominous flavour that he had not detected in the tree songs on the hill or in the lane. 'See us, Hear us, Feel us, Fear us.' Again. And again. Growing louder. The traces of impatience and frustration Baxter had heard on previous days were repeated, yet they were now overlaid with this mood of anger and threat. But it was the music Baxter most enjoyed. Never mind the menacing lyrics, the melody was sublime.

'You finished?'

Baxter jerked round. Mrs Pritchard was standing close behind him.

'Yes, ma'am.'

'Those roses want dead-heading.' She pointed.

'Right. Sorry. I'll do them.'

Baxter was annoyed with himself. He took pride in doing a thorough job. He had been distracted by the trees singing. Mrs Pritchard, it seems, had not. She had not heard the trees singing, had not heard their words. Baxter had not seen the woman's cats all morning. He wondered where they were and what they had heard.

Baxter's main income came from his work for the local Council. His duties took him around the various parks and gardens of the area. He would sometimes take Stella to work with him, when he thought he could get away with it, when he knew he'd be working alone. But not now, not this week. He wanted to keep Stella safe. This week Baxter intended to seek out the spots where the trees were. Stella wouldn't like it. He expected to hear more tree-songs. He was not wrong.

Throughout the week Baxter savoured a range of wonderful songs produced by the trees. One day he was working by the river and hearing the pitiful, melancholy songs from the willows brought tears to his eyes. Their

suffering imbued the bitter-sweet melodies with a

poignancy that spoke of waste and despair; there was an

added dimension that hinted at revenge and retribution. On

another day he was clearing weed from the reservoir and

the distant trees hummed a sonorous tune. Baxter

detected a mood of growing urgency within the connected

themes, yet still it was the beauty of the melodies that

Baxter most readily connected with, giving him a

heightened sense of ecstasy and bliss. He had never been

able to listen to music before. His hearing disability

interfered with any natural reception of tone and timbre.

He could not separate the pleasurable tones from the

discordant agony caused by his affliction. Now, here, and

apparently for him alone, the tree-music filled his heart

with joy. He disregarded the sinister warnings, lost himself

in the music. In the park he noticed, where previously

there had stood single trees, there now were small groups;

and the disparate copses appeared to be joining into larger

formations. Baxter didn't put it into words but he knew: the singing, talking, conspiring trees were now on the move.

Each evening that week he returned to Stella to be greeted with suspicion and fear. Stella's eyes carried accusation and disappointment, as though she were a wife greeting an adulterous partner. Baxter felt impotent. His messages of comfort, reassurance and solace failed to reach her. Favourite biscuits and soft toys, tempting bones and chase-me games: none of the usual devices worked. Stella remained aloof and distrustful, wary of Baxter's motives; she was sulky; she was scared.

At the weekend, Baxter resolved to help free Stella from the prison of her misery. She did not need to be afraid of the trees. She certainly did not need to be afraid of Baxter. He had to show her; he had to help her hear the beauty in the singing trees.

'We will go to Burton Wood,' he said, in the way he always communicated with Stella. 'It will be fine. You'll see.' Stella, safe in the basket where she'd spent most of the past week, lowered her head and curled into a tighter ball. She did not reply.

Baxter again put the loop of cord around Stella's neck. Her reluctance was apparent. He had to pull her down the two flights of stairs, through the swing doors, out into the warm afternoon. Once in the open air, Stella relaxed a little and trotted by Baxter's side, recovering some of her old energy. Her master continued to do his best to convey soothing words, calming feelings, to help Stella realise there was no cause for alarm, indeed there was enjoyment to be anticipated in this expedition into the company of the trees. They entered the wood along their usual path, and as usual they were alone. It didn't take long for the trees to find their voices. Forgetting Stella for a moment, Baxter turned around on the spot, trying to discern the different timbres and pitches of the tree-voices. There were proclamations and pronouncements from all sides, conflicting elements but with an underlying spirit of collaboration rather than confrontation. The ashes and beeches set up a particularly tuneful refrain, with a positive message of healing and reparation. An alder seemed to oppose this with a mysterious broken atonal wail. Rowans and yews sang of a future full of wonder and delight; a silver birch sang of love; elms and oaks combined in a chorus that overrode the others, asserting their ancient wisdom and authority. Baxter span around, arms outstretched, as though trying to absorb the breadth and depth of this choral collaboration, this musical conversation. The various disparate ingredients, the range from bass to alto, the rhythmic variation, the shifts between major and minor keys: all these elements combined into a glorious, powerful anthem. And then the song coalesced and the voices united into a simple rhythm and a simple message: 'We are coming. We are coming. We are coming.' As he span around, the denseness of the wood increased. The trees never moved when he looked directly at them, but gradually Baxter felt encroachment on all sides. They were coming for him.

Stella had gone. Baxter looked down at the cord hanging from his hand, the loop lying loosely on the ground. Somehow she'd managed to escape. He hadn't noticed. Where had she gone? Baxter called for her, whistled for her both verbally and silently as he stumbled through the undergrowth, thorns tearing at his clothing and scratching his bare arms, nettles stinging his hands. He pushed his way forward, through the foliage, not knowing in which direction to go but anxious to cover as much ground as he could as quickly as possible. Perhaps she's gone home, he thought. I hope she's gone home. She won't like it here. All these trees. All this noise. It's only her and me that can hear it. For me it's beauty, for her it's pain. I hope she's made it safely home. He floundered on through the thick vegetation, in the shadow of the branches, his nostrils full of the leafy aroma, the tree-songs reverberating around him. Then. Suddenly. Silence. Stillness. Baxter emerged into an area of open grass. He saw his dog.

Stella was lying on her side in the middle of the clearing. Her body was stretched out. Her mouth was gaping open. Her eyes were wide and wild. Baxter knew straight away, yet still squatted down by the body to check. He stroked her head, her neck, her back. There was no twitch of her tail, no flutter from her ears. There was no breathing. There was no heartbeat. Stella was dead. Baxter had no veterinary training, but he knew. Whatever the official verdict might be, Baxter knew what had killed Stella. She had been frightened to death.

Back home, Baxter's mind was blurred, his thoughts vague around the edges. He sat down on the floor next to Stella's bed. He placed his hand on her blanket. It was warm. He could smell her, part dampness, part shampoo, but also a soft sweetness, a warm fragrance that encapsulated her essence. He thought about Stella. He thought about trees. He thought about the heaven he'd glimpsed in the tree-songs. He thought about the hell Stella must have experienced. He thought of the way beauty and monstrosity can coexist. Was he right? Was Stella right? Was there such a thing as rightness when it came to trees singing, trees talking, trees conspiring? Rightness? Wrongness? Where would it lead?

He stood up and walked through to the kitchen. He opened the drawer by the sink. Underneath the tea towels and spare dishcloths he sorted through the candles, batteries, light bulbs, the electric plugs, fuses, two screwdrivers, the set of coasters with ships on them, a pack of playing cards. He found the matches. He rummaged further and, right at the back, he found the half-empty pack of small cigars. He lit one and inhaled cautiously. It had been a long time. Years. He looked down through the grubby kitchen window. Behind the hedge, the grassland sloped down to the river. The willow trees flapped in the wind. To the left he could see the outer edge of Burton Wood. More trees. From this distance, all innocently normal, a peaceful rural scene. He looked in the other direction where Finedon Hill rose up. He imagined the ancient oak tree at its summit. The leader.

Baxter shuffled back, picking up a saucer for an ashtray, and sat again on the floor by the side of Stella's bed. What used to be Stella's bed. He sat and he smoked and he thought. He picked up Gabby, Stella's cloth toy. He thought of it as a piece of Stella. He held it to his cheek. He thought about the trees. Their songs and their words. He thought about Stella. He flicked ash into the saucer. He blew on the cigar and studied the red glow at its tip. He thought of trees. He thought of wood. He thought about justice and fairness. He recalled, in soft focus, a TV news item about a forest fire. A curtain of red and orange flames dancing. Consuming. Burning, burning, burning. Revenge began to take shape in his mind.

The first local press story about the Burton Wood fire was factual, 'Blazing Inferno' the predictable headline. It reported that by the time the fire service had received the call, the fire was already widely spread and fiercely burning. Further delay occurred because the wood was located so far from any traversable road. By the time the fire engine had found a route across adjacent fields there was no prospect of preventing the devastation. Later reports included pictures of the remains, showing nothing but layers of ash and blackened stumps, like decayed teeth in the mouth of a decrepit corpse.

There was much speculation as to the cause of the fire. 'Mindless vandalism' was a popular theme; other possibilities, such as a campfire insufficiently damped down, or a childish prank that went wrong, were also suggested. That summer there were similar unexplained fires occurring at multiple sites across the country. It was that sort of year, hot and dry, and the countryside was ripe for burning. At the time, no other connection between the fires was sought or contemplated. Perhaps if it had, later escalation would have been averted.

Nor was there any connection made between the Burton Wood fire and the 'Hanged Man'. At first, the body found on the top of Finedon Hill was merely an unexplained suicide, with the small added spice that the authorities had been unable to identify the man. Then, later, more facts emerged. The man had not, in fact, hanged himself. His body had been found hanging from an oak tree, which is what led to the confusion. But the naked corpse had been supported not by a rope but by a freakish combination of twisted branches. The man had died of suffocation. His lungs had ceased to function. That was because his lungs, along with his other abdominal organs, had been subjected to intense and acute external pressure. The local press interpreted the medical evidence into terms their readers would understand. Their report stated that he had been crushed to death. He was the first one.

# Spaces

'What do you want me to say, Pete?' She was not expecting an answer. 'I have a strong affection for you. Of course I do, you know that. We've had some good times. I've enjoyed being with you. Most of the time.'

I noted the 'most'. And the past tense.

'It's hard to explain. I feel there must be more to life.'

'Sorry for being so insufficient.'

'Oh, grow up.' She took some deep breaths. She expected me to be impressed by her ability to keep calm. 'Look, Pete. I'm not criticising you. You've been a real good friend to me.'

How many clichés was she going to cram into this dumping speech? Had she prepared it in advance or was it impromptu? Either way, it was hardly a masterpiece of originality.

'I sometimes seem so …' She hesitated, obviously for effect. Or maybe she was trying to recall the relevant *bon mot* from an article in one of her women's magazines. 'Oh, suffocated. Drowning.'

'Sorry for being such a. Wet. Blanket.' I was quite proud of that. Accounted for both her claimed afflictions simultaneously.

'No. No, it's not you Pete, it's me.'

Oh dear.

'I need some space. Somewhere to breathe. I need more than…' Another hesitation. 'Darts and drinking. DVDs and drinking. Sex. And drinking.'

'I thought you liked darts.'

'I do. It's just ...'

'And so sorry for forcing all that alcohol down your pretty little gullet – most of it paid for, incidentally, by yours truly – and such a pity that you needed quite so much booze to relax you before you'd drop your knickers.'

'Oh, now we get to it. Your real interests. Well, if only you'd been just a *tiny* bit more considerate ...'

A thumb and forefinger indicated the scale of the tininess in case I hadn't grasped the significance of the word.

'A modicum more caring and a wee bit *less* of the *macho man* with your Wam-Bam-Thankyou-Mam, maybe, just maybe ...'

The conversation began to take on a life of its own. Independent of factors like communication, relevance, truth. Blow and counter-blow were exchanged. We were two ring-weary boxers, slugging it out. Supremacy was the aim. Winning was everything. A battle for power. Yet the punches thrown missed their target more often than they landed. Wild swings causing the puncher more hurt than the punchee.

'And what about our plans for moving in together,' I tried. 'Our future. A family.'

'Your plans, you mean,' she countered. 'I always said I was too young to settle down.'

'Oh, sure. And that's why you tramped around all those estate agents with me. Pored over the brochures for hours, discussing how many rooms we'd need, how big the nursery should be, what size garden would suit us.'

'I didn't want to upset you.'

'Oh no, of course not. Whereas deciding you don't want to see me any more. That's not going to upset me, is it? Well maybe – here's something for you to munch your pretty mouth on - maybe it isn't. Ha. Maybe you don't really know what I feel at all. Maybe I don't need you even more than you don't need me. Ha, and again, ha.'

Eventually we ran out of steam, Kirsty left and I opened a can of lager. Celebration? Drowning my sorrows? Hard to say which. I wasn't dumped. That's what she said.

It felt like I was. A pause in our relationship, that's what it was, according to her. A trial separation, you might call it. It felt more like a break up. A split. The end. I put on a suitable CD and opened another can. Cheers, Mr Cohen, I know how you feel. Felt.

\* \* \* \* \*

Saturday evening and I was single. I considered the options. One: stay in and wait for the tearful phone call: 'Sorry … all a big mistake … let's try again'. Two: go around to Kirsty's, armed with flowers and chocolates and a bottle of sauvignon cabernet … beg … say please … say sorry. I went for option three: get smashed on my own.

But I never made it to the pub. Round our way isn't exactly posh, but it is smart. Respectable, middle class. Nothing extreme, all rather saturated in blandness. We don't go in for things like buskers, sellers of The Big Issue, winos. So when I saw this guy in a scruffy raincoat sitting on the kerb, head bowed, he was hard to ignore. I did try. I walked past him once. Then I looked back. We were on a narrow road near the centre of town. It was busy. Laughing pedestrians sauntered past him. Ignored him. Car wheels whirled by close to his feet, splashing his trousers with rainwater from the gutter. I walked back and bent down close.

'You okay?'

He looked up. His dirty, stubbled face appeared to have a natural ingrained sadness. But this quickly vanished under a broad smile. 'Pete,' he said. 'You made it. I'd just about given up on you.' He looked at his watch. 'I've been here nearly four years. What kept you?'

'I'm sorry,' I said.

'That's okay, mate. Anyway, you're here now.'

'No,' I said. 'Sorry, but I don't know what you're talking about. You must have me confused with someone else.' I leant closer so he could see me more clearly. I spread my arms in a shrug. He stood up.

'Don't mess about, Pete.' He held out his hand. 'It's great to see you.'

I didn't shake his hand. 'No, really,' I said, backing away, hands raised defensively, palms outwards. 'You're making a mistake. Sorry.' I backed further away.

The man stood up with his coat draped across his shoulders. His arms were hanging loosely by his side. He looked like a soft toy discarded by a fickle child, in need of more stuffing. The smile had faded and in its place there was a scared look in his eyes and a sad turn to his lips. Rain was running through his lank hair, down his cheeks. He slowly sank to the pavement. He'll get wet knees, I thought. His mouth moved. I was too far away to hear him. It looked as if he was reciting the elements in the periodic table: hydrogen, helium, lithium, beryllium. The street-light created a halo effect around his head. I turned and ran home.

* * * * *

Given the number of beer cans I've opened over the years, you'd think I'd have got the hang of it by now. But opening my fourth can that Saturday evening, I managed to carve a chunk out of the tip of my finger. Blood flowed everywhere.

I washed the finger and stuck on a plaster. Later, watching some vacuous TV drama, I heard a dripping. I looked down, saw the red spots on the imitation leather of the pale yellow sofa. The plaster on my finger was soaked with blood. I wiped the sofa and renewed the plaster. Immediately, the finger began to bleed again. As quickly as I wiped the sofa it was covered. I walked into the kitchen, cupping my finger with the other hand. The blood dripped onto the draining board, and then accumulated into pools on the work-top and started to flow onto the floor. Trying to clean it up I found my feet sticking to the dark red puddles forming on the tiled floor. A few moments later I was wading ankle deep in the glutinous liquid. I squelched upstairs. The bedroom was flooded with an ever-deepening, swirling sea of dark crimson blood. The bed began to float. I sat on it to get my feet out of the gore. I ripped the plaster from my finger. The wound had healed. The cut had closed. It had left no sign. That's when the blood around the bed seeped away. It drained as quickly as it had come. The house returned to its bloodless state.

Apart, that is, from the grimy red tidemarks on the walls.

* * * * *

'Are you ready?'

Standing in the doorway, loosely wrapped in a dressing gown, clutching a Union Jack coffee mug in one hand and half a roll-up cigarette in the other, there seemed no need for me to give a verbal reply.

'Will you be able to kneel before the Messiah in a state of purity? She is coming for you soon. She could come today.'

Being a Sunday morning, I should have guessed who they were and ignored the door-bell. I don't know which particular brand of God Squad they represented, but the two elderly women at my door wore the usual uniform of head scarves, handfuls of literature and resilient smiles; they offered a persistent mix of promise and chastisement and made me feel simultaneously guilty and holy. I was still distracted by a dream memory. I don't usually remember dreams. I wake with the emotion intact but no context. I feel anger or fear, arousal or pain, but can't remember why. But this morning was different: I had both a visual memory and the emotion to go with it. I still felt the swiftly-inhaled gasp, and the accompanying tumbling void between stomach and loins. And I could still see, like the closing shot from some horror film, two empty trapezes, swaying out of sync with each other, one hundred feet above the circus ring.

And now the Messiah was coming.

I told them I was busy. I said I wasn't interested. I confessed to being a non-believer. But in the end I had to be rude, and closed the door on the two hopeful smiles.

I put down the mug and stubbed out the cigarette. I took the leaflet from under my arm. It had a picture of the coming Messiah. I expected a Mother Theresa style of image, perhaps with a Mona Lisa smile. Instead the picture looked rather like Jane who works on the tills at Tesco's. She must be pushing forty but she's still surprisingly fit. As I read through the five Steps to Salvation, the corners of the leaflet began to curl. They turned brown and smouldered and then the paper burst into flames. I

dropped it and, sucking my scorched fingers, I stamped out

the Messianic fire on the blood-stained carpet.

* * * * *

That morning I thought I'd experiment with a different

route to the pub for my Sunday lunch-time drink. It took

me, under the heavenly blue sky, through the cemetery.

Most of the graves were freshly open, piles of earth like

molehills lined up on either side. Between them a sequence

of blue ovals marked a path. The brisk wind gathered the

early autumn leaves into complex eddies, before piling

them in the crevices at the bottom of the church tower.

The leaves and open graves were looked down upon by a

swivelling CCTV camera. As was I. I sat down on a bench,

leaning back against the plaque, shiny and new: 'In

Memoriam: Pete and Kirsty'. I lit a cigarette.

At the sound of a nightingale, and a smoky bonfire

smell, I looked up into the leaves of the overhanging elm

tree. Through the branches I could see a speck against the

sky. I thought it was a micro light in the far distance, then realised it was far closer and far smaller: it was a model aircraft. It flew towards the park across the road and steered between two scarlet kites which were swaying out of sync with each other. The air filled up with jasmine perfume, mingled with body odour and the sour scent of rotten vegetation. Near the horizon I spotted several multi-coloured hot-air balloons, hovering like Christmas baubles. Overhead, dozens of low-flying airplanes buzzed around in formation, veering and climbing and diving. Flocks of birds and swarms of bees accumulated in vast numbers; the blue sky turned black from the multiplicity of mosquitoes, angels and strangers. I looked back to the church roof from which a line of vultures looked down on the CCTV camera. I felt the spider's web clinging around my face.

Through the dusk-like gloom, I saw Kirsty enter the churchyard from the far gate. She saw me and stopped. She was wearing her famous blue raincoat over a polka-dot blouse; draped around her head was a blood-red scarf. I watched her. She watched me. On her right, The Artist stood, legs astride, in front of his easel, paintbrush poised.

On her other side, The Pianist played old Beatles songs, as the snake slithered around his legs. Kirsty looked at me, shrugged and turned away. She mounted her milk-white steed and rode into the hills.

# Edifice of Deceit

The back view, as he stood at the bar, was promising. Dark

hair curling over his collar, broad shoulders, fitted shirt

over denim trousers. Tight buttocks. And when he brought

the drinks to the table, a lager and a white wine spritzer,

the front view also earned a mental nod of appreciation.

The boyish grin and the crinkly hair were the same as

they'd always been. The crinkly eyes were new, evidence of

a smiley life? Also the chin stubble: he hadn't had that at fifteen.

They chinked glasses. 'You're looking nice,' he said, grinning boyishly.

Marianne had not made much of an effort, jeans and a jumper and a bit of lippy, but she was glad she'd had her hair done a couple of days earlier.

'Thank you. Not bad yourself.'

'It must be … what?' He stared up to the corner of the ceiling. He always did that when he was working things out. She remembered. 'Fifteen years?'

'More like sixteen. Seventeen.'

'You haven't changed.'

'Liar.'

It used to be, when the love of your life dumped you at fifteen, that was the end of it. You might occasionally think back, wonder 'What if?' Wonder how his life had turned out, where he was and who he was with. But any revisiting, any reprise or resurrection, remained hypothetical. The relationship was dead. He might as well be dead, for all the difference it made. And you were dead to him. But now? Not so.

One click on *Facebook*.

A 'friend' request.

'Are you really that David Walker from year ten?'

A couple of 'pm's later and a meeting (f2f) is arranged.

Marianne is not stupid. She knows the risks. She knows people change. She knows, as a rule, dreams do not come true. She has learned a lot in her short life. And yet. And yet. What has she got to lose? They can meet up, chat about old times, then go back to their lives. Separate lives, intersecting occasionally and virtually on social media as they exchange pictures of cocktails and cute kittens. No harm done. But then again ... Maybe ...

They sip their drinks and the conversation stutters along like a reluctant old banger: this dull pub, the lousy weather, the latest terrorist outrage. What else? Then they begin to share memories of schooldays and the words flow more smoothly. Their memories are not entirely aligned: he remembers things she's forgotten; she mentions things that get a blank look from him. But still there's plenty of common ground. His impersonation of old 'Bagsy Bagshot' has her in stitches. She tells him how much Jane fancied him and he looks simultaneously both amazed and appalled. The shared laughter softens them, relaxes them both. The bomb scare and its aftermath are a vivid memory they share. They can't agree who got the blame for the false alarm but they remember how they'd taken the opportunity to sneak away for a kiss and cuddle in the 'Alley'. Ah yes, the Alley. The games and the giggles and the fumbles. They steer away from too much detail, each keeping their own personal memories intact.

It's all a long time ago, and there's awkwardness again as the memories dry up. Another drink helps.

'So what have you been up to Dave, all those years between then and now? Famous yet? Didn't you plan to make your first million by the time you were twenty-five?

'Not there yet. Not quite. Working on it.'

And the conversation begins to chug along again with this fresh burst of fuel. Talking about themselves comes easy. There's safety on these familiar paths. They take it in turns. How they progressed from schoolchild through adolescence into adulthood, jobs tried, jobs failed, faces adopted, clothes discarded, where they are now and what has brought them here. Plans for the future.

Afterwards, Marianne decides he's been rather cagey. He told her he was a 'businessman' but what precisely was his line? She can't remember. He may have said, but parts of the conversation are blurred in her memory. Not surprising as there were whole sections when she wasn't really listening to his words, being too busy focusing on his curly hair, his laughing eyes, his lips. Presumably he wasn't as successful as he claimed. People are bound to exaggerate, try to impress. She doesn't blame him for that. She'd not been entirely straight herself. She told him she 'worked from home' but didn't give any details.

They've avoided the topic for long enough: eventually, inevitably, they talk about relationships. Not their own, that childish one they shared. No, grown-up ones. Romances. Dalliances and commitments. The ups and downs, the good and the bad. Where the praise is due, where the blame lies, the pleasure and the hurt. Mostly about the blame and the hurt. Marianne wonders later how truthful Dave has been. As truthful as her?

They agree to meet again. None of this 'Call me,' or 'I'll text you.' No, a definite arrangement. Next week. Same time. Same place. Just one awkward moment remains, when Dave escorts Marianne to her car. She had decided that if he moved in for a kiss, she'd turn 45 degrees to the left and catch it on her cheek. As it turns out, he aims for her cheek, so that's okay. And he doesn't do that continental thing of following up with the other cheek. So not so awkward.

'See you next week.'

Shared smiles.

'Sure. Looking forward to it.'

That night, lying on her back in bed, eyes wide open in the darkness and staring towards the ceiling, Marianne thought about Dave. Thought about their date. It had been fun. He was a laugh. No surprise there. His cheeky grin set up a flutter in her stomach. He seemed to have calmed down a lot. Less cocky. He'd listened to her, shown real interest in the things she'd said. She hadn't expected that. He'd developed a caring side. Or maybe he was just a good actor. Marianne reminded herself that she didn't know him, didn't know this adult version of the boy Dave. But she wanted to know him, she was sure of that. She hugged herself and thought about the smile and thought about his lips on her cheek. The roughness of his chin. His smell, a mixture of soap and hair gel. Beer on his breath, but no smoke, no garlic. All good. She thought about the other good bits of the evening. Glossed over the awkward moments. It had been fine. She was already looking forward to next week. It was wonderful to have something to look forward to, something romantic. It had been a long time.

Next to her, the gentle snore turned into a rasping cough and was swiftly followed by a loud fart. Marianne turned over, away from her husband, and closed her eyes, sinking into romantic dreams.


And so Marianne's life took a turn for the better and her Thursday affair began. Their first date had been on a Thursday and that remained their day which was fortunate for Marianne because Thursday had been her Pilates evening. She'd even taken to sharing a drink with her friend Rachel after the class, so she had a ready-made excuse for going out on Thursday evenings as well as an explanation for returning with alcohol on her breath. Some things changed. Like her taking a make-up bag with her (and fixing her face in the car), like putting on matching underwear, like her Lycra kit remaining sweat-free. But her husband was not sensitive enough to notice such subtle changes, and even if he did Marianne thought he probably wouldn't care. They didn't have that sort of marriage. Not any more. The passion had lasted no more than two years, probably less. It had been followed by a period of bickering, quickly succeeded by a period of open hostility, irrational accusations, shouting and swearing and slammed doors. Then it had settled down to indifference. Mutual bare tolerance. It was that sort of marriage. Even so, there was a surface veneer, unspoken yet mutually accepted, involving appearances and pretences that had to be preserved. So Marianne said nothing to her husband about Dave, continued to pack her kit into a holdall and carry it to the car at 7.15 every Thursday evening, and carry it back in (unused) when she returned a little after 10. She didn't risk getting properly dolled up (he might have noticed that) which was a shame as she would have liked to have made an effort for Dave. So she stuck to her usual, jeans, jumper and winter coat. Dave didn't seem to mind.

Their Thursday evenings soon evolved from drinking dates into opportunities for illicit intimacy. Shared goodnight kisses in one of their cars became longer and deeper, breathing became heavier, hands began to stroke and explore and burrow under layers of clothing. By the occasion of their fourth or fifth date, the drink in the pub had become merely a preliminary, consumed (in some haste) out of a sense of propriety and the central purpose of the evening was to drive out to some discreet, secluded spot where they relocated to the back seat and fucked. Marianne didn't like to use that word, she never had, but she did now when she thought about Dave. When she thought about him she did use the word and it brought with it waves of delicious shivering and tingling as she relived their closeness and relished the pleasure of those magical moments. It was hard for her to believe but Marianne was enjoying life. It had been a long time since she'd been able to say that. Her life was great. Dave was great. Fucking Dave was great.

'Why don't we go back to your place?'

They'd nearly finished their drinks, the preliminaries were drawing to a close and they were about to move on to the featured event of the evening. This was a question Marianne had been expecting and had prepared her answer. She explained how she had to protect her son, Bertie. That she didn't want to upset the babysitter. The neighbours would talk. None of it was true, but it all sounded plausible. She could hardly say her husband wouldn't like it. She had also been expecting Dave to suggest going back to his place, but she didn't want that either. It wasn't that she didn't trust him. So she told herself, but it was a lie. That was precisely the reason. Fortunately, going back to Dave's wasn't on the agenda.

'I'm afraid my place is out, too,' he said. 'It's my mum.' He'd explained before about his relationship with his mother. When Dave had got married it had been much against his mother's advice. In fact she'd been set against it and made her opinion of his wife very clear before and during the short marriage. When they broke up after a year, Dave's mother took great delight in telling him it served him right, that she'd told him 'that woman' was no good and he ought to have listened. She let him move back home but seemed to think she now occupied the moral high ground and that gave her the right to control his life. She treated him like he was still a teenager. Gave him chores to do, chose the TV programmes they watched, decided when it was time for bed. Wouldn't let him go on a date without vetting the woman first. And Dave, still traumatised by the break-up of his marriage, didn't fight it. 'Yes, Mum.' Anything for an easy life. Thursday was the one night of the week when he was allowed out, supposedly playing darts at The Black Horse. Dave hadn't told his mother about Marianne.

'You can't carry on living like that,' said Marianne.

'No, of course you're right. I'll tell her. Just not yet. She's not well, you know. It's her heart. I wouldn't want to upset her. I need to keep her sweet. She is my mum, after all. And it was good of her to take me in.'

So the back seat of the car, parked in a dark lay-by, remained the location for their Thursday evening communion, and Marianne was content with that. Dave's relationship with his mother was weird, but she couldn't help thinking it reflected well on him. For all that she'd fancied him, Marianne remembered the teenage version of Dave as an arrogant, selfish boy. He'd always been unpleasant to the younger ones at school, teased them, liked to see them scared. Not exactly a bully, but not far removed. Always getting involved in scuffles and shouting matches. Loved the sound of his own voice. When he'd broken up with her he'd grinned like he was taunting her, enjoying seeing her suffer. That boy wouldn't have cared tuppence for the feelings of his mother. It was wonderful that he'd grown up into such a caring man, such a thoughtful son. And a caring and thoughtful lover.

Marianne did have a child. And his name was Bertie. Marianne often said he was the one good thing to come out of her marriage. She prayed he hadn't inherited any of the traits of his father. So far he was a kind, sweet little boy, everyone said so. Perhaps too generous in sharing toys at playgroup, not willing to stand up for himself. Marianne sometimes wondered if he'd turn out to be gay. No harm in that.

Marianne's weeks revolved around the bliss of Thursday evenings. During Friday and over the weekend she would replay the details of the evening in her mind, his smile, his caring eyes, the warm words he'd whispered. The way he made love to her, with such tenderness. Unselfish, generous. Then for the first half of the next week she'd be counting the days until their next meeting, then counting the hours, thinking about what she'd do, what he'd do, how it would feel.

She hated it when Christmas and New Year came around and she had to play the family game, with siblings, nephews, nieces, in-laws. Seeing the joy on Bertie's face on Christmas morning had been some compensation, but not seeing Dave for three whole weeks was hell. She got back to work as quickly as she could once January arrived, telling her husband how much catching up she had to do, locking herself away in her study with her computer and her thoughts of Dave. She longed for the first Thursday of the year.

Marianne worked from home, that much was also true. She was an Interior Designer, mostly on the commercial side - offices, shops, any workplace really. These days all you needed was a laptop and a WiFi connection and you could work anywhere. Her employer was progressive enough to recognise that keeping a mother sweet made good business sense and Marianne's conscientiousness ensured they got best value out of her by letting her devise her own work patterns. She was a valued employee. A little less so lately. The reduction in her efficiency over the last few weeks of the year had been noted and would be raised at her next appraisal. Nothing too serious, but it needed watching.

Marianne's husband worked in a hardware store. His income was significantly lower than hers but he made up for that by doing significantly more than his fair share of the spending of their combined income. He was out most nights (apart from Thursdays). Marianne didn't know where he went and didn't much care. He wasn't a violent man but he was an oaf. That was the word Marianne used. He was lazy, selfish and vulgar. He had no ambition, no interests beyond football and drinking (and probably sexual exploits: she had suspicions but lacked the energy or inclination to seek out conclusive proof). He had no redeeming attributes, unless you counted his height, his stature and his chiselled features and these had long ceased to work any magic on Marianne. When she'd first encountered him he'd stood out, a handsome man dominating the group he hung around with, and Marianne had been smitten. She was sure he'd have hidden depths which she would delight in discovering. He didn't. What you saw was what you got. He looked like an oaf, despite (or perhaps because of) his film-star features. He behaved like an oaf. He was an oaf.

Marianne didn't love her husband any more, if she ever had. But she did love Dave. She was certain of that even though she hadn't told him yet. Nor had he said it to her, but he'd showed his love in so many ways: 'It's in his kiss,' as the old song had it. After the drought of the festive season, Thursday evenings became an even more central feature of Marianne's life.

She sometimes wondered how she'd respond if Dave tried to take things further, to turn their affair into some sort of official pairing. What would she say? She'd have to tell him she was married, of course. That would probably put him off. Even if it didn't, Marianne couldn't imagine leaving her husband. No, it had nothing to do with any residue of feeling for that oaf, it was her love for her son that was the problem. At the moment Bertie had a stable life. He had a mother and a father and not all children are so lucky these days. His father, for all his faults, took him to the park to play football, to fly kites, to climb trees. Marianne helped him with his letters, cuddled him when he was hurt or sad, read him stories. Okay, it was crude old-fashioned gender stereotyping, but it worked. Even if her husband would give her a divorce (which was by no means certain, he could be an awkward cuss when it suited him), she wasn't going to ask him. In any case, would Dave be prepared to step up to the mark, to step in as a step-father? Marianne thought it unlikely. He didn't seem that sort of man, a family man. He was a lover. That's the relationship they had. They had an affair. They met on Thursdays and fucked. End of.

In any case, there was no sign of Dave wanting the relationship to change, to progress, to develop. He was as committed as she was to their Thursdays. He often texted her during the week, although his texts were always brief: 'Last night was awesome'; 'Missing you'; 'Can't wait.' She replied in similar fashion. But that was all. So there was no need to think beyond that: that was enough for Dave, and that was enough for Marianne. She enjoyed it for what it was, made the most of it, and was not interested in adding complications. She was having the time of her life. 'Don't mess it up,' she told herself. She pushed all thoughts of the future to the back of her mind. Enjoy the moment. Thursdays came and Thursdays went and Marianne's life was as perfect as it could possibly be. So long as she didn't do or say anything silly, everything would be fine, nothing would change.

But, of course, things did change, as they always do. She might have guessed they would. Happiness did not come naturally to Marianne as events of her past illustrated only too well.

February mornings can shimmer with promise. Promise that the dark days of winter are gone and lightness is emerging. This Saturday morning was like that. Blue sky, bright sunshine and bristling with potential. The 'promise' angle didn't concern Marianne: she didn't need to be optimistic about the future because the good times were already here. But she could still enjoy the day for what it was. It would be chilly out, so they wrapped up warm: overcoats, scarves, gloves and hoods. Bertie's father was still in bed (he'd come in late the night before). So Marianne had decided to take over weekend duties and mother and son set off together for park and playground. Marianne felt happy, light-hearted and wanted to share her pleasure with Bertie. They ran and danced a bit. Sang a silly song that Bertie had learned at playgroup. Changed the words to make them funnier. Laughed together. They entered the park and took the diagonal path towards the playground area, hand-in-hand, still singing, still laughing.

The park was practically deserted: a couple of dog-walkers, a slow, well-muffled jogger. And one man in the playground. Marianne recognised him as soon as she entered the park, the curly hair, the broad shoulders, the shape of his body, the multi-coloured scarf. She was about to run across to him, joy welling up in her heart. But something wasn't right; she hesitated. She squatted down by the railings, pretending to adjust Bertie's collar and hat. She pulled her hood up but looked sideways towards Dave.

He was standing at the bottom of the slide, gesticulating and shouting. She was too far away to catch his words. She could see a young girl sitting at the top of the slide, shaking her head, smiling. Then, with a squeal, the girl let go and whooshed down the slide. Dave snatched her up, swirled her (still giggling) in a wide arc, sat her on his shoulders and trotted off towards the gate. He put the girl into a pushchair. Strapped her in. He spoke to the woman standing there. They kissed briefly. He put his arm around her waist. The two of them pushed the buggy towards the far exit. They walked out of the park. Disappeared from view.

'Change of plan, Bertie.' Marianne grabbed her son's hand and marched him back the way they'd come. The boy protested. Marianne did her best to placate him but stayed focused on getting home as quickly as she could.

Her husband was up. In a loose-fitting dressing gown, he was leaning against the frame of the open back door, a coffee mug in one hand, a cigarette in the other.

'No smoking in the house,' yelled Marianne. 'How many times?'

'I'm outside.' The man stretched the hand with the cigarette through the doorway.

'Bertie wants to build that airplane he got for Christmas.'

'Can we, can we?' begged Bertie, running up to the man and tugging at the cord of his dressing gown. 'Please Daddy, can we?'

'I've got to go,' said Marianne. 'To see someone.'

Marianne gets into the car and drives up to the top of Finedon Hill, parks in a lay-by, gets out of the car and leans back against the bonnet. The area is deserted. The sun carries no heat but it casts a shimmering luminescence across the hilltop. Down in the valley, swirls of mist linger. Marianne breathes deeply. She closes her eyes. She feels tears seep out and begin to roll down her cheeks. Then she cries for real, lung-busting sobs that seem to come from her innermost core. She crouches down by the car, her head in her hands and cries and cries and cries.

Eventually the sobs subside. Marianne opens the car door and finds a box of tissues in the glove compartment. Wipes her eyes, her face, blows her nose. She wishes she could clean her mind as easily: her mind's a mess. It's full of random emotions but no connecting logic: hatred, love, grief, jealousy, hurt, resentment, anger, pain, sadness, hatred, love, anger, anger, anger. Then, bit by bit, her thoughts organise themselves into greater coherence, condense into questions: How could he? Why did he? What am I going to do?

Marianne has had more than her fair share of anguish in her life, so what is another catastrophe? She can cope; she will survive. Her half hour on Finedon Hill is the worst. The next 24 hours are still pretty bad as she stumbles through a day displaying normality on the outside while hiding turmoil on the inside and aches through a sleepless night. Then it gets easier. She is still suffering. She is still angry. She still has questions with no answers. But she is determined to cope.

In a period of clarity she tried to weigh things up. She had a husband who she hadn't mentioned to Dave. He had a ... wife was she? Partner? Whatever. He hadn't mentioned this person to her. So that made them even, didn't it? No, no and no again. Marianne's marriage was sterile, paper-thin, a thing of no consequence. Not worth mentioning. But Dave's, Dave's marriage if that was what it was, was another thing entirely. From the kiss, the exchanged glances and the gestures she'd observed, his was a loving, caring, rich relationship. Which meant that she, Marianne, as far as Dave was concerned, was nothing but an addendum, an extra. A casual bit of fun. He must feel nothing for her. She cried again. It didn't take much. That week she cried a lot.

It was Thursday again and she sat opposite Dave in The Black Horse, staring at her white wine spritzer as he sipped his half-pint of lager.

'You okay, M?'

'Sure.'

A pause. 'Only.' Another pause. 'You don't seem as ... you know.'

'I'm fine.'

A longer pause. 'Having a hard time at work?'

No response.

'Are you sickening for something? You look a little pale.'

No response.

'We don't have to ... you know. If you don't want to. We could just ...'

A few minutes later they drove to a secluded spot. They clambered over onto the back seat. They adjusted their clothing. They fucked.

Afterwards, as usual, Marianne's thoughts revisited the events of the evening. She hadn't known what she was going to do. She'd rehearsed several scenarios. She might have asked him directly: was he married? She might have told him she'd seen them, in the park. Asked who the woman was, demanded an explanation. She might have slapped him: a bit melodramatic but she was sure it would have felt good. She had done none of those things. And they'd ended up going somewhere quiet and making love. As usual. It was the same as it always was, nothing had changed. They were two people in love. She did mean something to him; all that loving couldn't be faked.

Then again, it was also quite different. Everything had changed. Because now she knew about him, she knew who he was, she knew about the part of his life he'd kept secret. She knew about her, his 'other half'. And his daughter. He didn't know that she knew. Not yet. That made a difference. That meant she had the power, she was the master. Or rather, she was the mistress. The tears pricked at her eyes and she fought them back. After the week of misery, that week of darkness, she glimpsed some light and she was determined to hold on to it. She could decide their fate. His fate. The future was in her hands. She could pay him back. Revenge and retribution figured prominently in her thoughts. As well as love.

Marianne had scanned Dave's *Facebook* timeline before, but now she returned to it with a different mindset. She scrutinised every detail, every 'share', every 'like', looking for something she could use. She wasn't sure what, but she'd know it when she found it. But there was nothing worth finding. He had a few friends who seemed to be work colleagues. A small number of old Uni friends and an even smaller number of ex-school friends, some of whom she recognised by name even if the faces looked unfamiliar. She found a link to someone called Sally Walker and her heart flipped, but this woman lived a hundred and twenty miles away and had a husband with a beard and three teenage children. Marianne eventually figured out she was Dave's older sister, using her maiden name on *Facebook* like some women do. So there was no wife. No partner. Dave's professed status was 'single'. Just goes to show how much of social media is fiction.

Marianne moved on to the wider web, but a *Google* search proved fruitless. There were too many Dave Walkers in the world. She tried to narrow down the search, using age, profession, geographical location; none of it helped. Her Dave Walker was either hiding in the same way as one tree can hide in a forest, or he'd managed to avoid leaving any e-footprints. Either way, she was none the wiser. She needed to find this woman, this wife-stroke-partner. Marianne didn't even know where Dave lived. They'd exchanged location information over their first drinks but all she could remember were vague phrases – he lived 'near the industrial estate,' 'one of those old houses,' 'over the far side.' She'd nodded as if she'd got it, but she hadn't. She didn't know that side of town at all. But if they lived over there, it didn't make any sense for them to drive all the way over here to Jubilee Park. There had to be somewhere nearer they could have gone. Marianne's local park is okay, but would hardly warrant a trek from the other side of town. When the couple had left the park, had they looked like they were heading to a car? How could you tell?

Most mornings now, after dropping Bertie at pre-school, Marianne walked to the park. She wandered around, hoping to catch a glimpse of Dave's wife. She stood by the railings where she'd seen her before. It's the only link she had: they'd brought their daughter here, whether or not they'd driven hardly mattered. She wasn't even sure she'd recognise the woman if she saw her. She'd only seen her from the back and there had been nothing distinctive about her: slim build, average height, shoulder-length brown hair. The daughter had been more distinctive. Long blonde hair. Fresh, smiley face. And that squeal. More like a screech. How old was she? No more than 3 or 4.

About Bertie's age. Marianne gave a small involuntary gasp and her heart quickened. Yes, it was possible. Of course it was. Why hadn't it occurred to her before? Maybe, just maybe, Dave's daughter went to *All Smiles*, Bertie's playgroup. If they lived close enough to use Jubilee Park it would make sense.

Marianne had found *All Smiles* through the internet: it was close by and had good reports, no negative comments she could find, and Bertie was the right age for their intake. Once Bertie had settled in, Marianne fell into a habit of dropping him off and picking him up as speedily as possible. She didn't talk to other mums or their children, she barely acknowledged the helpers. It was simply a necessary chore, not deserving of more than minimal attention.

But on this day she arrived at the hall a good ten minutes before pick-up time. Feeling somewhat self-conscious, she stood by the door and tried to look casual. She spotted Bertie on the far side, playing with some trucks. She nodded to the assistant who was with him and got a smile in return; she couldn't remember the woman's name. She cast her eye around the room. There were plenty of girls, most of the right age. Some had blonde hair. Any of them could be Dave's daughter. Then she heard the squeal. More like a screech really. She jerked her head around to the left. Long blonde hair. About Bertie's age. Pretty. That squeal again. Yes, it was her. No mistake.

Marianne lingered after most of the children had been collected, determined to be there when the girl's mother came in. But it was over in a moment. The woman came barely halfway through the door, reached for the girl's hand and they were gone. A woman of average height, wrapped up in a thick coat, gloves, scarf, like all the other mums: winter was still biting hard. The adjectives that occurred to Marianne were not flattering: drab, homely, frumpy. It was the briefest of sightings. But one thing Marianne now knew: the daughter's name was Daisy. 'Come on Daisy.' That's what the woman had said. In a plain voice. Common, coarse.

Marianne's life has an added embellishment, another one. She's still married to an oaf, still a mother to a gorgeous little boy, still an Interior Decorator by profession and a passionate lover every Thursday evening. Now she also has a friend, a friend called Lindsey.

The third time Marianne saw the woman that she later knew as Lindsey she was standing right beside her, near the door of the playgroup hall. As luck would have it, Bertie and Daisy were playing together in the sandpit.

'Don't they play nicely together?' Marianne had said.

Lindsey had reacted like a scalded cat, fir bristling, ready to spit. 'What?' she spat, loud and vicious, turning abruptly into Marianne's face, a scowl on her lips.

Marianne flinched backwards, but looked towards the children and tried to put on a smile.

Lindsey's face turned to follow Marianne's gaze. 'Oh,' she said, more softly. 'Yes. I see.' A hesitation, then: 'He's yours, is he?'

Since that rather unpromising beginning, Lindsey and Marianne had struck up an unlikely friendship.

Marianne hadn't even had to try: it was Lindsey who made the running. All Marianne had to do was turn up early at drop-off and pick-up times and Lindsey sought her out, engaged her in conversation. Marianne's first impression of Lindsey had been off the mark: she was calm and generous, a caring woman with a wicked sense of humour. The two of them exchanged information about their children. What Bertie was into, what Daisy was into, favourite TV characters, how many teeth they had, what they would and wouldn't eat, what great strides Daisy was making with her reading, how Bertie loved to draw. Then they discussed the other children, the helpers, *All Smiles* in general, the hall where the group met. They talked about the usual things. They talked like friends. And, within a few weeks, friends is what they became.

'Do you want to go for a coffee?' It was Lindsey who suggested it, that sunny spring Tuesday after they'd dropped off the children at *All Smiles* and were standing by the gate, about to go their separate ways. Marianne had nothing to get back for. Her latest work project was a long-term thing, the deadline weeks ahead. No rush. So why not?

They went to *Café Olé*, which was less posh than it sounded, situated on Conway Street, about halfway between Marianne's house and the playgroup hall. The premises were small and the proprietor tried to squeeze customers in by using small tables and leaving little space between them. At peak times it was claustrophobic, but Tuesday morning was not a peak time. Marianne and Lindsey had a choice of tables and settled for one in a corner, Marianne sitting against the wall, Lindsey opposite her. It became their regular location for cappuccinos and walnut cake. Away from the playgroup setting, their conversations spread more widely.

'So have you always wanted to be an Interior Designer,' asked Lindsey.

Marianne rolled her eyes and puffed her cheeks. 'It's a long story.'

'I'm not going anywhere.'

Marianne found Lindsey easy to talk to. In bits and pieces over the weeks, Marianne told Lindsey the story of her life. Most of what she said was true, although there were also a lot of true things she chose not to mention. As a girl she'd had such a passion for drawing and painting, she'd dreamed of being a famous artist: portraits, landscapes, abstract op-art, she'd been prepared to tackle any style. A succession of teachers told her she was good, encouraged her to enter competitions, and sometimes she figured in the prize lists. But as she got older, reality set in. Marianne blamed her parents for denying her the freedom to give full rein to her talents. Her sights gradually lowered, step-by-step. An illustrator was a more realistic aspiration, her parents said, children's books, or maybe novel covers. But nothing came of that either – it's a highly competitive business. Then the advertising world – advertisers always want artistic designers, don't they? Maybe they did, but they didn't want Marianne. Another potential career track led only to impenetrable buffers. Marianne relayed to Lindsey each step of her journey, how it felt, the way the optimism turned to disappointment then to misery, and the other woman listened with genuine understanding and sympathy.

'But you've done alright,' said Lindsey. 'It worked out in the end, didn't it? You've got a good job now.'

'A trained monkey could do what I do.

'I'm sure that's not so. You shouldn't run yourself down.'

'Well, I'll tell you this. It won't be long before some half decent computer takes over my job. Mark my words, if they can drive cars … No, it's all been a waste, a total waste. All that supposed talent, that 'flair' they said I had. Where did it go? Where has my life gone?'

Lindsey was the fourth person Marianne had been this frank with. Her parents knew the story but had their own perspective: no sympathy emanated from that direction. Her husband didn't understand: so long as she picked up decent money, what was the point of worrying about what she had to do to get it? Any concept of job-satisfaction was beyond his grasp. Lindsey was the first to truly get it.

On other Tuesdays, Marianne explained how, after a succession of disastrous boyfriends, she'd met her future husband and thought he was the love of her life. How quickly the marriage had turned sour as his oafishness became increasingly apparent. Marianne found Lindsey's sympathetic ear a great comfort. There were other men she could have mentioned, but didn't. She also didn't mention the man who linked them together. She didn't tell her how, now in her mid-thirties, she'd recently met up with an old love from her schooldays and how this had brought her such glorious and unexpected happiness.

Marianne wasn't the only talker on those Tuesday mornings, and Lindsey wasn't the only listener. As often as not the roles were reversed.

'Listen to me, prattling on like an old woman,' said Marianne, one time. 'What am I like?'

'I don't mind. It's good to get things off your chest.'

'But what about you? How did Lindsey, mother of Daisy, come to be here?' Marianne had spread her hands, encompassing the café, the town, this time of their lives.

Lindsey's story was even sadder than Marianne's. The picture she painted was of an eternal victim. She'd been, in her own words, a 'fat, spotty, specky' child. She was the youngest of three sisters, five years younger than the next oldest, and always, in various ways, the scapegoat of the family. She did all the fetching and carrying, the cleaning and the washing. Her parents favoured her older, prettier siblings in every way. They could do no wrong. Anything amiss and it was always Lindsey's fault. It made her feel worthless, of no value, left her with no self-esteem. School was even worse. She was always the butt of the jokes and the bullying, so much so that she got used to it, thought that was the way things were supposed to be. She learned to ride the punches, to suffer the humiliations in silence, to allow them to do their worst and act like she didn't care. She only cried when she was alone in her bed. She knew she should have done more to stick up for herself; she felt ashamed of her passivity; guilty.

'I'm only glad we didn't have social media back then. It was bad enough but the things you read about these days.' She shook her head and sipped her coffee. 'I worry about how Daisy might suffer when she's older.'

'I think it's okay if parents keep an eye on things. Provide guidance and advice. Support. You need to keep talking to them, understand their world, make them realise they're not having to deal with things on their own.'

'I hope so. I'll certainly do my best. And then there's boyfriends. I dread the time when Daisy gets into all that.'

When classmates started getting into boys, Lindsey had received further taunting as the last girl anyone would fancy. It was true: all the boys either teased her or ignored her. Then one of them realised how grateful she would be to be asked out, and, being desperate himself, took advantage of that fact. He soon spread the word and Lindsey acquired a kind of popularity. But she was popular for all the wrong reasons. Popular because she was easy to manipulate, willing and eager, because she was still playing the role of victim. She found a way to hang on to a boy, or thought she did. She was wrong. Her willingness made her even more popular for a while, but then they all wanted her for one thing only. Her sluttish ways made her even more an object for ridicule and gossip, a social outcast.

'I couldn't wait to leave school,' said Lindsey. 'I was sure that would be the end of my problems. But it wasn't.'

'Oh dear, Lindsey, poor you.' The sympathetic look on Marianne's face was genuine. 'What happened?'

Lindsey's mum had got her a job in an office, but office life proved to be just a continuation of school: the women continued to bully her, the men continued to take advantage of her. She didn't have the qualifications to get a better job.

'You feel trapped, don't you? I know the feeling. Your hopes and dreams slip away like water through your fingers. You can't see any way out of it. It's so hard.'

'Then I met Dave,' said Lindsey. Her face lit up.

At the mention of Dave, Marianne's stomach lurched. She kept her face impassive. Took a large bite of cake.

'I thought he'd be like the rest and I nearly turned him down when he asked me out. But he smiled that wonderful smile and I thought I'd give it a go. The best thing that ever happened to me. Marrying him. And having Daisy, of course.'

Marianne knew about the smile. She recognised Lindsey's ecstasy. She put her empty coffee cup to her lips, to hide the jealousy which she felt sure was spread all over her face.

Lindsey's description of her life with Dave and Daisy sounded wonderful. But it was at this point, when it came up to the present day, that Lindsey's tale faltered. Marianne could tell. Lindsey would take out her phone and scroll through her album. Show Marianne pictures of Daisy as a baby. Then one of her a bit older, in the sea on holiday in Ibiza. More pictures of a family Christmas. Pictures of Dave with Daisy, a selfie with the three of them. But there was a catch in her voice, a trace of sadness in her eyes. The smile was still there, but Marianne was sure Lindsey was hiding something. She took pleasure in recognising that her life with Dave was not perfect; yet she still felt sorry for her friend.

Marianne never needed to remind herself that Lindsey was Dave's wife, but no longer was that all she was. She was a friend, a good friend. Marianne looked forward to their Tuesday mornings of coffee and cake. One time when Lindsey had to cancel – she'd had a fall or something, needed some medical attention – Marianne had been really disappointed. Tuesdays had become a big part of her week. Almost as important as Thursdays. Her friendship with Lindsey hadn't changed her love for Dave. She was still meeting him every Thursday evening, still making love to him, still playing the part of the amorous mistress. Not playing a part, no. *Being* that part. She didn't need to fake her feelings for Dave. She loved him as much as ever. She knew who he was, how he'd deceived her, but it made no difference. When she was with him he made her feel alive.

But having his wife as a friend confused things. Why had she wanted to meet Dave's wife? Hadn't she had some sort of revenge in mind? Some idea of hurting him, of paying him back? Or had she meant to break up the marriage so she could have Dave for herself? She wasn't sure. She couldn't remember. None of it made sense any more. She found it impossible to think of Lindsey as a rival. She cared about Lindsey, wanted to care *for* her. If there was trouble in Lindsey's life, in her marriage, she wanted to comfort her, help her sort it out, no way did she want to exploit that trouble by running off with her husband. Yet running off with Dave was still a dream that made her heart soar. Marianne was confused and was about to become more confused.

She couldn't pinpoint the occasion when her friendship with Lindsey changed. When it began to change. It was well into the summer months. Marianne loved the warm weather and liked to discard her jeans and wear a skirt with bare legs whenever she could. On Thursday evenings she took to wearing a tee-shirt and her pleated green skirt with sandals. Sometimes she'd risk wearing stockings, hoping her husband wouldn't notice. Dave liked her in stockings. During the day she preferred to wear button-through knee-length dresses, sleeveless. She had several. She generally wore one on Tuesdays. It matched the carefree mood of those mornings.

Every Tuesday morning in the *Café Olé* Lindsey and Marianne continued to drink coffee and eat cake. Having shared their life stories, they sometimes had serious conversations about the world and its troubles, but more likely they'd laugh together over some perceived absurdity. They had a similar sense of humour. A customer with a funny hat; a misprint on the menu; a couple outside the window, arguing and gesticulating wildly: it didn't take much to set them off. They sat at their corner table, Marianne against the wall, looking out, Lindsey opposite her. Lindsey sometimes wore dark glasses: she had trouble with her eyes. The table was small and there was not a lot of room. It was not surprising that their feet occasionally bumped into each other under the table. So Marianne scarcely noticed the first time it happened, what she thought afterwards might have been the first time. It wasn't until the following week that Marianne became properly conscious of the action, when she felt Lindsey's bare foot laying across her own. She sharply drew her foot back, embarrassed. Then wondered why she'd done that, why that had been her reaction. Another week later and the two of them were sharing a humorous tale as they often did. Daisy had come up with one of those phrases, like kids pick up not really knowing what they mean, and then tried to use it but got it wrong: it was so cute. Marianne remembered Bertie doing something similar. She felt again the other woman's foot on top of her own. This time she left her own foot there, she didn't pull back. And Lindsey's foot moved onto her ankle. There was no doubt now. This was definite stroking. Marianne looked at Lindsey. She had taken out her phone, was checking messages, texting short replies. She seemed oblivious to what was occurring under the table. As each week passed, the stroking became more obvious and more daring. Marianne was amazed to find she was actually welcoming the contact, looking forward to it and speculating on how far the foot would progress. The foot stroked her shin, the toes snaking around her calf; then it reached her knee; then it ventured above her knee, creeping along her inner thigh. It was at this point that Marianne put her hand down and placed it over the bare foot. Lindsey looked up from her phone. The two gazed at each other. Now it was in the open.

Lindsey spoke in a voice far huskier than usual. 'Do you want to come back to mine?'

Marianne found out several things during those warm summer weeks. She found out that where Dave lived (a large house he shared with his wife Lindsey and daughter Daisy) was only a few streets from her own home, not on the other side of town at all. She confirmed that, as she suspected, there was no mother (ill or otherwise) living in Dave's home. She found out that Dave probably shared a bed with his wife although she couldn't be certain as she had other things on her mind whenever she was in the family bedroom. That's where she discovered that a woman can please another woman in ways a man never can. During these weeks, she was amazed to find out how many hours it was possible to spend staring at a computer with your thoughts flying wildly as the work piles up, the deadlines pass, the increasingly urgent demands of your employer go unresponded to. She was amazed at how blissful such a state could be.

Marianne tried hard not to analyse her situation; indeed it seemed beyond analysis. She didn't know how it had happened. When she looked back she saw her life had been in freefall since the first meeting with Dave. No, freefall was not the word. What was the opposite, not down but up? A life ascending? Whichever direction it was going, it was out of Marianne's control. Every Thursday evening she made love with Dave, Lindsey's husband. Every Tuesday morning she made love with Lindsey, Dave's wife. In between those times she continued to share a house, if not much else, with her lump of a husband, trying not to think about what Dave and Lindsey might be doing with each other when she wasn't there. She didn't ask them, either of them: she didn't dare. Nor did she compare the husband with the wife, or the wife with the husband. They were different. She enjoyed everything about each of them. She loved them both. She loved the strength and the hardness and the roughness of the husband; she loved the gentleness and the softness and the smoothness of the wife. She should have been in turmoil. She was not. Instead she was in ecstasy, on a permanent high: the high of sexual excitement, followed by the high of glorious aftermath, and then the heavenly high of anticipation as she waited for it all to begin again. Her life was blithe and breezy, wonderfully fulfilling, what did it matter that it was full of lies? Every word she uttered, whether to Dave or to Lindsey or to her husband, had to be chosen with care, chosen to create an impression of veracity however distant it was from the real truth, chosen to preserve the edifice of deceit that supported her world. She had no idea how long this could last, how things might work out, what would happen eventually. She didn't know and she didn't care. The future could look after itself. The present was everything. It was sufficient, more than sufficient: she wouldn't have been able to cope with more; her mind was full, her senses were full, her whole being was full. Overbrimming and splendid and brilliant. A world no amount of scaffolding could support.

'Do you want to come back to my place?'

By now Marianne and Dave's weekly assignations do not involve much conversation, apart from the words that accompany the actions, the whispered endearments that go with their backseat activities. Dave's invitation comes as a shock. What can Marianne say?

'What about your mother?' She hasn't revealed to Dave any of the information she's learned through her involvement with Lindsey: yet another ingredient in the fabricated web.

'She's gone away for a few days. Her brother's ill. They used to be close.'

Marianne admires the glibness with which the words slip from his lips. More lies. She doesn't hold it against him. You do what you have to do. We all do. She knows that.

'Okay then.' The double-thinking clicks into place: 'Is it far?'

'No, no. A few minutes. Let's take my car. I'll drop you back here afterwards.'

'Okay.' Marianne picks up her bag and follows Dave out of the bar. Something's not right here. She knows that. Why this sudden change? But what choice does she have? One false step and it all dissolves, this fragile existence, this delicate structure.

Dave stops the car in his driveway. Marianne tries to say the right things. 'Nice house. Big for just the two of you.'

'It used to be our family home. When we were little. You need a big house with four kids. By the time we were teenagers it didn't seem so big.' More lies? Probably. But

Marianne doesn't have time to ponder on them. Dave unlocks the front door and walks through. Marianne follows him and waits in the hall as he closes the door behind her. It's all so familiar to her. The striped wallpaper. The subdued lighting. The glimpse through to the bright, white kitchen ahead. The stairs leading up to the bedroom. The bedroom, the bedroom.

'I'll lead the way,' says Dave, taking the right door into the living room. Marianne's heart is beating fast. It's wrong, it's all wrong. She's trembling, trying hard to control her body. Her stomach is bubbling, she feels sick. She continues to try to look at her surroundings as though for the first time. Tries hard to maintain the pretence. Tries hard to hold everything together, her world, her life. It's hard, too hard. As she follows Dave into the room, her hand goes to her mouth and she can't hold back the gasp that comes from her lips. Lindsey is there. She is sitting on the edge of the armchair. As Marianne catches her eye, the other woman mouths something. It could be 'Sorry'. Or it could be 'Gotcha.'

Dave stands with his back to the TV screen that dominates one wall of the room. He stares at Marianne. There is a flicker of a smile on his lips. Presumably he is trying to judge Marianne's reaction. Marianne tries hard not to react in any way. She shouldn't be here. She doesn't want to be here. She can't cope with Dave and Lindsey together. They don't belong together, sharing the same space. She loves them both, separately. Now she sees them together and that love is seeping away. A bizarre memory comes into Marianne's mind, from a chemistry lesson years ago. Two chemicals. Both benign, inert. Then they come together. Devastating explosion occurs.

'Marianne,' says Dave, speaking very deliberately, stressing each syllable. 'I believe you know Lindsey.' A long pause. 'My wife.'

'I should go,' says Marianne, turning towards the door. Her brain can't assimilate this. What's going on?

'Oh no,' says Dave, quickly placing his body between Marianne and her exit.

His voice and his manner are different, so different. Menacing, sinister, full of threat. Marianne hardly recognises the man she has loved for all these months. Where is the caring Dave, the tender and loving Dave? This Dave is more like the stroppy teenager she used to know years ago. Strutting and arrogant. Aggressive. Relishing the power.

'No, Marianne. That's not what's going to happen.' He's still speaking slowly, commanding, dominating. Still smiling. He stares up to the corner of the ceiling. He always does that when he's trying to come to a decision.

Marianne takes her phone out of her bag and clicks on the speed-dial setting.

Before she can activate it, Dave has taken the two steps to her side and snatched the phone away. 'I don't think so,' says Dave. 'No-one wants to hear what you have to say.' He speaks sternly, but quickly the smile returns to his lips. 'Apart from us, that is, me and Lindsey. We want you to talk to us. Don't we, Lindsey?'

The woman on the sofa does not respond.

'And you're going to keep us company for a while. Perhaps a message to your husband is in order, to keep him from worrying.' He thumbs a quick text into her phone.

So he knows about her husband. How long has he known? What else does he know?

'Give me that,' says Marianne, making a grab for the phone.

Dave easily side-steps.

Marianne stands back. She's shaking. She feels the tears welling up in her eyes. Her heart's beating like it's trying to break out of her chest. What's going on here? 'What do you want from me? Why are you being like this?'

'I think you know that, Marianne. You're such a clever girl.' He glances at Lindsey and then looks back to Marianne. 'We've been waiting for you Marianne. Haven't we Lindsey? Waiting a long time. Preparing. We've got everything ready for you. We had the attic converted. It's real cosy up there. You'll love it. Everything you could possibly want. Do you want to see it?' He holds out his hand.

'No,' says Marianne. She can hardly get the word out. She shakes her head and takes a step back. 'No way. Let me go.' She tires to sound strong but knows she sounds weak. 'You have to let me go.' She thinks frantically. 'Bertie, my son ...'

'He'll be fine,' says Dave. A smooth, soothing voice. False. 'It's all taken care of. All you have to think about is yourself, Marianne. And we're here to help you do that, to take care of you. You're going to love it here.' And the smile returns. A wide smile, a grin, but totally devoid of humour.

It's the smile, that smile she always thought of as boyish, the smile that now looks more like an ominous sneer, a cruel slash across an ugly malevolent face, it is that smile that draws the choking vomit into Marianne's mouth.

\* \* \* \* \*

Edward Stephens sipped from a mug of tea. He was sitting at the kitchen table, enjoying a few moments of peace after a hard day at work. Every day at work is hard.

Irritated, he stubbed out his cigarette in a saucer. He hadn't wanted to be disturbed, but the ringing of the doorbell was persistent.

He opened the door to two uniformed policewomen.

'Mr Stephens? Mr Edward Stephens?' Edward nodded.

'May we come in?'

'Of course.' Edward stood aside, allowing the policewomen to enter his hallway where they waited as he closed the door. 'Go on through,' he said, indicating the door to the left. Edward followed them into the small, rather cluttered front room. Not real policewomen, he registered. PCSOs.

'Robert,' he commanded.

A boy in school uniform, sitting on the floor in front of a television screen, looked up.

'Homework.'

The boy stood up with obvious reluctance, slouched out of the room, picked up a rucksack from the hallway and stumped upstairs.

'Please,' said Edward, indicating the settee.

The policewomen sat side-by-side on the edge of the settee.

Edward used the remote to switch off the TV, brought an upright chair from the table and sat down opposite them. 'What can I do for you?'

'Mr Stephens. We'll come straight to the point. We've found your wife.'

Edward looked bemused.

The younger woman consulted a tablet she was holding in her hand. They don't seem to use notebooks these days. 'Marianne. Marianne Stephens.'

The man raised his eyebrows and gave half a shrug.

'That is your wife's name, isn't it? Marianne?'

After a pause the man responded. 'Well, yes. I suppose so.' Another pause. He still looked puzzled. 'This is all very confusing. I don't understand.'

'Why's that, Mr Stephens?'

The other woman took over. 'We've found Mrs Stephens … When I say 'we', one of our officers. He found her …' The policewoman appeared to be trying to choose her words carefully. 'In Jubilee Park.' She pointed in a rather vague way towards the window.

'Yes, yes.' Edward shook his head. 'I know where the park is.'

'She was …' Still that cautious selection of words. She consulted her screen, flicked her finger across it. 'The officer who found her used the term 'dishevelled.' He also said she was 'in a state'. She'd been reported to us, you see, as being a vagrant, drunk in a public place, but the officer couldn't smell any alcohol on her. Even so, she wasn't acting …' She checked her screen again. 'Like you would expect a woman her age to act.'

The first woman took over again. 'We don't think there's too much cause for concern. Long term. At least as regards her physical condition. There are some minor injuries. Some evidence of … an accident, maybe? She's weak, disoriented, confused. Possibly in need of a good meal. It seems she's experienced a … a trauma of some kind. We couldn't get much sense out of her. They've taken her to the Princess Alice. I expect they'll run some tests. See how she is after a bit of rest and some TLC. It's her mind that's more of a problem. Has she ever suffered any form of … mental illness, Mr Stephens?'

'This is all very confusing.' Edward ran his hand through his sparse hair. Shook his head. 'I still don't get why you've come here.'

'Let me get this straight, sir. Mrs Stephens, Marianne Stephens, she does live here, doesn't she? We found her ….' She checked on her tablet. 'I think they identified her from her driving licence. This address ….'

'No,' said Edward. 'That's the point. She doesn't live here.'

'But she is your wife?'

'Well, yes. Technically. We never divorced. But me and Penny … She'll be back soon. Penny lives here with me … We're not strictly man and wife, but as if.'

'So Marianne …?' It was the policewomen's turn to look confused. They'd come here expecting one sort of visit, to make an announcement which they'd assumed would come as good news. To ask a few routine questions. But it was turning into something else entirely.

'Let me explain.'

'Please do.'

'Marianne … I received a text from her, from Marianne. My wife. Out of the blue, it was. I'd no idea. Anyway, that's beside the point. This text, it said something like… I'll not remember the exact words, but this is the gist. 'I'm leaving you. Don't try and find me.''

'So your wife, Marianne, has left you?

'Yes. I assumed so. I did think it was a bit odd.'

The younger woman raised her eyebrows, encouraging.

'She didn't take any clothes, see. So I thought she'd be back. If only to pick up her things. And perhaps she'd explain. Perhaps we could talk about it. She was so fond of Robert. But she didn't.' Almost as an afterthought he added: 'Her car was gone.' Another pause. 'And a few days later her work phoned. They'd not heard from her. I got the feeling they weren't happy about her. The guy said something about her jumping before she was pushed.'

'Can you tell me, Mr Stephens. When was this? When did Marianne leave you?'

'Oh, it was ages. Robert was little. Must be ten years. At least. That's why it seems so strange, you coming here. I haven't seen hide nor hair of Marianne for ten years or more.'

Marianne is confused and tired and her body feels frail. She doesn't remember anything. She feels as though she's in a state of limbo. Pictures dance in front of her eyes, like frames from a film. Nothing makes sense. It's all blurred. Is this what dying is like? She doesn't remember her husband. She used to have a husband. She thinks. But she can't put a face to him, or a name. She remembers her son, Bertie. But some man who claimed to be her husband paraded some snotty teenager in front of her and said he was her son. Didn't look anything like. So what was that all about? What is anything about? Are they lying to her, trying to trick her? Why?

They keep using the word 'escape'. How did she escape? Escape from where? It makes it sound like she was in prison. She doesn't remember being in prison. Not before. Now, yes. It's here that's like a prison. They won't let her go anywhere, she's not even allowed to get out of bed. This is the prison she'd like to escape from.

So many questions. All they do is ask questions. The questions themselves are idiotic, so how on earth do they think she might be able to answer them? What happened to her? Where has she been? Who was she with? How did she get the bruises? The scars? That's the sort of thing they ask. And what did they do to her, what did they do, what did they do? Over and over again. Different people but always the same questions. Who's this 'they' they're always on about? Anyone. No-one. It's all a blur. There's no point asking her questions like that. She doesn't know. She's tried to tell them. She can't remember. She can't remember anything. She's so tired.

She remembers Bertie. Sweet, sweet, Bertie. Her son. And that other boy. Older. A teenager. No, not the one they dragged in front of her, all sulky and miserable. The boy she means was smiley, always smiley. He had crinkly hair and crinkly eyes and a lovely smile. Why don't they bring him here? She'd like to see him again. He was good to her. He'd save her. He'd get her out of here, out of this prison. He'd tell her what's what, make everything right. He wouldn't ask her ridiculous questions. He'd take her home.

# A Lesson in Go

'I should have connected,' I say, waving a vague hand across the now empty board.

He nods.

'I let you get too much territory over there.'

He nods.

'Then I blundered in the endgame.'

He nods.

It's getting late and we are the only players left in the dusty, dimly-lit hall. The old man opposite me is hunched over the board wrapped in his black jacket, a hood like a cowl over his head masking most of his face, his pointed nose and chin just visible. His breaths come as wheezes. He coughs intermittently, his shoulders shaking gently.

'Another?' I ask. I don't want to walk home brooding over that loss.

He nods.

I place nine black stone on the handicap points and wait. He usually begins each game with a few words of advice. On this occasion they're slow to come. His thin, gnarled fingers hover over the bowl of white stones.

'Persevere,' he says, eventually. His voice is soft and rasping. I lean forward to hear. 'Do not concede,' he adds. 'Fight on until the battle is over.' He places a white stone equidistant between two of my black stones. A game of Go begins.

I try to remember his lessons. I use my handicap stones to attack rather than simply surround territory. I keep my stones connected. I play away from thickness.

The contest heats up and the lessons fade from my mind: the struggle for success is everything. I push through and cut; I seek out eye-stealing *tesuji;* I play every *atari* I spot.

The position becomes complex. I concentrate hard. Where are the big points?

The main battles appear resolved and I scan the board. I have some territory, there and there, and a few more points in the corner. I have lost that group but it is not so large. I remember another lesson and count the game as best I can. I am still over ten points ahead. Maybe twenty.

I protect my territory during the *yose.* My opponent *hane*'s on the first line and connects; I defend. He undercuts my area with a monkey-jump; I block him. He exploits my shortage of liberties and I lose three stones. I curse under my breath. The game is close. I cannot count it.

A few more moves and the game is over, the *dame* points have been filled. My teacher sits slumped forward, his slender hands clasped together in his lap. He gets tired at the end of the evening. I re-arrange the stones for both sides and count the territories. I count again. I check for stray prisoners lying in the lids of bowls. I count again. I am certain. The game has ended in *jigo*. It is a draw.

I nod to my opponent and smile, thanking him for the game. I hold out my hand across the board. He does not respond. He sits as before, hunched forward, his hands joined together in his lap. He is quiet and still.

The paramedics arrive promptly in response to my call. They confirm that my Go teacher is dead. They say he has been dead for some time and ask why I didn't call them earlier. I have no answer.

'Persevere,' he said. 'Do not concede,' he said. 'Fight until the battle is over,' he said. I shall not forget his advice.

# At the Frontier

Any observer monitoring the beach at that time (if such there had been) would have been impressed by the style of the young man. He ran in a relaxed and confident manner, his easy stride generating a brisk pace. The sole blemish was his left arm which swung limply at his side, upsetting the symmetry of his gait. He followed the borderline where the sea met the sand. His bare right foot occasionally splashed in a shallow wave, his left foot sank a little into a soft patch of sand, but despite such slips he maintained a regular rhythm, his face portraying calm and measured concentration. He ran steadily along the beach; he was in tune with the sand and the sea; he was in his element, an integral component of the environment.

Then that act came to an end as though some off-screen Director had called 'Cut.' He stopped. He looked around. Our fictitious observer would now have noticed a dramatic change in the man's demeanour. All confidence had drained from his features; he looked instead to be shocked and confused, loose and frail, his wide eyes displaying bewilderment. To the man it felt like he had suddenly awoken, had at this moment gained consciousness, although paradoxically his surroundings were evoking an unreal, dream-like texture, on the edge of nightmarish. He was lost.

The Big Bang marked the beginning of the universe. There was nothing before it, even time itself, so the very notion of 'before' is an ill-conceived misnomer. Everything flows from the Big Bang: it is the starting point. This was the young man's Big Bang moment, although it wasn't until later that he conceived of the analogy. True, it was not a very precise analogy but it conveyed the gist of what had happened: a beginning, a birth. He felt disoriented, suspended, out of focus. He was here. That much was certain. But where was here? How had he got here? Where had he been before? Did 'before' even have any meaning?

He looked out to sea. The deep azure ocean spread out before him, flat, calm, apparently endless, stretching to the faraway horizon. To either side, the sandy beach curved around into the distance, shimmering and glittering with an almost rosy hue, but with no discernible feature beyond gently banking sand and more sand and more sand. At the back of the beach rose large dunes dappled with sparse rusty-coloured marram-type grass interspersed with rugged boulders, outcrops of bare rock. There was nothing else. There were no people. There were no seabirds. There were no boats. There was no evidence of human occupation, not even any signs of passing human involvement: no discarded litter, no roughly-hewn holes dug out of the sand, no crumbling sandcastles. The landscape was natural and simple. And beautiful, he had to admit. Although, not quite. To his heightened senses it all seemed a little too much. The peace was too absolute, the view too luminous, the air smelled too sweet. Only the sun seemed unexceptional: warm but not hot, so his skin was glowing but not burning. This scene felt like a caricature of a perfect day at the beach, a fictional version, too bright, too perfect: so perfect as to seem unreal and make a man fearful. And this man was feeling the fear.

Slowly his thoughts began to take shape. He began to analyse his situation and his reaction to it. Or at least to frame pertinent questions. Where was he and how had he got here? Certainly nowhere in the UK. If this were Europe at all it would have to be the Mediterranean. The Caribbean was more likely. Or Australia? A Pacific island? His knowledge of such places was ... He strained to remember. Had he travelled to any of those places? He knew he ought to know, but he didn't. He examined his memory but there was nothing there. He knew the names of some places – Basseterre, Palikir, Tarawa - but had no experience of them. He had, in fact, no experience of whether or not he had experienced them. He thought some more. Turned his thoughts towards more fundamental directions, but again came up empty. Who am I? What am I? What do I do? What did I do before the Big Bang? There should be something there, some memory of the man he was, his career, his life, but he couldn't get there. It remained near, as if hidden by a thin shadow, but tantalisingly out of reach. How can you forget who you are? He wandered up and down the beach, looking to the ground, looking to the scene around him, examining his hands, searching, searching, searching for clues. Some trigger. Some sign. His hands were soft and well-manicured, not a worker's hands. Apart from that, nothing.

For a long time nothing changed. The scene remained the same. The man remained the same, located in the same place. His thoughts did not progress. Then he became aware of movement in the distance.

Far away along the beach a figure approaches. Gradually he is able to discern greater detail. It is a dark-skinned woman. She is wearing a white bikini. He glances down at his own body and registers for the first time that his pale figure is naked apart from a pair of brief swimming trunks. The flight instinct overcomes him. He bounds up the sand, slowing as he reaches the heavy resistance of the steep dune. He scrambles over the rocks and ducks down. From this hiding place he can see through a crack between boulders and watches as the woman strides purposefully nearer. She is young and tall and not unattractive. She advances briskly with an air of authority. Her path takes her away from the edge of the sea, along the upper part of the beach. She soon approaches close to where the man is hiding. He holds his breath as she passes barely three metres from his location. Then she stops.

'Why are you hiding there?' she asks, loud enough for him to hear. She turns to face his hiding place.

The man hesitates for a moment, then stands up and, feeling rather foolish, clambers over the rocks towards her. He feels like a schoolboy caught out in some minor misdemeanour. The woman folds her arms. Like a school-teacher.

Before the man can think of anything sensible to say, the woman continues. 'Did you really think I hadn't seen you? I could see you from way down there.' She gestures. 'I'm guessing I saw you about the same time as you saw me.'

'That makes sense,' says the man. 'I don't know. I just wasn't ready. You know, to meet anyone.'

'No, clearly. Anyway. Now we've met. I'm Victoria.' She holds out her hand.

'Maxwell,' says the man, briefly touching her hand. 'How do you do?' He feels even more foolish. 'Are you …' He wasn't sure how to phrase it. 'Are you local? From around here?'

'No.'

'Oh. Visiting? On holiday?'

'No.'

Maxwell finds it rather disconcerting, the way the woman stares at him. Nothing unusual in that. He finds the gaze of most women disconcerting. But this Victoria, with her rather superior air and dominating manner, causes him more discomfort than usual.

'Right. So.' He waits, not being able to put into words what he wants to ask.

'I'm guessing, Maxwell, that you too are not from these parts.' She doesn't wait for confirmation. 'So what precisely are you doing here?'

That was the question he had wanted to ask. Maxwell shrugs and looks at his feet. He doesn't know what to say. He has a feeling he's somehow entered the woman's domain and that he is trespassing. Very soon two large minders with snarling and slobbering German Shepherds on leashes will appear over the dunes and 'escort' him off the premises. He is mistaken.

Victoria's features seem to soften a little as she looks out to sea and speaks in a gentler tone of voice: 'It's so wonderful here, isn't it? The sun, the sea. This sparkling beach.' She kicks up a cloud of pinkish sand. 'A paradise you might say. Utopia. Shangri-La. Garden of Eden.'

'Yeah,' says Maxwell, keen to join in. 'It's like a model of perfection, the prototype for an ideal holiday location.'

Victoria looks at him quizzically. 'Doesn't sound quite so wonderful the way you say it.'

Maxwell shrugs again. 'Sorry.'

They find things to say to each other, but it isn't easy. It's like *a pas de deux*, a duet for two voices, a duel even, a duel in the sun as the two of them verbally circle around each other. It might look and sound like small talk – to anyone who happened to be looking at them, listening to them - two potential lovers involved in a strange version of speed-dating. But it is more serious than that. They both know that. Their thoughts are winding around far more complex existential and ontological issues than is usual in a conversation on a beach between new acquaintances. The stakes are high. They both know that.

As they agreed later, it was inevitable that it would be Victoria who made the crucial move in this linguistic contest, in a triumph for intuition over analysis.

'It's the same for you as it is for me, isn't it?' she says. 'You know nothing.'

Maxwell looks at his feet.

'When you first saw me down the beach.' She gestures like she had before. 'That's when I'd just … woken up. Come to … Surfaced. However you want to put it. And I could remember nothing about how I'd arrived here, what I'd done before. I still remember nothing. My whole life is … indistinct, a blur.' She pauses, waiting for Maxwell to raise his head and meet her eye. 'And I think it's the same for you.'

With that, the pressure is released, the tension broken, and they begin to relax, to be more open with each other. Victoria more than Maxwell, but both to some extent. They compare their perceptions, their memories such as they are, and find a high degree of alignment. They are in the same boat, although, as Maxwell points out, 'on the same beach' is a more accurate description. Wherever it is, they are in it together. One thing they agree on is that they are scared. They also agree that in this situation, fear is an unhelpful sensation: for a start, they don't know what they are afraid of.

'Do you remember anything at all?' asks Maxwell as they walk side by side towards the shoreline. 'About who you are, what you do, your job?'

Victoria hesitates briefly, trying to make something of not very much. 'Earlier, when I flushed you out from behind the rocks...'

'Hardly that.'

'Well, found you then. I felt like I had, or ought to have had, something in my hand.' She holds her right hand out, palm up.

Maxwell feels perplexed and looks it. He waits.

Victoria takes a deep breath. 'A gun.' She crooks her finger as though there is a trigger there. This word and all its connotations dangle between them and around them.

'A gun?' says Maxwell. 'Like ... a gun?' Victoria looks towards him but adds nothing. 'So you're a ... what? ... A gunman? Woman. A gangster? Some sort of criminal?'

'No, no, nothing like that. The opposite. I'm one of the good guys.'

'You're sure? How can you be? Suddenly from knowing nothing, you're now so positive?'

'I'm only saying what I feel. But yes. Sure.' Hard and emphatic. Her eyes challenge Maxwell to call her a liar. 'Yes, I'm sure.' Softer this time. 'I just know. Know something about who I am, what I am, what it feels like. Something like a policewoman. Or the military. Army.' New thoughts seem to come into her head as she speaks, but hazy on details. 'Uniform. I'm sure I wear a uniform. In real life.'

This is progress. They both feel it and want to hold on to it for a while. It isn't much but it's all they've got. They stand in silence. Then 'What about you?' asks Victoria.

A quick response from Maxwell: 'Something scientific. My work involves science. There are pictures, scenes floating around my head and fragments of thoughts. The thoughts seem to be analytic. Like when I was thinking about the sun earlier, how it's not as hot as you'd expect, in a place like this. And that led me to think about … nuclear explosions … the sun's surface … radiation.'

'Whereas normal people would be like, maybe there's thin cloud. Or the wind's from the north. Assuming the north is the cold direction.'

'Right. And before you came I was looking at the sand. I wondered why it was so sparkly, and immediately these thoughts about minerals and crystals and chemicals came up.'

'So what's the answer?'

'No, no answer. Just snippets of data. Random morsels. Nothing coherent but it seems to be the way I think.' He pauses. 'Oh yes, and I've got this picture in my mind of what seems to be a laboratory – you know, test tubes, retorts, Bunsen burners. Of course, it could be some old school Chemistry lesson.' Maxwell looks at Victoria who is trying to adopt an encouraging face. 'It's not much.'

'But there's more than that, isn't there?'

'How do you mean?'

'Well, our brains aren't completely empty. We have some knowledge. Language, for a start.'

'How to walk, talk, all of that. Breathe.'

'Yes. Perhaps more will come back. Gradually.'

'Depends why we can't remember.'

'People who've suffered trauma sometimes have amnesia for years.'

'Not sure those are real cases. I think it's mostly fiction. Films. Makes a good basis for a story.'

'I wish this were a story. I wouldn't be so confused.' Maxwell nods but Victoria then contradicts herself. 'No, not confused. Helpless. That's the word. I don't like it. I get the feeling I'm not used to it. I'm used to knowing what I'm doing. Being in control.'

Without agreeing to, they sit down together on a small ridge in the sand and look to the far horizon across the flat, flat sea which laps against the edge of the beach, producing flickers of white foam.

'What are we going to do?'

'I don't know. It's not like there's much by way of options.'

'We walk that way,' Victoria points. 'Or that way.'

'Or we swim out to sea,' adds Maxwell. 'Or sit here and wait.'

'Wait for what?'

'Whatever. Whatever happens.'

'Do you think something will happen?'

'I don't know.' Loud and aggressive from Victoria. 'How do you expect me to know? We're just …' She bangs her fists on either side of her face and lets out a scream.

Maxwell knows how she feels.

* * * * *

Somewhat later, they're walking side-by-side along the beach, direction chosen randomly. They have both been thinking a lot and saying little.

'Can you think of any explanation?' asks Victoria. 'For why we're here, like this?'

Maxwell shakes his head. 'No.' His face says this is a dumb question. 'No. We have no data. There's no evidence.' He holds his right arm out, palm up. The left arm hangs by his side. 'We have no past experience to feed off. There's nothing to serve as the basis for any deductions.'

'Okay, then. Let's try this. Brainstorming. Make a wild guess. Implausible as you like.'

Maxwell doesn't say anything.

'Even if it doesn't produce anything at least it'll pass the time.'

Still no response from Maxwell.

'Please.'

Maxwell sighs. 'Okay then. To humour you. A plane crash.'

'Right. Good. So where's the plane? The debris? The other survivors? Or casualties?'

'You said it didn't have to be realistic.'

'But it's a start. Once we've dismissed all the impossible explanations, whatever's left must be the truth. Didn't some detective say that?'

'Probably Sherlock Holmes. Perhaps it's round the next bend?'

'What?'

'The plane. The wreckage. And all the bodies.'

'And why are we unscathed? No injuries at all. Apart from your arm. Plus we've lost our memories. Can a plane crash cause that?'

'Okay. Your turn. Can you come up with anything better?'

'A dream,' says Victoria, after a moment's thought. 'I don't think I'm here at all. Nor you. It's a dream and any time now I'm going to wake up.'

'You can be in my dream if I can be in yours. Who said that? These fragments of memory are weird. But I can't say I've ever had a dream this real.'

'You're not dreaming. This is my dream and you're an ingredient of it. You're not real. I'm imagining you.'

'But I know I'm real.'

'But nothing you say will convince me it's so.'

Maxwell gives this some thought. 'So it feels like a dream to you?'

'How do I know?'

'No need to shout.'

Louder: 'I wasn't shouting.' Then quieter: 'Once you remember a dream, it's over, so how you feel then isn't necessarily how it felt when you were actually in it. We have no way of knowing what it really feels like to be in a dream.'

'Complicated.' That is all Maxwell can think to say. 'Is it my turn again?'

Victoria says nothing.

'First thing I thought of was some sort of practical joke.'

Victoria looks across at him. They are walking a couple of metres apart. 'Ha, bloody, ha. Some joke.'

'But it happens, doesn't it? Like on a stag night. They strip the groom naked and leave him tied to a lamp-post, miles from anywhere. There must be something in my background makes me think that's the sort of thing they might do to me.'

'They?'

'People. Some people. Friends. I don't know.'

'The "miles from anywhere" seems about right. So they fly across this beach and drop you out as they pass. No parachute? And where do I come in.'

'Perhaps it was a joint stag and hen party. Hey, perhaps we're the bride and groom.'

'Not remotely funny. No. Absolutely not.' She crosses her arms and then spreads them rapidly, wiping away the very idea. The workings of her mind show on her face. 'And this may be as good a time as any to make things clear. In case you were getting any funny ideas, you and me – you know – it's an absolute non-starter.'

'Okay. No need to be quite so absolute. Since you mention it, my thoughts hadn't been going in that direction. Not all men are ...' He hesitates. 'But ... Is it ... ?'

Another look from Victoria. 'No. For God's sake, nothing like that. I think we've outgrown all that racist nonsense, haven't we? No, the problem with you is nothing personal, especially nothing about your whiteness. Your problem is you're the wrong gender. It wouldn't matter if you were white, black or green with orange spots, I could never fancy you all the while you were male.'

The two of them walk in silence for a while. A few ramifications are considered. Nothing particularly coherent. There is still nothing to see except sand and water and sky. Nothing to hear but the faint ripples at the water's edge.

'Prison,' says Maxwell. 'Perhaps we're in prison.'

'I see no bars. I see no guards. Funny sort of prison.'

'But we can't get away. And that's surely the definition of a prison – a state you cannot escape from.' Victoria looks out to sea. 'Unless you have an escape plan. A route out of here?'

No response.

'I thought not.'

'It wouldn't explain the memory loss. If our captors have somehow deleted our memories, for some reason we can only guess at, that must be illegal. Against the Geneva Convention. Or something. We could sue.'

'We'd have to get out first.'

'What about a reality TV show? Did you see that film? Ages ago. Can't remember what it was called. This guy thinks his living a normal life. Turns out all the people he interacts with are actors and the whole thing's being filmed and turned into a television programme.'

'Rings a bell.' Maxwell stops. Does a 360 degree turn. 'Those cameras are a heck of a long way away.' He walks on. 'And this would be the most boring reality TV show ever. Even worse than Big Brother. Especially since we're never going to … you know. Because of your …'

'I'm a lesbian and so we're not going to have sex. Just say it. Nothing bad happens if you just say it.'

'Doesn't come naturally to me,' says Maxwell. 'I've never been very …'

'Yes, I noticed. It must be my turn again. How about the end of the world? Apocalypse. Nuclear Armageddon? We're the only two left. Living through it was so traumatic our minds blocked it out, along with other major chunks of our past histories. This is the only location in the world where life still survives.'

'You should write fiction.'

'My sister does. Ooh. Another bit of memory. Her name's … No, can't remember.'

'One slight flaw in your scenario. To really work we'd need to be Adam and Eve, here in our Garden of Eden, ready to start the repopulation of the earth. We're back to you-know-what again.'

They walk for a while in silence.

Then everything changes. That is to say, everything stays the same.

They're still on the beach, yet with a sense of having transferred to somewhere else. For Maxwell it feels like some sort of mild attack, accompanied by unsettling fuzziness. It's a dislocation, a time-shift. He's about to ask Victoria if she felt it too when she shouts out.

'Look.' She points ahead.

Maxwell looks. He can't see anything, but then he can. A small grey dome protrudes out of the sand a few hundred metres ahead, where the beach bends to the right. 'What is it?'

'Can't tell,' says Victoria, shading her eyes with her hand. 'At least it's something.' Their pace picks up as they head towards the structure, then slows as they get nearer, the fear rising again. But it doesn't seem particularly dangerous or threatening. Just strange. Close to, the dome's a lot larger than they first thought. It's a precise hemisphere, as far as they can judge, reaching up well above their heads, maybe as much as five metres. It has a silver sheen to it. Maxwell runs his good hand across the smooth surface. 'I thought it looked metallic,' he says. 'Now I'm not so sure. More like some sort of plastic. But not like anything I've ever seen before. Thin but strong, self-supporting.' He raps on it with his knuckle. No sound echoes back.

Around the other side they find an opening, a doorway but without a door. It's a low arch and with scarcely any hesitation Victoria ducks down and enters the structure – the house, the vault, whatever it is. Maxwell follows. They expect darkness, but it's almost as light inside as out. The sunlight penetrates the skin of the dome which, from inside, has a translucent appearance. The space is empty. They walk slowly to the centre, under the highest point, turning around, studying and wondering. The floor is of the same material as the rest of the structure. It's cool on their feet, slightly soft but their steps leave no footmarks.

'What is this?' asks Victoria, her arms spread.

'No idea.'

'What do you think it's for?'

'Not much. There's nothing here. I can't see it can do anything, serve any purpose. Apart from being some sort of shelter.'

They walk around each other, studying the roof, the walls, the floor, all of which are moulded together, no signs of joins.

Victoria is the first to spot the pictures. 'What's that, over there?'

They walk across to what appear to be three pictures pinned to the wall, at head height. Not really pinned, though. Maxwell runs his hand across them. They're imbedded in the wall, carved into the surface, an integral part of the structure. They depict crude sketches that could be faces, like a child might draw. Each consists of an oval outline within which there are two ovals for eyes and a third lower oval for a mouth. There are no other features. The three drawings are identical apart from their colouring. The first is shaded a dark grey with a tinge of mauve. The second is a pale creamy yellow. They could be interpreted as one black face and one white. There is no mistaking the colour of the third face. It is green with orange spots. Victoria and Maxwell stare at the drawings in silence, sharing a slack-mouthed confusion. Their bewilderment is increased by the captions underneath each: they are labelled 'Victoria', 'Maxwell' and 'Gabriel'.

There's nothing else to see in the dome. By unspoken agreement they head slowly back towards the doorway. This space no longer feels as safe as it did. They feel cautious, tentative, waiting for something. They both prefer to seek the sanctity of the open air and the beach, the sea and the sky.

'I'm sure it was here,' says Victoria.

'Roughly opposite the drawings,' says Maxwell.

When something impossible occurs, it's natural to deny it, assume there must be an alternative explanation. That's why the two of them scour the walls for the opening, long after they've realised it isn't there. They stand together under the highest point of the dome.

'Prison was right,' says Maxwell. 'Now it does feel like a prison.'

Victoria is silent. Maxwell turns to her and sees tears falling across her cheeks. 'Hey,' says Maxwell.

Victoria's face crumbles and she crouches down, head in hands, and lets out a loud exclamation, a cross between a moan and a roar.

Maxwell looks across at the drawings. The black one is crying. The white one is frowning. The third one is impassive.

He crouches beside Victoria, strokes her arm and makes what he intends to be soothing noises. He doesn't mention the pictures. He thinks maybe he's more in need of comfort than she is. Bewilderment and curiosity have given way to a wild, intense fear. Where are they? What is happening to them? Where do they go from here?

* * * * *

How many Big Bangs have there been? A nonsensical question. It occurs to Maxwell that he's had a second Big Bang. But no, this time the analogy isn't even close. Not a beginning, not a birth, more a continuation albeit after a pause. So quantum jump is nearer the mark. A change of state without any connecting progression, a sudden jolt, a singularity. Whatever it was, Maxwell is now back outside, standing on sand under a black sky sprinkled with stars. Victoria stands beside him. They exchange glances that speak of another shared experience.

'What just happened?'

A shrug. A shake of the head. They stare at the sky. They're calmer now. The shift not only brought them out of the dome, but out of their mood of fear, into some sort of state of relaxation, almost an acceptance of their fate.

'Do you recognise any of the constellations?' asks Victoria. She's at ease. The stain of tears on her face is the only reminder of her previous condition of anguish.

Maxwell lets his gaze roam across the apparently unordered patterns of light. 'No.'

'If it's not Orion or The Plough I've no chance,' says Victoria. 'What about the southern constellations? Do you know them?'

'I don't know. I mean, I don't know whether I know them or not.' Maxwell turns and looks to the horizon, then looks back.

'Sorry about just now. Inside. Before we ... jumped. It all became a bit too much. It's not like me to be so girly.'

'It's fine. Don't worry. I'd be the same, except ...'

'But for your stiff upper lip.'

'Something like that.'

Victoria has spotted the moon, newly risen. 'It always seems so big, doesn't it, when it's low in the sky.' The moon casts its diamond light across the water. 'It looks like a road. A straight white motorway we could drive away on, skate away on.'

'If only,' says Maxwell.

Something clicks in Victoria's brain and her relaxed and soft demeanour turns to wild animation; she's hyper-excited. 'Hey. I just remembered. I once walked on the moon. I did, I'm sure I did.'

Maxwell does not react. It isn't that he's stunned by Victoria's pronouncement: that comes later. Now it's something else. He takes a deep breath. Then: 'That's not the moon.'

Victoria can't interpret the strange look on his face. 'What? What are you saying?'

'It's not the moon. Not our moon. It's another moon.'

Victoria looks back to the sky. 'It does look …
different. But, you know, out in the open like this, away
from city lights. The sky always looks unfamiliar.'

'Agreed,' says Maxwell, speaking slowly. 'But as a
rule – even in the wilds of the countryside – I've never
known the sky to have … two moons.' He gestures to the
right and Victoria gasps as she sees the hanging, silver
crescent, much smaller than the other one, but
unmistakably a second moon.

There follows another pause in their conversation.
It's not that there's nothing to say; the problem is there's
too much to say, and the thoughts of each of them tumble
around their minds in chaos and confusion.

It's Victoria (again) who breaks the spell. 'Do you
think we can get back inside?' She indicates the silver
dome, which is some fifty metres down the beach, glinting
in the starlight.

'Only one way to find out.'

'I do feel somewhat exposed.' Victoria spreads her
arms as they walk, emphasising her scantily clad figure.

'It's not cold,' says Maxwell. 'But I know what you mean. Doesn't feel like suitable clothing for a night under the stars.'

The archway into the dome has returned, or maybe simply re-opened, and they crouch through it like they did before. The inside has changed. The pictures have vanished. Towards the centre two pale-blue ovals, slightly raised from the floor, dominate the space. Maxwell tests one with his foot. It dips slightly, then returns to flat when he takes his weight off. 'Do you think these could be beds?'

By the side of each is a pile of blue rags. Rather tentatively, Victoria picks at one of the piles and discovers it's actually an item of clothing. Once she gets it properly oriented she is able to slip it over her head. It's a loose-fitting kaftan-style garment, long arms, knee-length, decorated with an abstract blue and white pattern. Maxwell puts on the other: it's the same. They take one 'bed' each and sit on it, cross-legged.

Victoria has noticed the doorway is no longer evident. This time, it doesn't seem so important; she has no feeling of being trapped. In fact she feels safe.

Comfortable. The dome is more of a protective cocoon than

a constricting cage.

Gradually the two of them try to put into words their

reaction to the recent events: the apparent entrapment,

the quantum leap, the two moons. Those are big things,

weird events to try and assimilate and make sense of,

another layer to add to the strangeness of their situation.

Victoria looks at the stars and moons through the semi-

transparent skin of the dome. Maxwell studies his

fingernails.

'Not some practical joke then,' says Victoria.

'Probably not.'

'Funny thing is, you know, it was the next thing I

was going to say, my next guess. Abduction by aliens.

Maxwell looks up. 'Is that what you think?'

Victoria shrugs. Sighs. Shakes her head. 'Yes. No.

Maybe. I don't know. What else? Any other ideas?'

Maxwell says nothing, but nods slowly. 'Certainly this cannot be earth. Those two moons clinch it. No explanation for that is consistent with this being our planet.'

'How far is it from earth to the nearest habitable planet? The nearest planet like this. How long would it take us to get here?'

Maxwell puffs out his cheeks. 'Ages. Many lifetimes. It's a huge distance. Thousands of light years. There was this Kepler mission looking for signs and they detected many earth-style planets, but they're all far, far away. If they even exist, that is. You see, nothing's ever guaranteed. They just look for minor variations in a star's trajectory, transits, things like that. It's all indirect and surrounded by 'if's and 'maybe's. There was a rumour that they'd found a planet of the right size and temperature orbiting Alpha Centauri. That would be closer. About four light-years.'

'Sounds like you're an astronomer.'

Another look up from Maxwell. 'Yes, I suppose it's possible. Once you asked the question it stirred things in my memory. Things I didn't know I knew. I started thinking and stuff sort of floated up to the surface.' He stares at the structure that surrounds them. 'What do you make of this dome now?' He gestures. 'In the light of ... Any more thoughts?'

'It changes,' says Victoria. 'Forces us to change. Manoeuvres us. That's why I thought aliens. Higher beings. Bringing us here and then controlling us. Making us afraid. Making us calm.'

'We need to think beyond simply highly intelligent humanoids. The next division up won't do. We're talking a whole different league here, a fundamentally different species. The technology to travel those distances. To wipe our brains and yet not damage our ability to think. To build something like this, whatever it is. We'd be nothing compared to them. Some poorly-developed sub-species. Primitive. Insects.'

These thoughts need a further pause to ponder. Then Maxwell remembers something. 'Did you really say you walked on the moon?'

'Yup. I have this set of pictures in my brain. A vision suddenly came to me. Bit like your remembering, I suppose, floating to the surface. Not much detail, but the gist is clear.'

'I thought all the astronauts that walked on the moon were male. And American.'

'I was the first female. And not American.'

'I don't remember that. But then I don't remember much.'

'I don't think it was on the news. It was secret.'

Now Maxwell frowns and shakes his head. 'How does that tally with you being a soldier.'

Victoria shrugs.

Maxwell tries a different tack. 'Look. What about this? You know you said before about a dream. About this being your dream. Well how about hallucination? Some sort of hypnosis-induced vision? You see, I can't get my head around standing on a planet that has two moons. I'd rather it wasn't real. It's all been too weird, everything, but the two moons is a step too far for me. It can't be true.'

'We're short on alternatives.'

'Perhaps we're simply mad. Insane. Imaginations running wild while we lie in some sanatorium being calmed with drugs and therapy.'

There's a lot more thinking out loud that goes on. They try out ideas, mostly fanciful. But they trust each other to take them for what they are. They end up revisiting old ideas, circling and getting nowhere.

Then: 'How long have we been here?' asks Maxwell.

'I'm not good with judging time.'

'Four hours? Eight hours?'

'Something between. Maybe.'

'Are you hungry? Thirsty?'

'No, can't say I am.'

'Do you want to … you know … use the conveniences?'

'Piss and shit, you mean?' She laughs and so does Maxwell.

'Yes, that's what I mean. You put it so delicately.'

'Since you ask. No.'

'So add that to the mix. We have no memory – at least, not much – and our bodily functions appear to have stagnated. Now it's dark and I don't feel tired. Maybe the orbit of this planet doesn't match our body clocks, but I'd still expect to be feeling tired by now. Especially given what we've been through.'

* * * * *

Neither Victoria nor Maxwell know for certain whether or not they've been asleep. If they have slept, they wake up at almost the same time. Maxwell quickly rolls away. Victoria sits up sharply with thunder in her face and lightning in her eyes.

'What the hell? You fucking moron. What you think you playing at?'

Maxwell holds his hands up, surrendering. 'No, no. It's not like that. I didn't. I wouldn't.'

'You sure as hell were too fucking close, buddy. I thought I made it crystal fucking clear …'

Maxwell continues to beg forgiveness at the same time as he denies everything, at the same time as he closes his ears to the torrent of abuse and waits for the storm to abate. Victoria continues to rant, full of justifiable (as she sees it) outrage and burning with hatred and disgust. But eventually she runs out of steam and Maxwell takes the opportunity to crawl back to the relative safety of his 'bed', his own blue oval.

Later still, despite occasional eruptions and aftershocks interspersed with extended periods of uneasy, festering silence, they manage to discuss, in some semblance of calmness and civility, what has happened. Or what has not happened. Since neither of them can remember anything of what occurred before or during whatever happened happened (or didn't happen), it's pretty much guesswork. But they agree it must be the 'Aliens' who are to blame, or whoever it was drew the pictures, sealed the door, caused the quantum leaps, whoever it is who's controlling them having brought them to this godforsaken planet in the first place, it must have been them that brought this incompatible pair together. It definitely was not at Maxwell's choosing. It even more certainly was not at Victoria's choosing. They both agree it absolutely certainly must not and will not happen again. Whatever it was that happened. Or didn't happen. And yes, with reluctance on both sides but more on one than the other, yes they can still be 'friends' and there are no hard feelings. Because there are no other options. They're in this, whatever this might be, together.

Later – and if she thought about it, she doesn't know quite how or when she came to arrive there, but such things no longer seem important – Victoria is sitting on a rock at the back of the beach. Maxwell is nearby, strolling back and forth along the borderline between sand and sea. He kicks through the top of the sand, sending particles into the air which sparkle in the sunlight as they spray across the surface of the shallow waves, then land, then sink, leaving bubbles, then leaving nothing at all. He wanders back to Victoria. Her chin is in her hands, her elbows are on her knees.

'There are no shells,' says Maxwell. 'No feathers, no seaweed, no fish bones. None of that debris you normally find on the tide-line.' Victoria looks at him, then looks away. If she heard him, she gives no sign. She gazes towards the horizon. 'What thoughts?' asks Maxwell. 'Anything new?'

'I've been thinking about the good things. The positives about our situation.'

Maxwell rubs his hands together and sits beside her. 'Oh, good. I'm going to enjoy this. I can't wait. I'll settle myself down here. This is going to take some time.' He stares at her with feigned concentration.

Victoria ignores him. 'The memory loss thing. That's good. Don't you think? You see, I've no idea whether I have a partner, a lover. I could have several lovers, for all I know. If I did, if I knew, I'd no doubt be missing them like crazy. Worrying about them.'

'Of course, they might be missing you. Worried out of their minds.' Maxwell's more serious now.

'Yes, but I don't know that, do I, because I don't know her, them, don't even know if they exist. So I'm not worried. And I don't miss – oh, relatives, friends, pets. Who knows?'

'You don't know what you've got till it's gone. Somebody said that. Sang it, I think.'

'But if you didn't know about 'before'. Didn't know you had it, whatever it was. Then you're never going to miss it.'

'You do have deep thoughts sometimes.' Victoria gives him one of her looks. 'Just saying. No criticism. You're the one with the imagination. Perhaps you're a philosopher in real life.'

'Funny how we've started saying 'real life'. Like this isn't real.'

Maxwell thinks about this. 'It's what they say when they get off their machines, isn't it? Kids. Contrasting reality with the virtual world. This feels a bit like that, semi-real. Some sort of limbo. Real in that we're here and breathing and thinking and talking, but otherwise it seems artificial, out-of-consciousness, between-time. And not particularly frightening any more. Not like it was at the start. Because really it's not so bad, is it? Nothing really bad has happened to us.'

'Apart from being kidnapped, you mean? Imprisoned? Memories obliterated?'

'Right. Apart from those things, we're fine.'

After the regulation pause in their conversation, Maxwell asks: 'What made you suddenly start thinking about lovers?'

'I don't know. After what happened back there ...'

'Or didn't happen.'

'Okay. After that. I got some sort of inkling. Something at the back of my mind. Not a proper memory but I suddenly felt like .... I don't think I live alone. That's all.' She turns to Maxwell. 'What about you?'

'I'm divorced, I think. Or separated. I remember a wife, or a partner at any rate. Long term. No face, nothing physically concrete, simply a vague concept. And she walked out on me. I remember it because it was the same day I won a Go tournament.'

'So the day wasn't all bad.' Victoria smiles.

'No, no indeed. In fact it wasn't a bad day at all. It was a good day. Because I wanted her to leave. I'm fairly sure about that. Finding she was gone was a relief.'

'So weird, the way these fragments of memory sort of filter back, bubble up from somewhere deep down.'

'Yup.'

'What about your arm? Do you remember what happened to it?'

Maxwell looks down at his arm, raising it to a 45 degree angle, the best he can manage. 'Some accident, I think. It got squashed. A car door, a gate. Something like that. A long time ago. When I was a kid.'

They lean back and stare at the familiar blue sky, with it's green tinge. The sun, pleasantly warm, not too hot. It's like being on a beach holiday, except they're not in control. They wait for the next thing to happen.

* * * * *

About now, this thing they're in – unreal life, or whatever you might call it – takes on a new dimension. The 'jumps' as they've taken to calling them, those sudden skips when snippets of time and chunks of space disappear and they seem to be transported from one place to another in an instant, these jumps start occurring more often. Sometimes they're in the dome and get jumped outside. Sometimes they walk out of the dome only to be jumped back inside. Whenever they enter the dome, whether through the doorway or as the result of a jump, some new scenario is presented to them. Something for them to interact with. They decide that the Aliens – they can't think of a better term, they did blame 'Gabriel' for a while, the name on the third picture, but that sounded too weird – they decide the Aliens are experimenting with them, testing them, even playing with them. Each of the scenarios seem connected to something they've said to each other, or sometimes it might be something one of them has thought about. The Aliens seem to react to them. Then they're required to react to what the Aliens present to them. Then they wait for the next event, the next experiment. They never have to wait long. It's interaction of a sort, but hardly a balanced mutually-dependent relationship. A gap more than a link; a space more than a bridge.

One time they're confronted with a guitar and keyboard, set up in the middle of the dome and ready to play. It doesn't take long to decide what to do. Victoria picks up the guitar; Maxwell sits at the keyboard. They improvise some music. It's not wonderful, but nor is it atrocious. It's recognisably music. They guess there must be something in their backgrounds by way of a musical history, some lessons, some experience. They stumble through a rendition of John Lennon's *Imagine*, the only song they both know, although 'know' may not be an entirely accurate description of their degree of familiarity with the song. They hope the Aliens are satisfied.

On another occasion they enter the dome to find piles of bank notes. There are pounds and dollars and euros, some yen, some rupees, some other sorts of dollars; also plenty of others they do not recognise. They're not sure what they're supposed to do with this hoard. They estimate that it amounts to the equivalent of many thousand of pounds, possibly millions, depending on exchange rates; some of the more exotic notes have very large numbers printed on them. But the irony isn't lost on them: in their current situation the value of this treasure amounts to precisely zero. Victoria makes up some sort of game of barter and exchange and Maxwell joins in. They have no objects to buy and sell so they have to imagine them. The game doesn't last long.

They're surprised one time to be presented with an easel with a blank canvas, a palette and a box full of tubes of paint. Two brushes. The surprise comes from finding out that neither of them has ever painted in their lives, that they have no expertise nor interest in art. They wonder what conversation between them might have stimulated this misunderstanding. In some small way they gain comfort from this sign of a flaw in the Aliens' decision-making. Nevertheless, they feel obliged to participate in this event, however misguided it might be, so they take a brush each and begin to paint. They both opt for rather crude outlines, stick people and box-shaped houses. Then the addition of different colours and some more confident swirling and daubing produces a picture in what might be described as an abstract impressionist style. Despite their misgivings, they admit to enjoying it. They leave the dome and wash the paint off their fingers and faces, submerging themselves in the warmth of the sea.

Almost as bewildering as the art equipment, another occasion sees them presented with a set of religious tomes. They recognise a King James Bible and the Quran, but the other volumes are mysteries, probably key texts for those practising those religions, whatever those religions might be, but unknown to both Victoria and Maxwell. They have no idea what to do with them. Maxwell suggests putting them into alphabetical order by title. That's what they do.

A more interesting event occurs as they arrive in the dome to find themselves standing in front of a thick wooden table on carved legs, with a pattern of squares on its surface. 'It's a Goban,' says Maxwell.

'I know,' says Victoria. 'And we have stones.' There are cushions to either side of the table and bowls with stones, one set made of shell, the other of slate. Maxwell is surprised to find that Victoria not only knows about the game, but has played it. This is a scenario they know how to interact with.

The two of them kneel on the cushions, sitting back on their heels. They agree that Maxwell is the stronger player and Victoria places five black stones on the board, four on the hoshi points near the corners, one on the central tengen point. The next hour and a half passes peacefully. They could be in a dusty hall in some corner of the UK; they could be in a Japanese ornamental garden; they could be on an express train hurtling through Korea; that they are, in fact, (perhaps) on an exoplanet multiple light years distant from earth is of no matter. They are absorbed in the playing of a game of Go.

Victoria is a stronger player than she had admitted, and Maxwell has rather exaggerated his level of expertise. As a result Maxwell's groups come under sustained and violent attack. Some are able to scramble a meagre sort of life, others have to be sacrificed. Maxwell's play becomes increasingly erratic as he seeks to unsettle his opponent, to reduce her big lead, but it is to no avail. When his final outrageous overplay is soundly refuted by his opponent, he resigns.

'Well played.' They shake hands. 'Perhaps we should try again with four stones.' However, the second game does not take place, as they are at that moment transported back outside, to the sea, the sand and the sunshine.

That is to be the last time they are 'jumped', and when a short time later they walk back into the dome, this is the last time they enter that space, the last time they come 'home' in that strange vernacular they have adopted.

They had begun to experience a heightened sense of anticipation each time they came home, each time they entered the dome. What will be here this time? What they see is a table and two chairs in the centre of the space. They're not like any furniture they've ever seen before, but their relative size and the flat surfaces make them instantly recognisable. They ignore the pale blue colour, the oval shaping, the bewildering complexity of the supporting mechanisms. There's no doubt: these are chairs and this is a table. They sit on the chairs. On the table is a pile of papers. Victoria pulls them towards her. They're pages of a handwritten text. It's in English. It seems to be a story, entitled 'The Peridor.'

'What's a Peridor?' asks Maxwell.

'No idea. Is it connected with a periscope? A periwinkle?'

'A peri is a fairy, isn't it? Something from mythology. A genie?'

'But this isn't a peri, it's a Peridor.'

'Presumably they want us to read it.' Victoria reads it first. It's not a long story. When she's finished she hands it to Maxwell. He also reads it.

'It's a bit odd,' says Maxwell. 'Not really my sort of thing. I prefer a bit more action.'

'The ending's strange. It doesn't seem to end properly at all. You're still left guessing as to what happened to the two children.'

'Not sure I can be bothered to care.'

'It's like something Sophie would write,' says Victoria, then gives a small gasp. 'I've remembered her name. Sophie. That's my sister. And I've got a picture in my mind. Young. Big hair. Laughing. Oh, I wish there were more.'

'But then you'd start to miss her. Remember what you said?'

'Yes. But I don't. She seems … I don't know how to say it. She seems distant. In another … It's as though that world isn't real. Oh God.' She puts her arms onto the table and lets her head fall onto them.

'Hey Vicky, come on.'

Victoria sits up. There are tears in her eyes but she blinks them away. 'No, no. Definitely not. Never Vicky. Vick, Tori, none of those. Always, always Victoria. Or nothing at all.'

'Okay. Sorry. Chill.'

'What?'

'Nothing.'

At the end of the script there are a number of blank pages. They also find on the far side of the table, two thin rods that they identify as pens, or what counts as pens on this world, in this version of their lives.

'I'm thinking they want us to write an ending to this story,' says Maxwell.

'Or two endings,' says Victoria. 'There are two of us and two pens. You take that one, I'll take this. Race you.'

'Hey, it's quality that matters, not who finishes first.'

'Who appointed you as the maker-up of rules? There. Done.' She puts the pen down.

'Don't care,' says Maxwell. He licks the end of the 'pen' then wishes he hadn't. 'This is going to be good.'

When they've both finished their writing, they have two pages left. Maxwell folds one into a dart and launches it with enthusiasm. It nosedives and lands at his feet.

Victoria makes more subtle folds with the other piece of paper and eventually a flapping bird emerges.

'Smartarse,' says Maxwell.

They're surprised they haven't yet been 'jumped' back outside, having finished their latest task.

'Shall we go outside, anyway?' asks Maxwell. 'I'm sure it'll be evening again soon. There might be a good sunset.'

'Problem,' says Victoria, and points. She points to a blank wall where the doorway should be.

They're sealed in. Again. Since the first time this has never been a problem, because usually they've been transported out so quickly they haven't had time to worry. This time the jump hasn't come. They begin to worry.

Maxwell looks up to the ceiling. 'Do you think this dome is always the same size?'

Victoria looks mystified. 'Er, yes. Why would it be any different?'

'Only, that top.' He points. 'In the middle, the highest point. It doesn't seem as far away as usual.'

Victoria looks. 'I see what you mean. Perhaps it's just the perspective. The light. I think it is getting darker, like you said.'

Maxwell stands up and does a 360 degree turn. 'It's in all directions. It's definitely smaller. Funny we never noticed before.' He turns again. 'When we first saw it we estimated its size as what? Ten metres across? Five metres in radius? I'd say it was now less than four metres high.'

Victoria looks. Nods her head. Starts to look worried. 'Could it be shrinking?'

'No, no,' says Maxwell. ''That wouldn't be possible. Whatever it's made of is solid and permanent. It couldn't change like that.' He looks again, in all directions. Yes, the ceiling does seem lower, the walls do seem closer. He checks again. Now there's no denying it, much as they wish they could. The dome does seem to be shrinking down on them.

A few minutes later, Maxwell reaches his right hand up and touches the ceiling. 'There's no doubt now. That's no more than three metres high.'

'What are we going to do?' Stupid question, but Victoria couldn't think of anything reasonable to say. It feels right to say something. Screaming for help doesn't appear a sensible option. But there's no way out of the dome and it's collapsing around them; help is what they need.

Maxwell pushes at the ceiling with his good hand. It is now barely higher than his head.

'Perhaps if we push together we can break through. It can't be very thick.' He knows that statement's not compatible with his earlier assessment of the strength of the material of the dome. But consistency is the first thing to go when panic sets in.

They push together. They make no impression. The ceiling simply moves a little closer. They sit back on the chairs. Soon the ceiling is pushing down on their heads and the walls are touching their backs. They crawl under the table. Perhaps the table will provide some protection. At least, temporarily. They cuddle together. Mainly because there is no space to do otherwise, but partly out of a need for mutual comfort.

'I'm guessing the Aliens have no further use for us,' says Maxwell. 'The experiment is over.'

'Cheerful.'

'Honest.'

'Perhaps …' Victoria can't think of anything optimistic to say.

'I wish I had someone, something to pray to,' says Maxwell.

'Well, pray anyway,' says Victoria. 'There's nothing else we can do. Apart from screaming.'

'Everything is always okay in the end. If it isn't okay, it isn't the end.'

'Did you make that up?'

'I don't think so. Another random memory.'

'There's only one apt aphorism comes to my mind right now.'

'What's that?'

'Shit happens.'

They hold each other tight as the dome closes around them, praying as best they can and trying not to scream.

# The Peridor - Epilogue I

A few months before my father died we were, to some extent, reconciled. At least we were able by then to be in the same room without hurling abuse or obscenities (or indeed physical objects) at each other. When he knew he was dying, he became more willing to talk about my childhood and his part in it. I encouraged him. But when I asked him about our last seaside holiday he made some excuse, bringing the conversation to an abrupt end.

When I visited him again later, his health had deteriorated further but that did not prevent me raising the subject again. I asked him why we never returned to that resort. After some prevarication he chose to answer me. He said the reason was because that holiday had been the cause of my problems. After that holiday I became fanciful and unstable. That's what he said. My version of the story, how I remembered it, was that soon after we got home he confiscated the peridor and that had made me angry. I had scoured the house trying to find it but could find no sign. I believed he had thrown the peridor away. That made me even angrier.

I cannot deny that he was right, that my life has been beset by certain 'problems'. I blame his overly authoritarian approach to parenting, but he never saw it like that. I became rude and uncooperative at home. I became ill-disciplined and disobedient at school. I was often awkward and angry and short-tempered. I turned into a deceitful, dishonest and self-obsessed adolescent. There was inevitability to the trajectory of my life. I gradually evolved into a delinquent, a hooligan, a vandal. I began to get into fights for the pleasure of combat and conflict. I had girlfriends that I did not treat well. Let me be honest: I have abused women. I was a bully; I enjoyed inflicting punishment both mental and physical. I became a member of the criminal fraternity and am not ashamed of that fact. I believe the weak and the ineffective receive the fate they deserve. Strength is the attribute that yields the success it warrants. To survive you must be strong. I admit my failings but do not apologise for them: I can be irrational, I often become hysterical, I am told I suffer from paranoia. I have spent more time drunk than I should have done, but so what? I enjoy drinking.

'Why did you confiscate the peridor?' I asked him.

He did not reply.

'Why did you throw it away?'

He did not reply.

'Why did we never go back?'

He did not reply.

'All I wanted was to see Sally again.'

He closed his eyes and sank down in the bed. His skin seemed to turn a shade greyer. His breath was coming in gasps. He was very ill, and this conversation was not doing him any good. But I was not prepared to let things be. I insisted that he answer me. When he did answer me he did so by posing his own question.

'Who was Sally?' he asked, in a weak voice, resigned, exasperated, but looking at me with a sting in his eye.

'You know who Sally was,' I said, trying not to shout, trying not to get angry.

'Who was she?' he asked again.

'The girl I played with. On that holiday. Her family stayed in the caravan next to us.'

He closed his eyes again. Took a deep, rasping breath. He seemed to be thinking, working something out. Or he could just have been gathering his meagre strength. Eventually, he gave me his version of that holiday, speaking slowly, his words coming in short bursts of quiet determination. 'No, Joseph. They didn't. I've told you before, but you didn't believe me. Listen now. I'm telling the truth. A family came. To the caravan next to us. They stayed for one day. Then they left. After that. There was no-one there. All that holiday, you played on your own.'

* * * * *

Tomorrow I will go down to the sand again, by the edge of the sea and under the sky, to savour that breadth and that openness. I will relish those precious hours spent on the borderline, the sun on my back, the breeze in my face. I will search for a heart-shaped crystal shell. If I look hard enough I will find it, I will find the peridor. I am certain of that. And the peridor will lead me back to Sally. I know you Sally. I remember you. Sally, oh Sally. I loved you then, I love you now and I always will.

# Running Away

About three miles into the London Marathon, I noticed this t-shirt ahead of me. It was unusual. 'RUNNING FOR TOM AND MAGGIE' it shouted in big red letters on white cotton. I ran alongside, then glanced across at the woman wearing it. She was a little shorter than me, a little older. In profile, her nose and chin appeared prominently pointed. Her shiny black hair curled under her left ear. Her left cheek (the one I could see) was red and blotchy. She was no beauty.

'How's it going?' I asked.

'Bugger off,' she replied. Fair enough. I could take that. I dropped back a little and gazed at her bottom - firm buttocks tightly encased in black Lycra. Good for her age.

A tall, gangly youngster dressed as 'Beer-and-Fags Man' came lolloping past, covered in bottles and cigarette packets. He had a can of lager in one hand and a glowing cigar in the other. Probably fake, but I wasn't sure. And he was playing to the crowds, kissing the girls, giving out plenty of 'Oggy, oggy, oggy'. Prat. Surely a first-timer. You can't joke your way round a marathon. With any luck I'd pass him at twenty miles, spewing his guts out.

Shortly after the five-mile marker I again spotted the t-shirt, the shiny black hair and the bottom bobbing along a few yards ahead.

'Going okay?'

She glanced across at me. 'Sorry about before. I was a bit ….' She didn't explain. I wasn't sure but I thought she might have been crying. Unusual that early. Later, yes. But not five miles in.

'Who are Tom and Maggie?' She looked puzzled. 'On your back,' I added with a nod of the head. It was quite a while before she answered. We were in a crowded section, coming up to the Cutty Sark, plenty of noise, and you feel like you ought to acknowledge all that cheering, give a wave. That early you still look fit and strong, can pretend to be confident. Perhaps that was why she didn't reply immediately. Or maybe there was another reason.

'Tom's my husband,' she said when we had run through onto a quieter stretch. 'Was.' I waited for more and eventually it came. 'He's dead,' she said.

'I'm sorry.' You have to say it. Maybe I meant it.

'We used to run together. One of hundreds of things we shared. Last time I ran the London was with him. I miss him so much. Soul-mates we were.'

We ran side by side without talking for a while. I thought about her sadness. I waved occasionally to the cheering crowds. She didn't.

Gradually I became aware of a change in the ambient odour. You don't realise it from watching on TV, but marathons are smelly events. There's always a pungent mixture of sweat, lubricants and vapour rubs of various flavours. Now added to the mix I detected a bad-eggs smell that signalled a digestion problem. A cardboard red pillar box that we were about to overtake was the source. From within it, along with the stench, came an elderly male voice croaking a diatribe to anyone within earshot. He cursed in rhythm both with his flatulence and his chopped stride pattern.

'That effin' 'ill's done me in, straight into the effin' wind an' people keep gettin' in yer effin' way so yer can't get no effin' rhythm. These effin' straps are cuttin' into me effin' shoulders. I told 'em they effin' would. An' yer wouldn't effin' credit it - at that last drinks this effin' twat in a wheelchair only runs into me effin' ankle, don't 'e? Effin' spazzes, why can't they 'ave their own effin' races? Keep out of our way. My time's all fucked now.' He was running very slowly. He soon dropped back, still fucking and farting. I shared a smile and a shake of the head with shiny black hair. I glanced back and saw the front of the postbox carried a charity banner: 'Caring for the Disabled.'

'And who's Maggie?' It was a while before she answered. Was I in for another 'bugger off'?

'Maggie's my name.'

This was getting interesting. I was intrigued. Was she also dying? Was it the same illness that had killed her husband? How long had she got? She didn't seem ill – fit enough to run a marathon, after all.

She asked me about the charity I was running for and I told her who and why. Not the whole truth. Just a version of.

Running a marathon ought to be boring. Three hours or more, four hours, five, doing the same thing over and over again. Left foot, right foot, left foot. But your mind roams over various matters and that helps the time pass, eats up the miles. The crowd in London is constant. Whistles, klaxons, drums; loud and boisterous. It'll lift you if you let it. A conversation with a fellow runner can also help get you through the down times. You take whatever you can get.

It was around ten miles when my red-faced companion began to tell me, in bits and pieces, some of her story. 'We married very young,' she said. 'Too young – we were just kids. Ran away together. Very romantic. Ended up in a village called Reston. Scotland, the borders. Barely a few pence to rub together. Just the clothes we stood up in, as they say.'

'Didn't your parents approve?'

'No.' There was a peculiar finality in this. I knew right away she wasn't going to expand or explain. She just said it again, firmly in spite of her laboured breathing. 'No.'

'So how long did this adventure last?'

'A lifetime.'

A little later, between heavy gasps for breath, Maggie explained how they'd scratched together a living, first simply by begging, then doing odd jobs in the village. Over the years this developed into a 'House and Garden' business with Tom doing house repairs and Maggie doing landscape gardening. Eventually they'd built up a proper livelihood. But she still didn't talk about her parents. Or his. Nothing about family at all. Nothing about children. I felt it was an important part of her story. The hole at the heart of it.

'Do you have children?' You don't have to be tactful in marathon conversations.

'No.' The same finality in that simple answer. 'How about you?'

I filled her in on my domestic details. A version of. Then we compared training experiences, intended finishing time, running histories. Usual stuff. Turned out we were pretty similar in most regards. And both having a good run. Thus far. We were at halfway, just over Tower Bridge, sipping from bottles grabbed at the drinks station when she dropped the next bombshell.

'He died in an accident,' she said. 'Drowned.'

'That's terrible.' Another automatic response.

'We were out on the lake. The boat capsized. Hit some driftwood. It should have been both of us. They managed to drag me out but never found poor Tom.'

Another period of silence seemed called for.

Now we were into the tough miles. Breathing had become difficult, limbs were aching, blisters had evolved from irritation, through discomfort, into centres of wince-inducing pain. All the runners around us were struggling. Many had resorted to walking. I noticed a huddle of St John's Ambulance staff crouching at the side of the road, tending to someone. Looked like it could be 'Beer-and-Fags Man'. I hoped he was okay. Yes, really. Marathons bring out your caring side. There, but for the grace of the marathon gods ...

Maggie and I ran side by side without talking. At this stage conversation is hard, breath is too precious. The mile markers and the drink stations become your main focus, often your sole focus. The distance between them grows longer, stretches, stretches. You tell yourself it's not so but that's what it feels like. It was at twenty-one miles, coming out of the Isle of Dogs, that Maggie stopped running. 'I'm knackered,' she said. 'You go on.'

'No, I'll walk with you. I'm not feeling great either.' It was a lie, I felt fine. But I was sure there was more to Maggie's story. I felt she needed to tell it and I wanted to hear it. 'We'll walk for a bit. See how it goes.'

A bit later, Maggie continued. 'It was nearly five years ago that Tom died. I still think of him every day.'

'You must have loved him very much.'

'Yes'. That same simplicity I had already become used to.

I glanced across to Maggie. Now we were walking I could see her face more clearly. It was smeared with sweat and tears, but looked quite cute in a homely way. Certainly softer, less angular and more attractive than I'd thought at first. 'Sorry for all the questions,' I said.

'It's okay,' she said, 'I like to talk about him. I cry a lot but that's just me.' She smiled a weak smile.

The Angel Gabriel trotted past, surprisingly sprightly, dressed in a tutu, carrying a limp wand and (who knew why, maybe he'd mixed up the biblical references?) a cardboard trumpet. A rhinoceros lumbered by, provoking particularly raucous responses from the onlookers. I knew from experience that the more weighty the fancy dress that overtakes you, the worse your time will be. Not that I was bothered any more. My finishing time was no longer a priority.

We walked along the embankment and then turned away from the river, under the shadow of Big Ben, and headed towards the finish. Awaiting us were the medals and the goody bags, the congratulations and the space blankets. The stiff-legged, sore-footed trudge home. Separately. We knew we'd never meet again. That's always the way with marathon friendships – they're like holiday romances only more so. Less so. Maggie looked at me closely for perhaps the first time.

'Thanks for listening,' she said. 'It's helped me get through.'

I think she was talking about the marathon.

She paused, weighing something up. 'Look, I've never told anyone this, but I'd like you to know. I need to share it with someone. I think it'll be safe with you. What I told you before wasn't quite true. Tom and I were never married.'

I wasn't shocked. 'I don't think that's such a big deal, you know. I suppose it may have been back then, but these days most people are not so bothered. Don't worry about it.'

'Oh, I don't. It's not that. Not only that. There's something else. The reason we didn't marry.'

'Let's jog to the finish line,' I said. We were passing Buckingham Palace. A couple of hundred metres to go.

'Sure,' she said. We broke into a steady synchronised shuffle, dragging our aching limbs through the last few strides. The cheering crowds make you feel special, even though ten thousand have finished before you.

'So why didn't you marry?'

'Because.' She hesitated. 'You see.' One last intake of breath and she let it out. 'We didn't marry because we couldn't.' She turned her face to mine and I could see she was crying again. 'Tom was my brother.'

# Strictly Sacred

There are just two of them left as we prepare for The Final. That's how it should be and precisely how the TV stations like it: two protagonists remain standing, and now they will be going head-to-head, trading blows, attacking and defending. Then, after the votes have been cast, counted and verified, the overall winner will be announced: one winner and one loser, a victor and a vanquished, a champion and a failure.

It's been a good year, perhaps not vintage but with all the essential ingredients to make for a vibrant series: some surprises, some disappointments and a modicum of controversy. This year, for the first time, TV coverage has been almost global. The UK took the lead and all the usual Eurovision countries were involved, but also there was peak-time distribution in the Americas, Asia (the Indian subcontinent participating with particular enthusiasm) and even some countries in Africa. Organising the voting on this scale in a fair and equitable manner has been a logistical nightmare, especially taking into account the various time differences, but despite a few glitches and the occasional complaint, the technology appears to have coped remarkably well.

Some of the early presentations came across as rather timid and tame, but the results-shows still managed to produce high drama right from the start. The favourites were playing it safe, doing enough to get through without playing all their aces too early. One or two others, what you might term 'mid-table' contenders, tried the same tactics but came unstuck, suffering early exits: it's a difficult balance to get right.

As everyone remembers, the *Jedi* were the wildcards in the pack this year. They were the bookies' favourites to go out in week one. The judges' collective condemnation seemed as though it had sealed their fate: 'Not even a proper religion, darling,' said one. Another offered a more thorough denunciation: 'A one-trick pony, my old son, relying on a pretty feeble joke from 2001 when you tried to persuade the British electorate to put you down as their religion in the census. You've had your day in the sun, now clear off to the dark side.' The great voting public, perverse as ever, kept them in for week after week. The *Jedi* did have one quite neat catch-phrase, 'May the Force be with you,' simple and accessible, but their platform of 'peace, justice and love' was insufficiently distinctive to separate them from their rivals. Ultimately, being fictionally-based meant their support was too fragile and could not be sustained; they exited in week six.

Returning to the start, many viewers probably don't even remember that the *Spiritualists* were in this year's competition: they were the first casualties. As the joke of the time had it, they were handicapped by the rule that dead people were not allowed to vote. Their main approach was to advise viewers to consult with their 'spirit guides' in order to find out who they should vote for: that didn't work out as well as they hoped it would. They had fore-grounded their belief in reincarnation, and as at least one social medium thread suggested that meant it was okay if they lost this time, because they would always be able to come back in the future and try again as often as they wished.

The first shock was that the *Hindus* had to go home in week two, despite a substantial Indian block vote. They'd had a warning in week one when they'd finished in the pray-off, the voters perhaps having been influenced by one of the judges who described their mantra of honesty, patience and compassion as 'boring, boring, boring'. Though they upped their game in week two, it was perhaps a mistake to try and teach both Dharma and Kama almost simultaneously, causing confusion in some quarters. But surely their fate was sealed through being so ill-prepared: 'You have to do your homework' was one judge's accurate piece of advice. When faced with the most predictable question, 'Is there or is there not a God?' they appeared to have no answer; or rather they had too many answers – maybe, maybe not, maybe one, maybe many, all possibilities appeared acceptable and the floating voters couldn't accept such procrastination.

*Buddhism* had come out strongly, second on the leader board in week one, but as a result they probably became complacent. Despite being another contender with a strong base in Asia, stretching from Mongolia to Sri Lanka, they failed to pick up sufficient votes elsewhere. The 8-fold path was widely seen as too complex, their lack of a creator a major deficiency, and the Middle Way – ridiculed by one judge as 'Namby-pamby liberal fence-sitting, not good enough at this level' – left many viewers cold. One judge scoring them 'two' didn't help, adding (not the only time he used this joke), 'My friends: you need a miracle to survive.' Week three saw their departure.

Week four brought the first major controversy. It was Hallowe'en week. There were threats of boycott from those contenders who saw this theme as favouring the *Christians*, it being a Christian festival. Yet ironically it was the Christian group which was most opposed to the supernatural connotations inherent to this theme and threatened to walk out. The organisers tried to appease everyone by asserting that the origins of Hallowe'en were *Pagan* and as there were no *Pagans* participating this year, that was all right. In the end, it was a very watered-down and superficial version of the ghostly, spooky, other-worldly spectacle that went to air. The *Rastafarians* triumphed on the night. The dreadlocked Rastafaris, dressed in their familiar red, gold and green, treated the whole event as a major *binghi*, singing and dancing their way through their presentation (the sections showing the smoking of cannabis having been edited out). Apart from the glorification of Zion, much of the content was incomprehensible, but that didn't seem to matter: it was clear that everyone had a great time and that was all that mattered. Then, in the third major surprise of the season, they were voted out: all straw polls showed their set to have been a huge triumph, so voters must have thought they were safe and therefore used their votes to prop up other groups considered more vulnerable. An unlucky exit.

The exotic flavour of *Shinto* is believed to be the reason for their good run in this year's series. The oriental ritual inherent in this Japanese religion, contrasted as it was with the informality of 'folk Shinto', provided a broad church, accessible to many beyond the true believers. Hence, although never serious contenders for the Glitter Chalice, they did well, finally leaving in week five. That left six contenders still in the running when we arrived at Jerusalem week.

Of course, the choice of Jerusalem for the venue that week caused more controversy and dissension, but those with grievances were soon appeased; ('None of the religious histories of the city will be mentioned or even alluded to,' assured a spokesperson for the production company). The boycott threat soon fizzled out and everyone chose to continue in the competition. Many observers had begun to believe that the *Zoroastrians* could go all the way and their odds had shortened considerably. It had been very astute of them to emphasise the fact that their religion pre-dated (and so, by implication, was superior to) the more mainstream of their rivals; this approach drew in votes from across the religious spectrum, in addition to non-believers. Who could argue with 'Good thoughts, Good words, Good deeds'? This message was reinforced by the judge who paraphrased it as: 'Good slogan, Good argument, Good luck!' But the other contenders were all upping their game by this stage of the competition and the *Zoroastrians* were squeezed out in week seven. *Sikhism* suffered a similar fate a week later: they had also used the 'all-inclusive' tactic, asserting that *Sikhism* was compatible with other religious traditions, that it provides a framework, an all-encompassing scenario of a disciplined way of life. But being all things to all people wasn't going to work in the closing stages: it was 'make-your-mind-up' time, in the words of one aged judge; 'To Sikh is not, apparently, to find,' added another.

So to the semi-final and the one group who had defied the bookmakers and survived the pray-off three times: *Candomblé*. Perhaps their success has no rational explanation. 'A – ma – zing' and 'OMG' had been two of the more memorable comments from an otherwise normally harsh judge who continually scored them highly, and this seemed to catch the mood of the moment. This is a popular religion in South America, especially Brazil, so they had a strong base vote, but they drew support from far wider afield. Perhaps it was the natural tendency to root for the underdog that underlay their success; perhaps the references in their presentations to aspects of both *Islam* and *Catholicism*; perhaps the links with Africa: any of these could have aroused the enthusiasm of the neutrals and earned them the votes they needed to outlast many of their more fancied rivals.

But at the semi-final stage, *Candomblé* was deemed to be too obscure a religion to survive. 'Can do? Can't do! Won't do!' was one judge's final denunciation, scoring them just six, low for this stage of the contest. *Judaism*, suffered from the opposite problem: it was too well-known. So those viewers not born to the faith could not be won over and regarded it, of the remaining contenders, the easiest to reject. The *Judaism* cause wasn't helped by the supposed wit of the judges which continually emphasised all the well-known Jewish clichés, with much cruel negativity hiding behind Shylock and Fagin impersonations. There were several protests submitted on the grounds that these were anti-Semitic comments and went beyond acceptable playful banter: the rejection of the final protest was surprisingly harsh in its criticism of this group's overall approach, asserting that the Holocaust had been used over-zealously and inappropriately and therefore (through some rather obscure logic) the group had invited ridicule. So these were the two religions which fell by the wayside at the final hurdle and that left the two favourites, the two usual suspects, to contest the final.

So who will win the final? The *Christians* have played a blinder this year, highlighting a few miracles but repeatedly playing the Christmas card, with the virgin birth and the magic of the nativity scene proving particularly popular. They are presumably saving the crucifixion and resurrection and promise of salvation for their showpiece in the final. In the beginning, commentators had felt that the *Islamists* were faced with an insurmountable problem: how could they explain away and distance themselves from the Western media's portrayal of their religion as dominated by terrorists, suicide-bombers and Jihadists? Their strategy was masterly: they simply ignored that extreme wing of Islam altogether. They kept their message simple and positive, returning repeatedly to the Quran and the Five Pillars of Islam, to love and to peace. One idea floated on the web page suggested that some neutrals were perhaps not even aware that 'Muslim' is the name given to followers of Islam; therefore the post 9/11 anti-Muslim prejudice had less effect on their vote than predicted. Be that as it may, they are widely regarded as worthy finalists. All the current rumours confirm that the Islamic showpiece in the final will centre around the 'Day of Resurrection' and the promise of a heavenly eternity supplied by that event.

So Resurrection, Heaven and Hell have been chosen by both the remaining religions to be the final battlegrounds. How appropriate is that?! Now, as we await the culmination of the series in this fascinating duel, we are all anticipating the battle ('Armageddon' as it is being heralded) with bated breath. There remains just one thing we can do to try and influence the outcome and that is to follow the oft-repeated advice of the presenters of the programme: we must all …. 'Keeeeep praying.'

# Another Bad Day for Jane

'All men are rapists.' Many people have said that. I used to think it was Andrea Dworkin who started it (American feminist of the 70s/80s), but then someone told me that was a misreading of her work. What she really said was … What she meant was … No. It's gone. Faded into the muddy past along with so much else. I'm surprised I can even remember her name. Remembering my own's hard enough. No idea what she really meant. Or said. I ought to know, used to know, but I don't, not any more. That was a different world, back then. A world of knowing, of certainty and optimism. Things seemed to matter. Everything was exciting and new and … And yes, I was happy. Happier than I realised. Happier than I am now.

No, that's silly. Rose-coloured spectacles and all that. Where does that sort of thinking get you? Pull yourself together, woman. Hankering after the past never helps with the present. I don't want anyone to start feeling sorry for me, pitying me. I'm happy, I am. Life's good. Anyway, not so bad. Some people might see me as a full-time loser, a woman whose life's a constant nightmare, every day packed full of disasters. But that's not how it is, not always. No really, it's not like that. I've been unlucky, that's all. In between the troubles, as you might call them, we've had some good days.

For instance, a couple of weeks back I took the kids to that farm, on the other side of the motorway. That was a good day. It hardly rained at all and Rachel and Mickey had a whale of a time. It was only the cows that Rachel said were gross. We got really close to the pigs and the kids loved how the little pink piglets squabbled and scampered around and were poked by their mum, and nobody minded the smell too much. We sat through the sheep-shearing demonstration which was fascinating, even if it did get a mite boring towards the end. Well it went on a bit and the puns began to wear thin: 'ewe' know what I mean (oh dear). We all enjoyed looking for the eggs and what did it matter that the kids didn't actually find any. And then we got to feed the orphaned lambs and though Rachel had one of her funnies, Mickey loved it. We had to catch them first, the lambs that is, and Mickey, a bit too enthusiastic as usual, managed to get his arm squashed when that devil-child who'd been causing mayhem all day – why can't parents control their children? - slammed the gate on it. He didn't cry for long, considering. All in all it was a good day. So there. And we've had other days just as good. I'm sure we have.

But yes, some days are like today: things spiral out of control, go from bad to worse. Not good. Days like today I wish I'd stayed in bed. Fat chance! Rachel was up three or four times last night, throwing up and complaining of stomach pains. Probably eaten something she shouldn't have. I gave her some of that pink medicine, rather more than you're supposed to at her age but eventually it did the trick. I got her up and ready for school this morning, but she turned her nose up at breakfast which is never a good sign. I was thinking she looked a bit pale when she clutched her hand to her mouth and ran upstairs to the toilet. She nearly made it.

I couldn't let her go to school after that so she went back to bed. Fortunately Wednesday's the day Mickey goes with Kevin and his mum because of football, so that was one less problem. But I had to go shopping so had no choice but to get Rachel up again and take her with me. She wasn't happy getting in the car, still feeling queasy, but I gave her some *Kwells* and crossed my fingers. I needed to get Mickey a new geometry set – he's 'lost' the last one, but I'm sure someone nicked it off him, even though he says they didn't. I hope he's not being bullied. I also had some things to get from *Boots*. Then I went to

*Asda* to pick up a couple of days worth of meals and bits and pieces for the kids' lunch-boxes. I know I get my discount at *Tesco*'s but sometimes the rebel in me says I owe them nothing so why shouldn't I shop somewhere else? They always want me to do evenings and weekends but I can't because of the kids, unless they happen to be at their dad's. They're so petty – *Tesco*'s, not the kids – they cut my hours because I wasn't 'flexible' enough as they put it, so now it's only three mornings a week.

*'I swear by almighty God that I will faithfully try the defendant and give a true verdict according to the evidence.'*

It was in *Asda* that Rachel threw up again, right in the middle of the yoghurts and fresh cream. Fortunately they weren't too busy, but it was still embarrassing. I could have died. They were very good. They let her sit down for a while in an office out back, brought her a glass of water, offered me a cup of tea. She soon brightened up a bit, began to get her colour back, but my timing was all screwed. By the time we got back to the car there was a ticket on the windscreen. Sometimes I think the world's got it in for me. I was only a few minutes over – okay maybe 10, certainly no more than 15, but even so. Anyone else would have got away with it. £60 was the fine, but when I read the small print I found it was only £30 if you paid right away. Woo-woo! Still, that's £30 I can't afford. I'll have to borrow it from the Christmas tin, which'll leave it a smidgen away from empty.

This afternoon, social services came calling. I didn't realise that's who it was at first. There were two of them. A small chubby woman, forty-ish, fuzzy hair, glasses, stern face. She was wearing a thick brown overcoat – well, it was quite chilly this morning – and when she took it off she had underneath a longish pleated skirt over dark green woollen tights and a bright orange cardigan. Nice! The man with her was younger, younger than me, wearing a suit and tie and an inane grin that seemed painted on. And – yes, really – he was carrying a clipboard. I assumed they were doing a survey, probably they were going to try and sell me something I didn't want or need, or maybe it was religion. Same difference. But then the woman showed me some sort of ID. I didn't look at it. She told me her name and that didn't register either. Then she said they were from social services. That's when I took notice.

There's no good time for social services to drop by, but I ask you, what's my luck like? First, I'm in my dressing gown caked in heavy make-up at three in the afternoon. I'd been upstairs on the webcam. Well, like I said, *Tesco*'s have cut my hours and I have to get money from somewhere. Jim pays the mortgage but other than that how am I supposed to bring up two kids? So that didn't look good.

I have no choice but to ask them in. Then I start seeing things through their eyes. I do try and keep the place presentable, but you know how it is. This morning's breakfast things were still in the sink. Yes, okay, so were yesterday's dinner plates and some cups and glasses ... you get the picture: they certainly did. Speaking of glasses, there were empty bottles on the side, five of them. That didn't look good either. I wished I'd got around to fixing the kitchen door, then maybe I could have kept that clutter hidden.

'You live on your own?' asked the woman, her eyes on the bottles.

'With Rachel and Mickey. The children.'

'Right.'

The front room wasn't much better. In the corner was a pile of ironing. Alongside it was the ironing board with the iron on it. I'd been going to get stuck into that later, but this morning I only had time to iron Mickey's school shirt. In between clearing up after Rachel. There were magazines on the floor – mine and the kids – the Hoover (another chore on the to-do list), a dishcloth, discarded clothing, empty crisp packets and half-empty Coke cans, a disorderly pile of mail (mostly bills) I'd been meaning to have a go at. Just everyday stuff that accumulates the way it does, but I'm sure to them it looked slovenly.

I offered them a drink, making it clear I meant coffee or tea, not alcohol. The man had a black coffee, the woman a sweet tea. I had tea with no sugar: I'd much rather have two spoonfuls but you have to try, don't you? I was pleased to find three mugs that matched (nearly) and even some biscuits that had somehow survived last week's binge.

I asked them what it was all about, why they were doing me the honour of a visit. That was the point at which Rachel took it into her head to start playing up. She's usually fine when we have guests but – I suppose it was because she was feeling poorly – this time she was a major pain. She was tugging at my arm and whining – 'Can I have a drink?' 'Where's the TV control?' 'What's the time?' Give me this, give me that, she kept wittering on, even when I was talking to the 'guests', ignoring my attempts to shush her. I didn't slap her but I got mighty close. I probably would have if they'd not been there. Sometimes you have to. What I did do was shout at her, very loudly. Dragged her out into the hall and told her to get up to her room and not come out till she was ready to apologise. I heard myself through their ears. I sounded freaky, out of control. I saw the man write something on his clipboard.

'She's normally so good,' I said, sitting down again and trying to sound calm. 'Just sometimes. You know. She's not herself today. And she's still so young. You sometimes forget because she looks so grown-up. Tall.'

'Yes,' said the woman, giving nothing away. 'That was ... Rachel.' I saw she had a folder in her lap and had flipped it open. 'Shouldn't she be at school?'

'She's been sick,' I said. 'This morning. Vomiting.' I didn't sound convincing even to myself. Why do these people make you feel so guilty?

'Actually, it's Michael we'd like to talk to you about.' She looked at her file again.

'Oh, Mickey. What's he been up to now? More murder and mayhem.' It was supposed to be a joke but they didn't laugh. The man grinned but by then I'd realised that meant nothing, it was just the shape of his mouth.

'Well,' said the woman, a sort of throat-clearing word. From the look on her face I was guessing what was to follow wouldn't be good 'We've had a report.'

'All good, I hope. In line for a medal.' Another joke, as flat as the first.

'Mrs …' Another glance at her notes. This woman wasn't exactly blessed when it came to memory. 'Mrs Henderson.'

'That's me,' I said, holding my hands out palm upwards. 'Da-da.'

'This is a serious matter, Mrs Henderson.'

I nodded. I didn't trust myself to say anything. I can't help it. When I get nervous I lose control over what comes out of my mouth.

'According to …' I could see she was trying to resist the temptation to look again at her notes. 'According to his teacher, Michael has a large bruise on his arm. Do you know how he came by it?'

I shook my head. 'No.' I stared out of the window. Nothing out there to help me. 'No. I can't say I do. But you know what kids are like. Always falling over. Especially boys.'

'So you don't consider this bruise to be important?

'No. Yes. I didn't mean that. It's always important. That's what we're her for, us mums.' It occurred to me that she probably wasn't a mother so using the 'in-this-together' tactic was another blunder by yours truly. 'Pick them up. Dust them down. Send them off to their next disaster.'

And so the conversation stumbled on, as conversations do when you feel out of control, out of your depth. I tried to say the right things, to make a favourable impression, but the more I tried the more I seemed to achieve the opposite. It turned out this wasn't the first time school had noticed bruising on Mickey. Well no, I could have told them that. There was the twice he'd fallen off his bike – no, make that three, - the time he ran into the corner of the shed playing football in the garden, oh and he got a heck of a bump from banging his head on the table when … You get the picture. If it's there, Mickey will find a way to fall over it, bump into it or cut himself on it. I remembered the gate squashing his arm at the farm, that would have been what caused the latest bruise, but because I'd only just said it I could see they thought I'd made it up. I wondered if I should mention the bullying. Well, I wasn't sure. Had no proof. I didn't say anything.

Then they asked about Jim. They knew about the children's father: presumably that was on the school records. They knew I'd married again but didn't know me and Jim had split up, soon to be divorced. They made me feel guilty about that. If they'd known about his violence and his affairs they might have seen it all rather differently. But hey ho. It's the man what gets the pleasure, it's the woman gets the blame. That's just life, isn't it? Then they asked about my mother. That made me mad. I couldn't see what she had got to do with anything and I told them as much in no uncertain terms. Another black mark.

Best part of an hour and a half they were here. I tried offering them another drink after the first hour in the hope they'd refuse because they'd got to go somewhere else. No such luck. Once they left (eventually) I did two things. Number one was opening a bottle of Sauvignon Blanc. Just a sip. Then I went up to see Rachel. She'd been asleep but woke up when I went in. I gave her a hug, asked how she was feeling, told her I was sorry for shouting. I think she'd forgotten. She seemed better, more colour in her cheeks. I asked if she wanted something to eat. When she came down I made her toast and jam. Funny how she likes that. Most food that they think of as 'old-fashioned' they won't touch with a barge pole.

*'I swear by almighty God that I will faithfully try the defendant and give a true verdict according to the evidence.'*

I drank another half glass of wine. Blurred the edges a bit, made the world look a little softer, less sharp, more tolerable. I know what you're thinking. But when you're ... what's the euphemism they use? ... 'On a budget'? Let's call a spade a spade: when you're poor. The important thing when you're poor is getting priorities right. Sorting out the luxuries from the essentials. And (I'm sorry) an occasional glass of wine is essential. For me. I don't think I could get through the week without it, now I've given up smoking. Certainly not weeks that include days like today. I felt like I'd been sitting through an examination. That's a feeling I do remember. *Time's up*, they say, and you ought to feel better because it's over, but that only signals the start of the real stress, through the long wait for the results. They didn't give me any 'results', those people from social services, no verdict, no conclusion. They said they'd be in touch. Lord knows what that means, what the 'subtext' is. I just know it's not good. It's as if they're stalkers and they're going to pounce again any time. While pretending they've got my best interests at heart.

We walked down to pick up Mickey from Kevin's. He was on great form, bouncing around like he does, full of everything the day had brought, the footie especially (he'd scored a great goal), but also wanting to share everything else, relishing living it all a second time. Once we were out

of sight of Kevin's house I gave him a hug. Not too tight.
He soon pulled away. The bruise on his arm did look bad,
all brown and purple, but it didn't seem to be bothering
him.

*'I solemnly, sincerely and truly declare and affirm that I will
faithfully try the defendant and give a true verdict
according to the evidence.'*

It's early evening now and I'm heading for Debbie's. I do
sometimes feel guilty, the way I use Debbie. But she knows
I'd be there for her if the boot was on the other foot. Only
lately it never seems to be: it's always me in pieces and
Debbie doing the putting back together. The last two
bottles of wine are in the carrier and they keep chinking
together. Fortunately there aren't too many people around.
They'd have me down as a wino, due to the jangling of the
bottles and the tears running down my face. It's not Rachel
I'm crying over: kids get sick all the time and then get
better. It's not the parking fine. What's money anyway? It's

not even those bloody social workers and their poncey, patronising, judgmental, smarmy voices and ugly faces. Although I am quite annoyed with them. No, the tears are because of the letter that came this morning. I knew it was coming. Jim and I had agreed it was time we got divorced. First thing we'd agreed on for years. He'd said it would be painless. A clean break so we could get on with our lives. Huh! I should have guessed that rat, that scheming, lecherous, arrogant rat, wasn't to be trusted. I still had to read the letter, the letter from his solicitor, three times. I so couldn't believe it. That fucking bastard only wants the house. Okay, a share of it, half-and-half, all so reasonable. But there's no way I can buy him out. That means we'll have to sell up. And with my half – or the fraction left once the mortgage has been paid off – I might have enough to buy a garden shed. We'll be homeless, me and the kids. Out on the street. More tears seep from my eyes as I think about it. Debbie will know what to do. She'll have an answer. I'm sure she will. I can depend on Debbie.

I've taken the kids to Karen, down the road. She's always happy to have them for a bit. The four of them – Rachel, Mickey and her two – get on like a house on fire. They'll sleep over at hers and she'll take them to school tomorrow. So there'll be no rush. As I told her, I just need a bit of space. I didn't have to go into details. She's good like that.

I walk up Debbie's drive. It's getting chilly now the sun's gone. All I'm wearing is sweat pants and a sloppy jumper. I should have brought a coat. Maybe she'll give me a lift back later. The bottles are still chinking. I ring the bell. Straight away I know it's not Debbie coming to the door. Through the glass I can see a dark shape, plenty of height and broad shoulders. The door opens.

'Hi Jane, come on in.' He steps aside. It's Frank, Debbie's better half. I go through into their front room and notice the signs. The signs are not good. There's a pint glass on the side table half full of beer. Beside it there are three unopened cans alongside the open one, a king-size packet of crisps and a remote for the DVD. There's an easy chair and a footstool pointed towards the TV; the screen is static but flickering, the action on pause.

'Debbie not here?' I ask. I've already worked that out, I'm not stupid, but I need to make it clear it was her I'd come to see.

'No, I thought she told you. She's taken the kids to her mum's for a few days.'

I'm bemused for a second, then remember. 'Your half-term's different from ours, isn't it. We're not off till next week.' I'm standing in the middle of the room, handbag over my shoulder, clutching the carrier bag and feeling stupid, wrong place, wrong time. 'Sorry to barge in,' I say. 'My head's all over the place. It's been one of those days. I'll leave you in peace.' I look towards the beer. 'Looks like you're well settled in for the evening.'

He laughs in a conspiratorial sort of way. 'Making the most of a few hours of freedom,' he says. 'The dancing girls are booked for 8 o'clock.' He places a finger to his lips and whispers: 'Don't let on.'

I make it as far as the hallway. 'Don't feel you have to rush off,' he says from behind me. I turn. 'Having trudged all the way up here. At least stay for a cuppa.'

*No,* is what I should have said. Right then. And left. Gone home. But I'm feeling awfully weary, from the events of the day and the climb up the hill. The thought of a few moments' sit down is appealing. I look at my watch for no good reason. Nothing to get back for. 'Oh, alright then. You've twisted my arm. I won't stay long.'

I hear him put the kettle on and then he comes back into the front room and swiftly re-arranges the furniture, turns off the TV. I sit down on the sofa, put down the carrier bag and I can tell he's heard the bottles. 'Would you rather something stronger?' he asks. I sheepishly pull out my two bottles of Sauvignon Blanc and he smiles as he takes them. 'From the look of you I think you could do with some of this.' I ineffectively wipe at my tear-stained cheeks with my thumb.

*'I swear by Allah that I will try the defendant and give a true verdict according to the evidence.'*

I've known Frank for almost as long as Debbie has. Actually, it may even be longer. We were all in the same crowd, back in the day. Then the two of them got together at that New Year's Eve party, when I somehow got landed with spotty Brian. They make a great couple, same crazy sense of humour, both into films in a big way, and they've grown into wise parents after those early glitches. We've stayed close through the years. Ended up living in the same town and that wasn't entirely a coincidence. They've been good to me, through my ups and downs. Mostly downs. Of course, it's mainly been Debbie – there are some things only women can share – but Frank's been there in emergencies, especially lately since Jim left and I've been on my own: ferrying children around, finding the stopcock when there was all that water, repairing the broken window (one of Mickey's little accidents). This evening he soon has me relaxed enough to talk about my latest woes, the social services, the letter from Jim's solicitors. It's a different version from what I'd have told Debbie. She knows me so well. On the same wavelength. But Frank is a good second best. He listens, says all the right things, keeps the wine flowing. The main difference from Debbie is that Frank doesn't offer solutions. Debbie has that knack of understanding exactly what's needed to solve a problem and gets it solved. Frank is altogether lower key, more easy-going, favours the slow and steady approach. Still, talking things through with him, even in the careful way you have to with a man, I begin to feel better. He re-assures me it's not as bad as I fear. That things will get better. The drink helps as well. No surprise there.

Frank puts on some ancient CDs and we talk about the old days. As students we seemed to spend more time in pubs and clubs than lecture rooms or libraries. That's what our memories tell us. We used to go out as a foursome, that was with my first husband, before the children. Now I come to think of it, we weren't even married then, but already an 'item' as they say these days.

Frank and I recall some of the good times. He says how he used to fancy me more than Debbie, back when we were all free and single. I'm not shocked. He's told me before. I laugh it off, like I always do. It was all a long time ago. Bucketloads of water under the bridge. And a fair few bottles of wine.

The CD is packed with songs from our youth. They bring back good memories. Frank stands up and reaches for my hand, extravagantly polite, all gentlemanly elegance. 'Would you do me the honour of joining me in a dance?'

'Ooh,' I say, coyly placing a hand over my mouth and fluttering my eyelashes. 'Enchantée.' I carefully get to my feet. Later I'll regret drinking so much, but right now I feel good.

He places his hands on my waist and we dance slowly. His arms wrap around me. I can feel his strength. It gives me a powerful sense of security. I feel safe, protected. I close my eyes and lean against him. Some tunes have that knack of triggering memories. I'm trying to remember the singer's name. She used to be in

*Eastenders.* Oh yes, Martine McCutcheon. *Perfect Moment.*

The next track is *Flying Without Wings.* Is that Take That?

Westlife? Some boy band. Frank kisses me full on the lips. I

kiss him back.

'No.' I jump back. 'Sorry.' I'm confused. 'Sorry

Frank. No. We shouldn't have done that. I shouldn't have.'

He just stands there, smiling. He shrugs.

I'm flustered. I put my hand to my mouth as though

to wipe away the kiss. The illicit kiss. My best friend's

husband. What was I thinking? 'I think I should go,' I say

shaking my head, looking around for my handbag. 'That

wasn't … It's not right. Too much booze.'

'Come on Jane,' he says, gently, soothing. 'No harm

done.' He takes a step towards me, holding out his hands.

'I'm sorry. It was just … Felt like a moment. Didn't it?'

I don't say anything. I'm trying to calm down. It's

not easy.

'You don't want to be going back. Not like this.

Relax. Deep breaths.'

There's an echo of a memory in that phrase. I smile, in spite of myself.

'I'll make some coffee,' he says and heads for the kitchen.

I grab my bag and scuttle out into the hall. I fumble with the front door catch. Eventually get it open. Stumble down the steps, nearly fall. I haven't got any shoes on. It's dark and the cold makes me catch my breath. Then strong arms grab me from behind.

'Jane, Jane. Don't be like this. There's no need to go. Look at you, you're shivering. I'll give you a lift, get you home safely. But first, come back in for a bit. Warm up. You haven't even got any shoes on.'

It makes sense. I go back inside. I'm feeling whoozy. No fit state to be walking the streets. Certainly not barefoot. I usually hold my drink better than this.

'Sit yourself down,' he says. There are two cups of coffee on the low table. 'Cheer up,' he says.

I smile weakly. I take those deep breaths. Gradually feel a bit better. My heartbeat's steadying back to normal.

Why was I so panicky? There's nothing wrong here. Everything's normal. It's okay. I'm beginning to calm down. To get back on an even keel. He's right. What's the big deal? There's no real harm done. I like Frank and he likes me. Two friends. Sometimes these things happen. Doesn't mean anything. I ignore the coffee and take a sip of wine. Then I drain the glass. Tastes good.

*'I swear by almighty God that I will faithfully try the defendant and give a true verdict according to the evidence.'*

Why didn't I leave? I don't know. Nothing to go home for, I suppose. And it is dark and cold out there. I've been enjoying myself. Enjoying the reminiscing. Enjoying the music and the wine. Enjoying Frank's company. He's fun to be with. It has been a long time since I've enjoyed myself. And once I've calmed down, we're okay again.

We chat some more about old times. Frank has a better memory than me. And he doesn't mind being the butt of the jokes. In lots of his stories, he doesn't come out smelling of roses. One time we were in a crowd having a bit of a singsong in the street. It was late. I guess we were drunk. This policeman tells us to quieten down. It was Frank who nearly got arrested, for giving him an earful he shouldn't have. Then there was that holiday together, the four of us, a villa in Spain. What a great two weeks that was. One night Frank fell into the pool, drunk as a skunk. Took us ages to drag him out. Pissed ourselves laughing. Then Frank remembers the argument with the locals in that bar where they were showing the football. Nearly turned into a fist fight. Men, eh? He can even remember the names of the teams. When we were coming back through customs Frank made some stupid joke about carrying a bomb. We nearly missed the flight while they made us jump through all sorts of hoops. Idiot. Then there was some tale about a traffic cone, but even he can't remember the details. Lots of stories. Lots of laughs. We drink more wine and the coffee goes cold.

One of my favourite songs comes round on the CD. Ricky Martin. *Livin' La Vida Loca.* I sing along, remembering some of the lyrics. Frank suggests dancing to it. It isn't a slow number so it's safe. We prance around like crazy things. Some distorted version of the way we used to dance, though goodness only knows what we look like. I get a bit dizzy and end up collapsing full length on the sofa. Frank tumbles on top of me and we're laughing ourselves silly when suddenly the mood changes. I can see it in Frank's face. In the set of his lips and the whites of his eyes. Intensity. He is lying on top of me and tries to kiss me again. I turn my head away. Then I realise his hands are on my body, places where they shouldn't be, places I don't want them to be. His knee is pushing between my legs.

'No,' I say. 'Stop it.' I try to get up. 'Get off. Let me get up.'

I hit him on the shoulder with the palm of my hand. Push against him. Nothing has any effect.

He has me pinned down and I realise he is not going to let me get up however much I plead with him, however much I struggle. His face has changed. His breathing has changed. Frank has changed.

One thought comes into my mind. 'All men are rapists.'

**One year later**

**In the court room**

Judge: You should retire now and consider your verdict. The clerk will show you where to go and explain the process.

**In the jury room**

- I don't get why she left it to the next day to report it – That prosecution lady explained, like it's the trauma, they can't sometimes think straight, takes a while to sink in – Or takes a while to think up a story

- If I was raped I'd shout for help right afterwards. No, during.

- Two failed marriages and she'd not even forty. Tells you all you need to know.

- She was drunk, asking for it. Deserves what she got.

- You know the type. Had her bit of fun, then felt guilty, thought better of it.

- I mean, her best friend's husband! How low is that?

- She knew her friend would find out. Made sure she got her excuses in first.

- All men are rapists. Someone said that. And it's true. All they need is the opportunity. If they think they can get away with it.

- She admitted to dancing with him! Both drunk, on their own, in his house. And she dances with him. What else can you say?

- There was this other business, with the garage mechanic. What did you make of that? No smoke without fire, that's what I say – Shows what she's like. You know, puts it about.

- Doesn't go to the police till the next day. Why was that? – Seems to me she sobered up and then realised what she'd done.

- The neighbours didn't hear anything. No screams. No cries for help. Funny sort of rape.

- He's not the type. Businessman. Respectable, you can tell. His boss said what a decent chap he is. He'd never do something like that. She led him on.

- Lives up on the Blackhouse Estate. You know what they're like up there. All on benefits.

- Well, I believe her. All that hassle she's had. Nightmare, and none of it her fault. I feel sorry for her – You can feel sorry for her all you like. Don't mean she was raped.

- Because of all that bad stuff in her life, she took the opportunity for a bit of fun. I don't blame her, but I don't believe he raped her.

- He admits she didn't say 'yes' – She said she said 'No'. But we've only got her word for that – You don't have a discussion every time you have sex.

Sometimes the signals are there and you just go for it. You don't wait for written permission.

- Did he 'reasonably believe' she was consenting? That's the question we have to answer. It's on the sheet - Right. Someone comes into your house when they know you're alone, gets drunk and dances with you. Lets you kiss her. I know what I think.

- Why did it happen on the sofa? If it was consensual they'd have gone upstairs, found a comfortable bed. That's what I'd have done – What, his wife's bed? Her friend's bed? I don't think so.

- She should never have gone to the house. She must have known he was on his own. And she took wine with her. She was setting him up.

- She knew her friend was away. Grabbed the opportunity.

- She'd been separated for ... what was it? A year? She'd not been getting any. She was desperate.

- He was as drunk as she was. Four bottles they found. He didn't know what he was doing – Being out of it is no defence. He's still guilty.

- She trusted him. Her best friend's husband. She'd known him for years. She thought she was safe with him. All men are bastards.

- He'd been waiting his chance. He knew she was lonely, borderline desperate. Bet he'd been planning it for a while. Pretending to be a helpful neighbour. Grooming her, that's what it's called.

- She tried to run away. She wouldn't have done that if she'd been up for it – Did she try to run away? I don't remember them saying that – None of the neighbours saw her run out. Or him run after her – Anyway, she soon went back. That's not the action of someone who's scared of what might happen – He admitted she tried to leave and he had to persuade her back in. Said she was hysterical. He had to calm her down – He didn't know the neighbours hadn't heard. He needed to have a plausible story.

- Why'd he say 'no comment' when the police first questioned him? If he'd nothing to hide, he'd have explained right away – I expect that's what his lawyer told him to say. Don't think we should read too much into that – He said he was trying to protect her reputation.

- He's a wanker. All men are wankers. Only after one thing.

- Her pants were torn. They showed us – Well, you know what they're like, these days. They rip as soon as you look at them. I bought some the other day. Once through the wash and they're ruined.

- The medical evidence didn't say anything about cuts and bruises. How do you get raped and not have any injuries?

- Can you give consent when you're drunk? – Allowing yourself to get drunk. That's a sign you're up for it, seems to me. When I've had a few, I'm anybody's.

- The medical evidence said she was over the drink-drive limit. That was the next day. At the time she must have been barely conscious – You can drink yourself sober, you know. If you get really pissed, then keep drinking, you sober up - Is that really true? – Yes, happens to me all the time.

- I don't know what happened. Both of them sounded so believable. How do we know? We're supposed to be certain, but I don't see how we can be – 'Beyond all reasonable doubt,' that's what they say – No, the judge said ignore that. Just 'be certain' he said.

- He'd spiked her drinks. You don't do that if your intentions are honourable – We've only got her word for it, that her drinks were spiked – Did she say that? – She said about the strange taste. And feeling more drunk than she normally would. She didn't sound too sure – So drunk she couldn't remember.

- If we convict him, that's the end of his life, his marriage, his career. Hefty jail sentence – We shouldn't think about that. Nothing to do with us.

- Her friendship's over anyway. That Debbie will take her husband's side over her friend. Bet you.

- What about that porn site? I didn't get that. Is she on there? – Yeah, you can get money. Blokes send you money to take your clothes off – What's that got to do with anything? – It's what she's like. You know.

- She admits she kissed him. I tell you, she wanted him. It's always the woman who does the choosing. Maybe later she thought better of it, but at the time there was only one thing on her mind.

- She got rid of the kids for the night. Why'd she do that? Pretty sure I know.

- If it wasn't rape, why did she say it was? If she'd kept quiet, no-one would have known. Why'd she want to deliberately hurt her friend, spoil her friend's marriage? – Jealous, maybe. Her friend had something she didn't. Some people will do anything – She had two failed marriages so was envious of her friend's good one. Decided to break it up. She's a devious cow.

**In the court room**

Judge: 'Have you reached a verdict upon which all of you are agreed?'

Foreman of the Jury: 'We have.'

Judge: 'Do you find the defendant guilty or not guilty?'

Foreman: 'Not guilty.'

# The Peridor - Epilogue II

I live in that caravan permanently now. The same caravan we stayed in for our holidays. I'm supposed to leave in the winter but I don't. Nobody notices, or if they do they don't say. They switch off the electricity and the water but I still manage. I think of it as camping. I am a resourceful man.

It's not that time of year yet. It's still the open season. When I get back to the van after my day on the beach I make a cup of tea and two pieces of toast with marmite. It's been a good day. It always is when I can relive that holiday with Sally. I didn't find a peridor. Not this time. But there will be other days. There will always be other days. It's a pity I remember Sally's proclamation as so tentative: 'I think I might love him.' Only 'think', only 'might'. But I don't hate her for that. I could never hate Sally. She didn't know.

I've kept the cuttings. I don't get them out often because they make me sad. But today seems a good time to read them again. They say there's a storm coming so it could be several days before I can go back to the beach. Once winter comes I rather lose hope. I'll still search, I'll always be searching. But finding a peridor never seems so likely when winter takes hold.

I reach up to the top of the wardrobe and bring the tin down. I take it through to the living room. I've put the fire on and it's warmed up nicely. I clear the table of the empty mug and the plate with the toast crumbs and open the tin. The fragments of newspaper are getting old now, the print fading and the corners curling. The pages feel fragile to my fingers. I unfold them carefully and spread them out on the table. The large one is the one I like best.

It has a picture of Sally. Only black-and-white, like they were in those days, but that curly hair frames her pixie face and I remember its golden colour. She's smiling in that cheeky way she had.

I know the headline off by heart: 'Fears increase for missing schoolgirl.' The text tells the story of the 999 call, the lifeboat being launched, the hours it chugged up and down the shoreline while the police combed the beach, everyone searching, searching, searching. And finding nothing. The article ends with a plea for anyone with information to call and gives a phone number. Nowadays it would be an email and a *Facebook* page.

The other cuttings are follow-up stories. I think they call them 'human interest'. They had found friends of Sally and family members who were willing to talk about her, say how pretty and bright she was, how lively and lovable, how much missed. Her parents wouldn't talk to the press and I remember my father telling me to say nothing to anyone. Apart from the police. I told them everything.

They never found her. I do not believe she died. I do not believe she is dead now. Before we became separated she was laughing and splashing me and still telling her stories. We'd made it to The Island and she told me all about it. It was her idea that we should have a race to see who could get back quickest. I won. I wish I hadn't. I was sure she was right behind me all the way. When I walked out of the sea onto the beach I turned around and she wasn't there. I waited and waited. I waited too long. If I'd gone back sooner, told them she was missing, perhaps they'd have found her. But I didn't realise she was missing. Not like that.

I still don't think of her as missing, not lost. I believe the peridor keeps her safe. Perhaps not safe like the rest of us, not safe like we think safe should be. She's safe under the sea, safe in her world, safe and sure with her stories and with *Gabriel*, the peridor. If I had a peridor I'd ask it to take me to her. It's not too late. It's never too late. She'll be waiting for me, as always. Waiting for me to come to her. Once I find a peridor I'll go to her.

# Revenge

I was late and wet and out of breath when I arrived at the door of the restaurant. I hadn't been able to find a parking space and ended up using the multi-storey from where it's quite a hike to *Ricardo's.* And it was raining.

'Table for one, sir?'

'Yes. No. I've booked. For eight o'clock.' I looked at my watch. The black waistcoat took my name and made me wait the customary thirty seconds while he (presumably) checked it against a list. I took off my raincoat and the penguin hung it on a hook by the door.

'Please follow me, sir.'

'Is my companion here yet?' I spoke to his back. He didn't hear, or if he did he didn't respond. He led me by a circuitous route to a distant table in a dim and cramped area of the restaurant. It was set for two but Alice wasn't there. It was already 8.15.

'Anything to drink, sir?'

I hesitated. 'I'll wait till my companion arrives.'

'Very good, sir.' He bowed stiffly and walked away.

I checked my watch again and looked towards the distant door. The restaurant was busy but not full. There was a large table of women close to my left. Office do, I guessed: too old for a hen party. To the other side sat an elderly couple. Probably many years married given their solemn faces and silent eating. Further over, an animated couple, lots of laughter and smiles. Sounded false. First date? A smart and stern-looking male group of four on the far side were conducting what looked like a serious/boring business meeting.

It was nearly 8.30. I signalled to a waiter and ordered a beer. He listed several and I selected one in a manner intended to suggest an informed choice. When he brought the drink (which was an insipid lager rather than the bitter I'd hoped for) he asked if I'd like to order.

'I'm expecting someone,' I said, indicating the empty place. 'I'll wait.'

'Very good, sir.'

I wondered why Alice was so late. I checked my phone: no messages. She could have been caught in traffic. Diverted by a family emergency. Had an accident. Anything. I checked the phone again. I could call her, but that might seem too … What? Too needy? Too caring? This was not the first time we'd spent time together but it was our first proper date. The first pre-arranged evening, the first dinner. We'd had lunchtime drinks together twice. Three times if you count the first one, but that had been in a group. Somebody's birthday. I knew Alice well. We'd worked together for over a year. Not 'together' exactly, but in the same office. I suppose I shouldn't really say I knew her well. I knew things about her, the sort of things you learn incidentally, in slack times at work, during tea breaks; the output from the inane mutterings of minor cogs in the company machine. About families. Pets and hobbies, favourite TV programmes. Glimpses into a past. I never gave away too much about myself. Emphasised my quiet life, leaving her to infer that I was lonely. But we got on well, considering. Shared a liking for puzzles, horror movies and quizzes. Helped each other finish crosswords. Laughed together. I liked her because she could be amusing without being silly. It was a fine line, but of all the girls in the office – all the women – many were young and light, some were old and heavy, but Alice was just right. Should have been called Goldilocks. She'd do.

It was nine o'clock, I'd finished my second beer (which wasn't as tasteless as I'd feared) and I decided she wasn't coming. I could have stayed and ate alone, but where's the fun in that? I settled the bill. The cost of the two drinks was extortionate, to which was added an equally exorbitant booking fee and service charge. But then I had blocked a table for an hour, so I suppose they had to get their retribution somehow.

I picked up a portion of rock and chips on the corner. I had to wait for the rock to be cooked, which was why I chose it. That way you can be sure it's freshly fried. I took the paltry meal back to the car and ate it in the car park. I sent Alice a text. 'Sorry we missed each other. Some mix up, I suppose. Hope you're ok.' I thought of adding, 'Call me', 'Let me know you're alright'. But those sorts of phrases sounded too paternal, too serious. Also, no 'xx'.

I drove back home, back to my flat. It looked unusually tidy. I'd spent some of the previous evening smartening it up. It's not that I'm slovenly, but when you live alone you don't have to bother. So I'd tidied things away, had a bit of a dust round. I'd picked out some CDs I thought were appropriate. Stocked up the drinks cabinet. Well, the cupboard, I should say. Some of the grander ideas from my previous life still stay with me. I'd bought some half bottles of spirits and some mixers. I'd put clean sheets on the bed. It all seemed so much wasted time now. I made myself a black coffee and checked my phone again: no reply.

I gave it another half hour and then thumbed Alice's number. It rang three times before switching to voicemail. I didn't leave a message. Where was she? Why didn't she have her phone with her? Or why wasn't she answering it? Should I check the local A&E department? I knew there couldn't really have been a mistake. *Ricardo's* had been her suggestion and we'd both been there recently. We'd compared what we'd eaten. Agreed it was a good choice. So where was she? Why hadn't she called me? She wouldn't have stood me up. Or if she was going to, she'd have called with some sort of explanation, a plausible excuse. She was like that, Alice. Thoughtful. Kind. She wasn't the type of girl – woman – to mess around. I'd wasted an evening but I shouldn't rush to blame her. It may not have been her fault. Once I'd found out what had happened I'd take it from there; I could forgive and forget as well as the next chap.

Before going to bed I phoned her once more. This time I left a message. 'Hope you're okay, Alice. See you tomorrow.'

When I got into work next day I immediately registered her vacant desk. She was always there before me. Something about building up flexi-time so she could get away by lunchtime on Fridays. To meet her mum. But today she was late, later than me. In fact, she didn't come in all day. There was a lot of work on and nobody mentioned her being missing so I didn't ask. We hadn't let it be known that we'd fixed a date. We agreed it was for the best. Well, they'd only talk. You know what offices are like.

She wasn't there the next day either. Then it was the weekend.

When she didn't come in on Monday, I grabbed a word with Steve. He's the boss. Well, office manager I suppose you'd call him. The real bosses had offices upstairs where they hibernated, pretending to be too busy and too important to mix with the likes of us. I made my enquiry sound casual.

'No idea Jim. Nobody tells me anything. If she's called in sick HR would know, but they won't tell me until I can get a temp in. That'll be another couple of days at least. They expect me to cope if it's less than a week. Unless they know it's something serious, you know, hospital, long term, that sort of thing.'

'So you haven't heard from her?'

'Nope. That's what I said. Why're you bothered? Linda'll pick up her work. It shouldn't be coming to you.'

'No. That's okay. Just wondered. You know.'

'Right.'

At the end of the day I stayed at my desk as the others left. I sometimes do that. You get more done when it's quiet. Once the office was empty I stepped across to Alice's desk. She'd left it tidy, as always. A photo of an elderly couple had pride of place. Her parents, lived in Bristol I think. Somewhere like that. No, that can't be right because she met her mother on Fridays, didn't she? I must have misunderstood something somewhere along the line. No big deal. I checked the drawers but found nothing significant. Her diary was on her desk. We all use *Outlook* for office appointments, but I knew she kept a written record as well. The marker was in the page for last Wednesday. Three asterisks filled the space. Looked like our date had been a significant occasion. No indication of why she hadn't shown. Or why she'd not been back to work since. I flipped through the diary but there was nothing interesting, just birthdays, some phone numbers, a few cryptic symbols. I was amused to see she'd recorded that anagram. I remember her telling me she'd discovered that 'ambidextrous' was an anagram of 'must aid boxer' and she took delight in that sort of thing. In the front of the diary she'd written her address and I copied that onto my phone. I tried to log on to her computer but didn't know her password. Had she ever mentioned her mother's maiden name? If so, I couldn't remember. Anyway, Alice would be more subtle than that. I went back to her diary and flicked through it. Came back to the Wednesday entry, the asterisks, the three stars, and thought about anagrams. I guessed at a password. No good. I switched it around. Bingo! But then a page came up with one word on it. The word flashed for a couple of seconds before the screen went blank. No amount of clicking or typing produced any further reaction. Her computer had gone down. Odd. What was that all about? Oh well, they can't say I didn't try.

Back home, I opened a beer, fired up my lap-top and started streaming a film I'd been meaning to watch for a while. But I couldn't concentrate. I kept wondering what had happened to Alice. None of my business, really. We were nowhere near being a couple. Far short of that. But it irritated me to think she'd maybe got one over on me. I'd tried calling her three more times over the weekend. Left a message each time. I'd thought of asking someone at the office but there was no-one who you'd actually say was her friend. It wasn't that she was disliked. We all got on well. At that level it seems the norm in any workplace. But she came and went on her own, had lunch on her own apart from when she met her mum or there was a special occasion. I phoned her again. No answer. I texted. Waited a few minutes. No reply. It was no good: I had to visit her. Not that I was running after her. I'm not that desperate. But I had to find out. Whatever it was, I wouldn't get angry. I'd grown out of all that.

I rang the bell. I remembered the last time I expected to see her, at the restaurant. I was at another door, not so wet this time because I'd brought an umbrella, but out of breath again. That was because the lift wasn't working. Four flights of stairs had taken it out of me. I needed to get fitter, lose a bit of weight. The door opened.

'Hello,' I said.

A woman with a pale face stood there.

'Is Alice in?'

The woman turned around and walked into the flat, leaving the door open. I followed, closing the door behind me. I propped the umbrella in the corner of the tiny hall; a left turn led into a living room. First impression was of chaos, a jumble of objects in all directions as if a litter bin – several litter bins - had been randomly spilt, clutter on every surface. Including the floor. Especially the floor.

'Sorry it's such a mess,' she said as she moved a dirty plate from the sofa to the table, shifted a pile of clothes with her foot, picked up a couple of paperbacks and dropped them on the floor. 'Wasn't expecting visitors.'

She was middle-aged, forty-something, long straggly auburn hair, dressed in some sort of patterned kaftan, abstract blue design. Thick-rimmed glasses, no make-up. White lace gloves up to her elbows. Weird.

'Have a seat.' She indicated the end of the sofa, a small area now empty.

I brushed the crumbs off and sat. She made some space and sat down opposite me, on the floor, leaning against the wall. She raised her knees to her chin, without troubling to tuck her skirt in. I could see her underwear. She didn't seem to mind. I tried not to look.

'You must be Jimmy,' she said.

'Jim,' I said. 'Or James. And you are?'

'Phil.' She saw my look. 'Short for Philomela.'

There was an awkward pause. At least, I felt awkward. I didn't like it. I like to be in control. I looked at the broken flowerpot on the windowsill, the pile of earth on the carpet, the drawers in the sideboard overflowing. The corner lamp had fallen over and nobody had bothered to put it right. There was a stale smell in the air: old food, dirty clothes, ashtrays. 'So,' I said, injecting a tone of authority into my voice. 'Is Alice here?'

'No.'

'Are you expecting her?'

She didn't answer immediately. Eventually she shrugged. 'Maybe.' Another pause. 'Couldn't say.'

'Is she … okay?' I felt I was losing more ground.

'Far as I know.'

'Only … She's not been at work. For a while.'

'No.'

I kept expecting this woman, this Phil, to tell me more, to explain. It didn't seem like she was going to. She took a pack of cigarettes from a bag slung round her neck and lit up. As an afterthought she held the packet towards me. 'Smoking Kills' said the label. I shook my head. She tilted her head back and blew smoke at the ceiling.

'Do you want something to drink?' she asked. I hesitated. 'Coffee? Or maybe there's a beer?'

'No, no,' I said, holding my hand up as she seemed on the point of getting to her feet. 'I'm fine.' She sat back down. Her knickers were pale pink. She puffed on her cigarette. She seemed relaxed. I wished I was.

'We share this flat,' she said. 'Alice and me. Not cohabiting, you know. Just flat-mates. We share the rent, share the bills. Otherwise she does her thing, I do mine.'

'So you don't know where she is. When did you last see her?'

Phil gave this some thought as she puffed on her cigarette and blew more smoke. 'Before the weekend. She wasn't here on the weekend.'

'Have you seen her since Wednesday?'

'Wednesday. Last Wednesday? Like last week?' She looked at me in an appraising sort of way. She stubbed out her cigarette in a saucer and stood up. 'I need a coffee. Sure you won't?'

'I'll have a tea. Milk, one sugar.' An afterthought: 'Please.'

The tea came in a cup without a saucer. I fished out the teabag with a pen and dropped it onto the greasy plate on the coffee table. Phil sat back down against the wall, her legs now flat on the floor. She had bare feet. Her toenails were painted blue. She held a mug of black coffee in two hands and sipped cautiously.

'I tried to phone her,' I said. 'No answer.' Not sure if Phil heard me. She didn't react. Seemed to be mulling something over.

'I'm not going to let you sleep with me,' she said.

It takes a lot to throw me. My first instinct was to respond with an insult involving a barge pole. I went with my second thought: 'That sounds like a challenge,' accompanied by a shrug and a lecherous grin.

'No.' she said, 'a fact,' but I thought I detected a small smile. She sipped her coffee. I finished my tea, which was bitter, no sugar, and put the cup down on the plate. I thought I ought to leave. There was nothing for me here.

Phil stood up and left the room. She came back almost immediately and threw something towards me. I caught it. It was a mobile phone.

'Alice's?' I asked. She nodded. I found the 'on' button and scrolled down her missed calls. Mostly they were mine. A couple of others. Likewise the texts: unread. 'Why didn't she take her mobile with her?' I dropped the phone onto the cushion beside me.

'It's not the first time. She's a bit random. Like me.' Phil was still standing by the door. That didn't sound like the Alice I knew. I'd describe her as careful, precise, organised. In control. But then, what did I know? Did I even care? Not really.

'Don't you think someone should contact the police?'

Phil didn't answer. She sat down on the floor again. Raised her knees. Lit another cigarette. 'She knows about you,' she said.

'What?' A reaction more than a question. 'Well yes,' I added. 'We work together. We're … friends.'

'No,' firmly. Then more slowly: 'She really knows about you.' She emphasised each word, pointing at me with her cigarette.

I picked up Alice's phone. Went to her contacts. Perhaps I could get the number of her mother. There was nothing under 'Mum' or 'Mother'. Nothing under 'Phil'.

'She knows you're married.'

'Well, that's not true.' Too quick.

Phil raised her eyebrows.

'Okay. Maybe technically. But we've been separated for … oh, ages. Soon to be divorced. Any day now.'

'And you've got children.'

'Step-children. They live with their mother. Nothing to do with me. Not any more. Anyway, what's this got to do with anything.'

'I'm just saying. She knows you. Better than you know her.'

'So she talks about me, does she?' I was still trying to get onto the front foot. Phil puffed on her cigarette and didn't answer.

'She knows you got the sack from your last job. And why. An affair with your secretary, wasn't it?'

Back home again, I opened another beer and tried to think things through. What that woman had said, what Alice had told her, was all true. When they sacked me I knew I'd struggle to find another managerial position with no reference from my previous employer. I had to move out from Jane and her kids anyway: it had been running out of steam for a while, like they do, so her finding out about the affair wasn't such a disaster. A change of scenery seemed the best option, and I decided to plump for a simple clerical job. A bit of creativity in the CV, playing down my qualifications and salary scales (they weren't going to check carefully at that level); a good interview performance, I've always been a good talker; and that was that. A fresh start. A chance to take stock. I could get by on the low income for a while. Nobody knew me around here, so I could keep my past life secret.

Alice had started at the company a month or so after me. I was pleased, mainly because it took the pressure off. I was no longer the 'new boy', feeling that every move I made was being monitored, people waiting for mistakes they could pounce on. That may have been paranoia – they were a friendly bunch even if they were boring as hell – but I hadn't felt entirely accepted. When Alice came along and she became the focus I could blend into the crowd. I was also glad Alice had arrived because she was more attractive than the rest of them. I didn't want to rush things – it took me nearly a year to ask her out – but I knew from early on there was something there and I'd be able to win her round. Sometimes you need to play a long game.

So how had Alice found out about me? Who had told her? Why hadn't she let on? I would have told her eventually. At least about the wife (soon to be ex) and her kids. No reason to go into details about getting the sack. And there are other incidents from my past that are nobody's business but mine. Anyway, she can't have been put off by my dark past because she agreed to go out with me. On the other hand she'd then stood me up. Had she? Is that what had happened? If so, why? Why hadn't she told me she knew I was married, and that I'd been fired from my previous job? Was she intending to reveal all over dinner? Was she planning on blackmailing me? Well, it wouldn't have worked. I'd walk out on that job at the drop of a hat; meant nothing to me. You can't blackmail someone who has nothing to lose. I'd have merely moved on and picked up something similar elsewhere: no sweat.

Could arranging the date and then not showing up have been part of some grand scheme? I couldn't see how. It didn't make sense. And what I'd found on her computer. One word. A worrying word, but confusing: I didn't get it.

I had another beer and went through it all again. Where was Alice? No change. No progress. Still as much in the dark as ever. I was annoyed at not understanding; I don't like mysteries, puzzles I can't solve. I was even more annoyed that I was letting it get to me. Letting *her* get to me, that little provincial nonentity.

When I'd said to that Philomela about going to the police, I'd almost been serious. I was worried that something had happened to her. Yes, there is a caring side to me, despite what they say. But going to the police was a big step. I was less sure now, now there were these complications. The safest bet was to keep my head down. Yes, I decided to leave it for a while. Forget about it. If Alice still hadn't shown up in another week or so, maybe I'd go to the police then. Or maybe not.

In the end, I didn't need to go to the police. They came to me.

First they came to the office. I could tell something was up as soon as I got in. Tension crackled all over the place. They didn't make any grand announcement, not the police nor senior management, but the rumour soon went around that the police were here and they were asking about Alice.

It had been a fortnight or so since Alice had last been in and Steve had hired a temp who was occupying Alice's desk. She was called Becky and she was blonde and quite attractive even though she was middle-aged and plumpish. Didn't seem to know much but could cope with some of the grunt-work. The stuff from Alice's desk had been put in a box in the storeroom and that's where the police started, going through her things. Then they interviewed each of us in turn, using Steve's office. When Christine came out I asked her what they'd asked her. 'You'll have to wait and see,' she said. 'They said not to talk about it.'

When I went in, the first thing they said was that Alice had been reported as missing. I asked if it was her mum who'd reported it. Given how they looked, I guessed the answer was *No.*

They seemed confused. 'Do you know Alice's mother?' one of them asked.

'No, no,' I said. 'But Alice mentioned her. Once or twice.'

'Really?' This was the other one.

There were two of them, both young, both male, virtually indistinguishable. They exchanged glances I couldn't read. Why were they so interested in Alice's mother?

'What did she say about her? About her mother?'

'Not sure. Nothing really. Just. You know. Office chat.'

They waited for me to say more. I felt I'd already said too much. It wasn't as though I really had anything interesting or relevant to tell them. After a pause, they launched into what I assumed was the prepared interview programme. The things they'd be asking everyone. Like, when had I last seen her? What had she said? Did she say or do anything unusual? I gave what I hoped were all the expected answers. Having decided to keep my head below the parapet, the interview hadn't started well but I thought it ended okay. I felt I'd come across as suitably anonymous, simply one of the office group.

A week later they came to the door of my flat. One was a youngster; may have been one of those who'd come to the office, he was as blandly anonymous as they had been. The other one was older, not in uniform, smart grey suit. He showed me ID and told me his name. I wasn't taking anything in. It wasn't a speeding fine, or parking: that would have been a letter in the post. So something more serious. An incident, an accident, a death. My parents in Australia. My wife – ex-wife – or her children. It was none of those things. I stood aside to let them in.

'We'd like to ask you a few more questions, Mr Henderson. Concerning Ms Alice Curtis.'

The older one asked the questions. He was wearing glasses and a permanent frown. When he took his hat off I noticed his baldness. The younger one, the uniform, seemed to be the note-taker. They sat on the sofa, perched on the edge like jackals about to pounce. I sat in the armchair, leant back, crossed my legs.

'Perhaps you could tell us, in your own words, about the events of the evening of Wednesday April 29th.'

I shrugged and looked blank. 'I presume I came home, had dinner and drank some beer in front of the TV.'

'Are you saying you did not leave your flat that evening?'

'Yes. No. Look.' I uncrossed my legs and leaned forward. 'I was just saying. That's what I usually do on a weekday evening. Days, evenings, they're all much the same. What's special about this one?' I sounded unaware and innocent.

'It was the day Ms Curtis last attended her workplace. Your workplace. The last day she was seen.'

'Ah, right.' There didn't seem any point in stalling. I told them about the disastrous dinner date.

'Let me get this correct,' said the suit, turning to his colleague who'd been writing as I spoke. 'You're claiming you went to the restaurant, to *Ricardo*'s, but that Ms Curtis didn't.'

'That's right, yes. She never showed. I sat there … must have been nearly an hour. Maybe more. Then I gave up and left.'

The lead policeman, detective I suppose you'd call him, seemed to sit himself a little taller and pull back his shoulders. 'I want to put it to you, Mr Henderson, that you are … mistaken. I want to suggest that Ms Curtis did indeed come to the restaurant. That you shared a meal, or at least half a meal.'

I tried to interrupt but he held up a hand.

'Please allow me to finish.'

I sat back, looking suitably angry, and crossed my legs.

'During your meal you had an argument. Quite a heated argument, it appears. Then Ms Curtis left and you threw some cash onto the table and followed her. As you left the restaurant you grabbed her arm rather forcefully.'

He paused. I waited to make sure he'd finished and that he'd now allow me to speak. I shook my head. 'Can I speak now?'

He gestured with his hand, palm uppermost.

'This is all absolute nonsense. You must have me mixed up with someone else, another couple. That did not happen. None of it. Who told you all this?'

'The staff at the restaurant and other customers. You seem to have created quite a stir. They all remember it very well. And they've given us accurate descriptions of you and Ms Curtis.'

I shook my head. Couldn't think of anything else to say. 'I don't understand.'

'Well Mr Henderson, if it occurs to you that you may have misremembered that evening and want to revise your statement, please feel free to do so.'

He gave me time to say something, but I kept quiet.

'Meanwhile, let's try another tack. Have you ever been to Ms Curtis's flat?'

I hesitated. 'Yes,' I said, eventually. 'One time.'

'Let me be clear here. When we spoke to you last week, you described Ms Curtis as someone you only knew through work. He looked to his colleague who flipped some pages over on his pad. ' "Just a colleague" was the precise description. Yet you've had drinks with her.' He counted off on his fingers. 'At least one dinner date. And you've been to her flat. Rather more than colleagues, wouldn't you say?'

'No, you're getting it wrong. Okay, I quite fancied her. That much is true. And I hoped we might. You know. Become friends. Close friends. But we weren't an item. No way.'

The suit interrupted. 'You're using the past tense, Mr Henderson. Why would that be?'

'Yes. No. It's what you said. She's missing. Presumed ...'

'I think you'll find we've said nothing at all about the whereabouts of Ms Curtis.'

'Okay. Fair enough. I was jumping to conclusions. If she comes back to work, I'll be delighted. Lovely girl. Woman. And I hope we can be friends. Maybe more than friends.'

'So tell us about the time you met Ms Curtis at her flat.'

'No. You've got that wrong too. I didn't meet her there. It was after she'd not been at work for a while. Several days. I was worried.'

I told them about my visit to the flat and the conversation with Philomela. I couldn't read the look on their faces, but sceptical may have best described it.

When I'd finished, the suit sighed and then looked over to his colleague's notes. 'So tell me about this Philomena.'

'No. Philomela. With an 'l'.' The uniform amended his notes. 'What do you want me to say? A bit odd. Sort of old-fashioned hippie. Not young. Alice and her shared the flat. Share the flat.'

'Only according to our information, Ms Curtis lives alone.'

'That makes no sense,' I said. 'She was there, in the flat. She let me in. She lived there.' I tried to think how I could convince them I was telling the truth. Nothing occurred to me.

'We seem to be at cross-purposes here, Mr Henderson. Your report of your actions rather contradicts what we know. Let me tell you what we think, Mr Henderson. We think that you went to the flat when no-one was there. You used a key, perhaps Ms Curtis had given it to you, or maybe you acquired it by some other method.'

Here he gave me his concentrated stare. I shook my head and tried to interrupt but like before he wouldn't let me.

'We have found your fingerprints and Ms Curtis's fingerprints, but no-one else's. What we did find is that the flat had been trashed. Why did you do that, Mr Henderson? Trying to cover something up?'

'I didn't. Honestly. You have to believe me. I went there. Yes, the flat was a mess. But I had a conversation with a woman calling herself Philomela.' I remembered. 'She was wearing gloves. That's why you didn't find her fingerprints.'

'Convenient.'

He didn't believe me. He nodded to the uniformed policeman, who drew out some photos from a folder.

'We'd like you to look at a few photographs, Mr Henderson.'

They showed me two photographs and I identified my raincoat and my umbrella. I was feeling sick.

'Where are your coat and umbrella now, Mr Henderson?'

'I don't know. I lost them.'

'The good news is that we've found them for you.'

He looked pleased with himself. I wanted to hit him so hard.

'The bad news is that we found them in Burton wood. It looked like there had been some attempt to bury them, but it had not been very successful.'

He paused. He was definitely enjoying this.

'The other bad news is that we found spots of blood on both items. The blood belonged to Ms Curtis.'

I slumped forward, my head in my hands. How was this happening? Then I realised I was looking guilty, and sat up again, shaking my head vigorously. 'This is all so much nonsense. Someone must be out to get me. I'm being set up here.'

'As I'm sure you realise, Mr Henderson, we're going to have to ask you to accompany us to the station. You may need to think about calling a lawyer. But there are a couple of other things you may wish to comment on. We know you rifled through Ms Curtis's desk? Why did you do that? Did you take something from her desk? Something that might have incriminated you?'

I shook my head. Any explanation would have seemed weak.

'And in the wood. Alongside your raincoat and umbrella we found one other item.'

He showed me a third photograph.

'This is Ms Curtis's mobile phone. As I'm sure it will not surprise you to learn, it has your fingerprints all over it. Along with more spots of Ms Curtis's blood.'

I closed my eyes. I felt like I was going to faint. How had it come to this?

'Where is she, Mr Henderson? What have you done with her? Have you killed her? Where did you bury the body?'

The only answer I could give was more shakes of my head. 'No. No. No.'

He seemed about to get up, then asked, 'You're not averse to bullying women are you Mr Henderson?'

I didn't know what to say. 'I don't know what you're talking about.'

'I'm talking about your wife. There are certain incidents. On file. Let's say you have a certain amount of previous in this regard.'

'No, that's not right. I explained at the time. It was all a misunderstanding.'

He raised his eyebrows and spoke slowly, for added effect: 'More than one misunderstanding, apparently. And maybe with dear Alice, Ms Curtis, the bullying got out of hand? Accidents happen, we know that, we understand. The sooner you come clean, the better it will look for you. Honesty, Mr Henderson. The best policy.'

I put my head in my hands.

The two policemen stood up and gathered their paperwork.

In the police car, on the way to the station, my mind was in fragments. I felt adrift, helpless. A cork in a stormy sea. No control. I had no coherent thoughts. Apart from one: re-living that moment when I sat at Alice's computer. It was the one thing that was now beginning to make sense. I still didn't know who Alice was, where she was, nor why she'd done what she had. But her message to me was clear. I had recognised that 'Three stars' – not three asterisks - was an anagram of 'Here's start,' but that didn't work as a password into her computer. But then 'Starts here,' did work. She knew I'd look for it and she knew I'd work it out. 'She knows you,' is what Philomela had said. She did know me. She knew everything about me. So she knew I'd be the one to read the one word that came up on her screen and flashed twice before disappearing. Now I knew what that word meant, that it's simple message was aimed at me and me alone: 'GOTCHA.'

# The Peridor - Epilogue III

Today, among the seaweed, rags and feathers and other detritus that lie along the high-water mark, I found a heart-shaped crystal shell. It fitted into the palm of my hand. It sparkled in the sunlight and vibrated slightly causing my fingers to tingle. I have found a peridor. Now I am taking it home.

We live in the caravan now, the same caravan we stayed in on that first holiday. The same caravan we stayed in every year for several holidays after that, while Sally and her parents stayed next door. After the first year we didn't need the peridor: we had each other. Eventually Sally told me she did love me. For certain. I told her that I loved her. I repeated it often through the years.

We moved here permanently after our children had both left home. We had such plans. Things we would do, places we would visit, adventures we would share. But it was not to be. Sally became ill and despite my endeavours she has gradually deteriorated. I do what I can but she is very sick. I know what she needs. I have always known and now I have it.

It is good news. I am bringing home a peridor for Sally. It is what she needs, what we both need. The peridor will cure her, make her well. I am sure of it. Then the peridor will take us again on wonderful journeys. The two of us.

I hope Sally will understand. I hope she will remember. She doesn't always remember things, doesn't always understand. But I'm sure she will see the peridor and understand. If I name it *Gabriel* she will remember.

# The Murmuring and Tumbling of Waves

The sweet, luminous air hangs over the rooftops, seeps down into the tranquil neighbourhood, collecting hopes and dreams, offering life and space in return. And the world turns and turns again.

The lacemaker sat by her window. She arranged her pillow at the precise angle so her work might catch the diagonal rays of sunlight and yet she could see past it to the scene below. The window was open a crack. The gap let in a cool draught, the warmth of spring having yet to arrive, but the lacemaker needed the sounds and the smells of the street to enter her world. That way she felt a part of it, a part of the community and not the secluded maiden some of them imagined her to be. She was called worse things: aloof, haughty, arrogant; and some were even less polite. They did not know her. That is the way things were.

Katarina worked a line of half-stitches, inserted a pin, angling it slightly towards the top of her pillow, and covered the pin with another half-stitch. Her fingers worked with the skill and precision that came from years of practice. The sunlight touched the tips of the brass pins and turned them gold, slid off the white thread and streaked it with silver. Katarina crossed the bobbins and twisted the thread and gradually the pattern emerged like a blossoming snowdrop.

In the street below, the time for the change of shift was approaching. With steps both reluctant and eager, the miners, in twos and threes, left the café and headed out of the village, turning up the hill towards the mine. As they walked into the rising sun, shielding their eyes, their shadows stretched out on the tarmac beneath their feet, dragging them back, urging them on: either or both. They laughed and hollered and occasionally jostled against each other. Old men, young men, strong men, their Cyclops helmets glinting in the sunlight, their orange overalls as vivid as marigolds, some exuding brash confidence, others turned inward with quiet caution: a team.

An hour later the team from the previous shift would lumber down the hill in fragments, walk through the village and file into the café. The stride of the returning men would be heavy. They would trudge in weary silence, one behind the other, their overalls dusty and grey, the whites of their eyes fixed and shining against the blackness of their faces.

'Katarina.' The voice of the lacemaker's mother echoed through from her bedroom.

Katarina hesitated for a moment, reluctant to leave the peace of her lace, her street, her morning sunlight. Then she called out: 'Coming.' She brought her mother a glass of water. The woman in the bed sipped at the glass. Katarina stayed close, wary of the trembling hand: was it getting worse? The mother leant back on the pillows and the daughter placed the glass on the bedside table. The nightdress of the aged invalid was hanging loosely around her neck. Katarina bent forward and retied the cord, making her presentable for the doctor's visit. They sat in silence in the gloomy, heavily-shrouded room. The mother's eyes closed. Her cheeks were grey and hollow. Her sparse hair hung limply against her damp forehead. Her breathing was rapid and shallow.

'Can I get you anything else?'

No response.

'Would you like me to read to you?'

With the curtains drawn there was insufficient light in the room for reading, but there was a lamp that could be lit.

The mother gave her head a slight shake.

'We'll have some lunch in an hour or so. Is there anything particular that you'd like?'

No response.

The two sat in brittle silence.

The next morning the lacemaker sat in the sunlight that slanted through her window. She began a whole-stitch trail that would loop across the pillow. She watched the miners leave the café and walk up the hill. Later she watched the others walk down the hill and enter the café. She brought food and water to her mother and sat with her for a while.

The following day, the lacemaker watched the miners come out of the café and walk up the hill. She watched the previous shift traipse down the hill and enter the café. She worked on an area of honeycomb, separating the tessellation of oval spaces with twisted thread. Her thoughts settled into the spaces and she found comfort there. She made lunch for her mother, cheese and salad, and later brought her dinner, a little pasta, a little sauce.

Another day. More lace. Another shift. The mother. The daughter. The world turns and turns again.

Day by day things changed: the angle of the sunlight increased, the lacemaker's mother grew weaker, patterns of lace evolved on the lacemaker's pillow. Sometimes, breaking away from her shifting bobbins, Katarina played the piano. *Für Elise* was her favourite piece. She lingered as long as she dared over the hesitant passage before releasing the tension, rippling through the flowing arpeggios. Once a week her old school teacher visited and they sat on the floor and played a game of Go. Katarina always took the black stones and she always lost. She did not mind losing. Her teacher could not understand her lack of competitive spirit. For Katarina, the game was a joint enterprise, a cooperative venture in the creation of a beautiful work, the black and white armies abutting and interlocking in a fluid and complex dance. She viewed the process of playing as an act of creation and it brought her joy. The ending of the game brought her nothing but regret at its conclusion. Who wins? Who loses? It does not matter. She returned to her window, to her lace.

Daniel was always the last miner to leave the café. This tradition began when he was a newcomer to the shift, when he first came to work at the mine. He needed to follow the others: they knew the timings, the direction, the protocol. Now it had become a ritual, a superstition. He had to be last to leave the café, he had no choice. The others ensured it was always so.

Katarina studied Daniel, the last man to leave the café, from her window high above the street. She first noticed him several weeks ago and had been watching him for days. Now she studied him. The young man carried his helmet loosely in his left hand. His fair hair, long and dishevelled, was lifted by the breeze and he raked his right hand through it. He kept his eyes down, on the heels of the men who walked ahead of him. When they turned, laughing, and playfully punched at his shoulder, he swayed to the side with ease and his face came alight with a coy smile.

Striding out of the village, Daniel was able to look out of the corner of his eye, and without turning his head he could see the girl at the window. He caught sight of the white of her lacework glinting in the sun, the paleness of her face and the redness of her lips. He glimpsed the yellow of her hair. Shuffling back down after work, aching and exhausted, he longed to look up to the window again, but could not do so without turning around. He kept his eyes on the road; he did not turn around.

One morning Katarina left her room, left her lace, left her mother and walked across the road to the café. She ducked through the low door. The air in the café was thick with the smells of fried cooking, the stench of burning fat and the claustrophobia of testosterone. The walls and floor were dark and greasy, the tables were bare wood, the chairs small and unstable. The room was filled with the hefty bulk of hungry miners, sitting before plates piled high with bacon and bread, tomatoes, sausages and eggs. The early starters were already leaning back from empty plates, replete and content. In one corner games were being played: dice and dominoes and chess, accompanied by argument and debate; money changed hands. In another corner, Katarina saw Daniel sitting alone. She carried her croissant and double espresso to his table and sat opposite him. He was eating toast smeared with a thick, dark spread, drinking from a mug of brown liquid. He did not raise his head to Katarina. But he had seen her. He had seen her lace cap, lace gloves and lace shawl over a long green dress. He had seen her long blonde hair. He had seen her pale face and her red lips.

There was laughter from the next table. A big man turned on his chair and grinned in Katarina's direction, gesturing crudely. She did not react. She ate her bread and drank her coffee. Once she had finished, she took the gift from her small lace clutch bag and slid it across the table towards Daniel.

Daniel hesitantly reached out and placed his hand on the card.

'It's for you,' said Katarina.

Daniel picked it up. It was a playing card. The ace of spades. But the central portion had been cut away and there was a fine lace insert, an intricate design with swirls of spiders and leaves, part abstract, part floral. It incorporated a curly letter 'K'.

'It's for luck,' said Katarina. Daniel held it in both hands. 'For you to keep. Keep it safe and it will keep you safe.'

Daniel tucked the card inside his bulky overalls. For the first time he raised his eyes to Katarina. 'Thank you,' he said. He wished it had been the ace of hearts. He didn't say this to Katarina.

Spring eventually arrives, followed by a short summer and before long the evenings are drawing in. Daniel is now working on the night shift, so Katarina makes sure she is at her window as dusk arrives so she can see him, the last to leave the café, following the other miners up the hill. They lean into the wind and rain. Sometimes she catches him as he looks up at her weather-stained window. He never smiles or waves. She wishes he would.

Katarina's mother is moving towards the end of her life. The priest is now a more regular visitor than the doctor. The doctor says it is only a matter of time. Still Katarina makes her lace. She watches the miners through the window now securely closed against the violent weather. Sometimes she plays the piano. Sometimes she plays a game of Go: she always loses but never minds.

Katarina is in bed, half asleep, when she hears the rumbling, the resonance echoing through the labyrinth of her mind, through the darkness of the room in which she lies, through the sweet dream she is dreaming still, yet cannot quite remember except that it involved pleasurable matters, rumbling, rumbling matters that Katarina strives to recall because she believes it to be vital to do so, to hold on to that sweetness, but she cannot, the details slip away and drown in the reverberation, the beating, the throb of the rumbling, the source of which Katarina cannot quite discern as it may be a murmuring of tumbling white waves from within her dream, it may be a rasping coming through from the other side of the wall, from her mother's room, a death rattle, a symbol of the final step before her mother's journey reaches its conclusion, or perhaps the rumbling, rumbling, rumbling is of thunder in the hills, heralding a storm, a storm to end all storms, or maybe, maybe, maybe the rumbling comes from underground; perhaps it comes from the mine.

Katarina folds her body tight, clutches the sheet between her hands and her knees, bites on a corner of the pillow-case.

Then.

Relaxation engulfs her. She licks her lips, turns onto her back and frees her mind. Daniel will be safe: he has her lucky gift. Her mother will be safe: she has her faith. The world will turn and turn again: it always does. Katarina breathes deeply, softly, quietly, closes her eyes and returns to the peaceful patterns of her sweet, uncharted dreams.

# The House

The house was hard to ignore. I didn't ignore it. I noticed it, registered it, began to walk away, turned back. I was susceptible. If there was ever going to be a time, this was it. The house stood out, bold and proud, confident in its own identity yet with a hint of ambiguity, coyly shielding secrets. Eccentric was the word that came to mind. Its demeanour suggested it had once been grand, a house of stature, although signs of decay had bitten into its facade: it was grubby, stained, dog-eared.

I was in a distant part of town, away from my usual habitat. Late afternoon. I had been counting lamp posts, shuffling the pack, stirring the soup. At a loose end, you might say. Touched by unfocused sadness, my collar raised against the wind. Needful. It had been a long day; a long year; a long life.

The house offered itself, welcoming as well as intriguing, attractive in its eccentricity. The front gate was open, hanging from one hinge; the path, a sequence of blue ovals like stepping stones, signalled a route between clumps of vibrant, tangled foliage leading to the imposing front door. The door itself was painted red, a bright shiny scarlet, at odds with the solemnity of its intricately carved brass knocker. The sign on the door – a blue oval sign – said 'Knock and Enter'. How much more welcoming could a house be?

Storm clouds were gathering, hanging low as though considering settling on the roof of the house. Light from the uncurtained windows on the upper floors flared like headlights through the evening gloom. A few heavy drops of rain had already landed on the tarmac, heralding the deluge that had been forecast. I needed shelter. All the signs pointed one way. I walked up the path, knocked on the door and entered the house.

I expected to find myself in a mahogany-lined corridor, dimly lit, with faded portraits on the walls. Or an extravagant entrance hall with gold chandeliers, a luxurious russet carpet and a sweeping staircase. A sterile hotel foyer? Truth to tell, I didn't know what to expect. As the door clunked shut behind me I observed my surroundings. The room resembled an office, the sparsely furnished space dominated by a desk and a chair. Low ceiling, bare walls, no windows. Not so much an office, more a cell. Reminiscent of another place, another time. As well as the apparent desk and chair, there was another chair, occupied. Someone was seated behind the desk: a small, dark figure, shrouded in dark clothing, a hood over his face. Or her face. I sat opposite, in the vacant chair.

'Are you prepared?' The words came from within the hood. An old voice, a whisper, barely audible; I couldn't decide whether it was male or female.

I held out my hands, shrugged my shoulders, raised my eyebrows: 'As ready as I'll ever be.'

'The right answer.' I wondered what a wrong answer might have sounded like.

Silence stretched like elastic. When would the breaking point occur? It felt like a nightmare of an interview. Or rather, the nightmare you have on the day before the interview when you imagine yourself unable to think of anything to say, unable to remember the question, but certain that nothing will happen unless and until you find your voice. I waited, saying nothing: I had nothing to say. I sat poised, ready to react when the moment came.

A calendar was pinned to the back wall. Some dates deleted, others circled in red. On the other side of the clock was a notice. It looked like an advertisement but there were too many words. More a message than an advert. Or an advert that needed better design; some colourful pictures would have helped. My eyes roamed across the words as I tried to pick out the gist. It seemed to be promoting a women's refuge, an escape for battered wives. But no, that's not what it was offering. Not only safety. Maybe not safety at all. I found the crux of the piece. It was offering revenge. 'If you're a suffering wife, come to us. We will exact retribution.' There was a phone number to call. And an email: missnightingale@gabriel.com.

'I hope you find what you are looking for.' The voice spoke slowly and drew me back into the room. 'Better still, I hope you find something you are not looking for.'

'I have an open mind.'

I was instructed to empty my pockets. Wallet, keys, phone, watch, ring. Lucky heart-shaped shell. I placed them in a pile at the corner of the desk.

A bell rang. Doors to left and right opened simultaneously. 'Your choice,' said the figure.

'Does it make any difference?' I asked.

'Of course.' I waited for further elaboration. None was forthcoming.

I stood up and walked through the door to the right, but I looked over my shoulder, at the calendar, the clock, at the advert, then towards the other open door and I wondered.

I am in a narrow passageway. It's light, with white walls and no pictures. No calendar, no adverts. Like a hospital. Or a prison. I step cautiously. I do not wish to hurry. I want to make the most of this experience, to relish it. My feet tap on the tiled floor. No other sound. I peer into the distance. It's a long corridor and I can't see to the end, my eyes failing to pierce through the misty blur, the imprecision, the uncertainty of the future. But still I step forward. The pleasure will come as the details are revealed. I believe this to be so. Then I hear the sound of a piano, close at hand. Two more steps and I discern a door to my left, half-open. The music comes from there. I push the door open wide and stand in the doorway.

A woman is seated at a grand piano, her back towards me. She is dressed in white. Her long blonde hair hangs down her back, tied with a neat red bow at the nape of her neck. She is playing a Beethoven piece. I believe it is called *Für Elise*. I stand and listen, allow myself to soften, to melt into the music. Through the slow section she lingers as long as she dares, drawing out each note to its limit. It's like being perched on the edge of a precipice, or occupying the space between the lightning and the thunder. I feel as though I am leaning forward, barely balanced, as she hesitates a further moment, a kitten with one paw raised, then falls through the rapid sequence, the notes rippling over themselves, a waterfall, a tumbling downstairs. My thoughts fall too, with the pianist, with the water, with the music. I see the long fingers travelling across the keys as the woman's right hand stretches to the high notes, her left to the low. Her head nods a little. Otherwise her body is held quite still.

The pause at the end of the performance hangs in the air. I hold my breath. The pianist begins another piece, a familiar lilting refrain this time, releasing the tension: a popular song, simple and hypnotic. She sways gently to the rhythm. It is the introduction to John Lennon's *Imagine.*

When she sings, her voice is fresh and fragile. As always with this song I find myself drawn in, complicit, compliant. I quietly close the door and move on. I feel soothed and refreshed. I'm not the only one.

This new corridor is different, shorter. The view is clearer, the mist has lifted. The air is warm, it holds a shimmering, comforting glow. I can see to the end of the passage. It's not far. I walk slowly on the patterned blue carpet. I hear more music. From behind a door to my right come the unmistakable sounds of a circus. I imagine dancing horses, jugglers and clowns, a pyramid of acrobats. I don't go in. It's that old fear, the fear of empty trapezes, swinging out of sync.

From behind the next door I hear a jig played by a fiddle and a flute and an accordion. I can picture the swaying kilts and skipping ghillies of a group of Scottish Country dancers. It sounds like fun. But now is not the time. Maybe later.

I walk to the final door before the corner. There's more music. Elvis Presley. *Jailhouse Rock*. I push open the door and enter. A low ceiling. Dark furnishings and dim lights. It takes my eyes a while to adjust; then I recognise the familiar features of an old-fashioned pub. The music comes from a jukebox in the far corner, where two youngsters lean inwards, heads together, studying the options. There are two oldish men playing darts and a group of four (two younger men, two giggling women) playing pool. A few solitary drinkers sit at tables. Chuck Berry comes on the jukebox. There's a smell of old beer and pork pies with, surprisingly, a whiff of seaside saltiness.

'Come and join me.' It's a middle aged man, clean-shaven, receding hairline, casually dressed. Normal. He's sitting on a stool at the bar, a newspaper open in front of him and a half-full pint glass in his hand. He indicates the stool next to him. I climb up. I'm nervous. 'What'll you have?' he asks.

'That's very kind of you.' I glance towards the pumps. 'What would you recommend?'

The drink supplied by the barman is rather bland for my taste, but I'm pleased to be sharing a drink with this man. I think I could relax here. Perhaps this is what I need. Perhaps my sadness can be abandoned here.

'I wasn't expecting this,' I say, indicating the bar.

'No,' he says, nodding.

'In fact it's all been rather unexpected. So far.' He raises his eyebrows, questioning. 'This house.'

'Ah,' he says. 'Yes.' We sip our drinks. I'm feeling less anxious. 'So what were you expecting?'

'I don't know. Just not this.' We drink some more.

'I think it all depends on who you are.'

'Pardon me?'

'What you bring. What you were before.'

'I'm sorry. I'm not understanding you.'

'You asked about the House.' The way he says it, it sounds like it has a capital letter. 'The way it appears to you, what it gives to you, how it operates, it's all dependent on what you bring to it. That's what I'm saying. Only that.'

'Oh.' This still isn't making any sense. But I begin to feel the lack of sense is my fault, not his.

'Tell me about yourself,' he says.

'Well,' I say, 'there's not much to tell. I'm rather ordinary.' So I tell him about myself. A version of. I put a favourable slant on it. The split with my parents, their disappointment in me. The failed career, well two failed careers if you count the attempt at teaching. A failed marriage. If I tell it straight it comes over as a failure of a life. So I concentrate on the positives. My survival. My free spirit. The pleasure I derive from my independence. My achievements in amateur sport, such as they are. I don't mention the sadness. Nor the needing.

'So not so ordinary,' he says. 'Rather special.'

'I wouldn't say that.'

'But you are. Like we all are. Unique. In our ways.'

I think this through. It's clearly correct, but where does such thinking lead? What are the implications, the conclusions? I wonder about his status, whether his views and opinions can be trusted. Is he an expert?

'Are you a keyholder?' I ask. He gives me his questioning look again. 'A caretaker, a guide? To this house. Someone who answers questions. Explains things. Gives directions.'

'Oh no. That wouldn't be right. Someone like that. No, there's nobody like that, certainly not me.' He raises his glass. 'I'm just the man at the bar.'

'Right.' I drain my glass. This meeting, this conversation, this episode seems to have come to an end. Buddy Holly is singing. *That'll be the Day*. 'So which way should I go? Can you at least tell me that?'

'Your choice.' He sips his beer.

I wait, hoping for more.

'But don't go backwards. A good motto, that is. Never look back. That's what life's taught me.'

I look towards the door I came in. There is no longer a door there, only a wall.

He points to the far end of the bar. 'Try that way.'

I leave the pub.

In place of lightness, there's now darkness. A chill has replaced the warmth. The air is sour. I'm at the bottom of a spiral staircase, with steep stone steps circling around a cement pillar. Bare outside walls are scarcely visible but I feel the curved, rough brickwork on my fingers. As I climb I keep my head up, peering towards the unknown, the ambiguity. I cannot imagine what awaits me at the top of the stairs. My heart beats fast, my breathing comes in shallow gasps. I'm nervous, cold, but through some sort of double-think I manage to separate myself from the fear. I watch myself climbing and imagine how brave that person might be, or how scared. How stupid. What is he doing there, that chap? Where's he going? Doesn't he realise? I'm reminded of an interactive computer game. The safe thrill of it. But this is not a computer game. This is real life. A version of. What awaits me at the top of the stairs is a sturdy wooden door with black metal hinges. I expect it to be locked. I expect it to be an impenetrable barrier, but, as I push against it, it yields and, with my fear rising to a head-splitting crescendo, I step through into …

A circle of seated lacemakers occupy the centre of a plushly furnished drawing room. There are long, crimson, velvet curtains at the windows, a deep-pile carpet, scented candles scattered around; there's a hint of lavender in the air and in the corner there is a string quartet playing *Vivaldi*. There is a lot of music in this house. Among other things. The ladies concentrate on their lacemaking, their heads lowered, fingers dextrously shuffling their bobbins as they twist the threads and firmly tighten them. The air is tranquil. Saturated in concentration and contemplation. Serenity. My heart rate and breathing return to normal. But there's a legacy from the climb. My thoughts are ill-defined. My mind is untethered. I need to absorb the tranquillity of the circle, bathe in the peacefulness of the lacemaking. I wander around the outside of the circle, peering at the complex designs.

'You must have such patience,' I whisper to one old lady.

She smiles.

'How do you know what to do?' I ask of the next.

Her pillow is a forest of pins that partially obscures an elaborate-looking pattern. She does not reply.

A large spectacular piece, with intricate leaves and scrolls, covers one lady's pillow. The work of weeks, months, maybe years.

'I never realised lace could be done by hand.'

'What happens if you go wrong?'

'My mother used to do a lot of knitting. She also did crochet. Is that the same?'

The circle remains unbroken, like a clock face, like a calendar. The labour is constant and continuous, like ticking, like the turning of pages. I'm being tolerated here. Not welcomed but neither am I rejected. The sadness is seeping away.

I smell the smoke before I see it. It's pungent an irritating. It's not the candles: their perfume is sweet. I breathe through my mouth. I can't believe someone would be smoking in here. They're not. The smoke floats up behind the ladies like rising mist in the fenlands. Then I hear the crackle and see the flicker of flames at the bottom of the curtains. The fire will soon engulf the room. No-one seems to have noticed: the musicians continue to play; the lacemakers continue to make lace. There is only one way to save them. I turn around and leave, firmly closing the door behind me.

I want to understand this house. This house is alive, organic. It shifts and bends and adapts. It grows. I want to piece its ingredients together. I am experiencing it but failing to discern a purpose. Yet as these thoughts form in my mind it comes to me that the house is its own purpose. My quest is to explore and there is no need for any mission beyond that. No need for a Grail (Holy or not), no need for treasure, no need for any Beauty to find (Sleeping or not). The notes are the melody. The words are the sentence. The rooms are the House. I am a catalyst, an agent. It is through me that the House is growing. My decisions contribute to its structure. I make the House. And yet I do not appear to have any choices. I am being led. I am a passenger. That paradox is what defines the House, and prevents the House being defined.

The next room is empty. It has warm, wooden panelling around the walls, cold stone on the floor, a high, intricately-carved ceiling. Shafts of sunlight enter from lofty windows. Dust motes dance. The air smells stale, musty. This could be a church. It could be a courtroom. Those could be choir stalls, or the seating for the jury. There could be the lectern from which the sermon is solemnly delivered, or the judge's bench from which the final sentence is pronounced. Those rows of seats are for the congregation or for family and friends of the accused, or casual observers. I think about trials and verdicts; I think about prayer and salvation. I think about spaces, spaces around, spaces between. I wander down the central aisle, listening to the tap of my feet echoing through the room. I sense potential here, embryonic promise. This is a room waiting to be used; I have no use for it.

The next room is also empty. Empty of people, but full of things. It looks like a chemistry laboratory, rows of benches covered by flasks and pipes and bubbling liquid in retorts. An alchemy experiment? No, it's more like an old-fashioned school classroom, and it's not only for chemistry: there are other sciences catered for here. There's a shelf with geometric objects – spheres, cubes, cylinders, a sliced cone displaying conic curves like circles, ellipses, hyperbolae, a model of a Klein bottle. There are plants growing in pots near the windows. An exercise in photosynthesis? Then there's a physics section, with electronic circuitry, a spring balance. weights in a box, some lenses arranged in an intricate configuration. But where are the computers, the keyboards, the TV screens? This is a schoolroom stuck in the dark ages, the pre-electronic era. Or someone's memory of how it used to be. Like other rooms in this house, it echoes with nostalgia whilst coaxing me forward. The theme is contradiction. Don't look back the man said, the man at the bar. Go forward. Don't undo the lace. Never regret. Move on.

At the end of the room, behind the largest bench, there's a blackboard. It's an ancient roller-board which displays some sections and keeps others hidden. Two boxes of chalk stand on the bench, one of white, one of colour. A dusty board rubber. A problem is written on the

board. It's labelled Л.

'Imagine a circle of cord wrapped around the equator of the earth,
all along the ground (ignore mountains and oceans).
Now insert an extra metre of length and raise up the
lengthened cord all around, spreading it out evenly.
How large is the gap under the cord?
Big enough for an ant to crawl under?
A mouse? A dog?
Which?
Now imagine the same experiment conducted on the moon
(ignore the lack of atmosphere).
What is your answer now?
What about if the experiment were conducted on some
distant exoplanet?'

Under the problem is written in capital letters:

## THE ANSWER

with a downward arrow. I spin the board around, looking

for the answer. But all that is written in the next section is

what appears to be an exam question:

'In Greek mythology, Philomela is transformed into a
nightingale: Discuss.'

The other sections are blank.

I look through the tall windows that run along the side walls of the laboratory. Outside I see trees. A lot of trees, a forest. Mixtures of evergreen and deciduous, various sizes and shapes, tall and sparse, short and bushy, leaves of bottle green and silver and orange and brown and a million shades between. And I'm there, here, among the trees, surrounded, engulfed, inhibited by trees. Controlled. There's a sprinkling of snow on the ground. It's cold. I duck my head and twist my torso as I struggle to keep to the frozen path which winds between the immobile, statuesque trunks. The path is narrow, it's poorly-defined, it splits and fades. I slip and reach into the undergrowth for support, stagger on. Is this the way? Am I sure? I'm nervous. Is this where I am supposed to be? Am I being led to safety or into danger? The forest hides secrets, it hides bright eyes, it hides the whispering movement of predators. Am I still inside the House? If so, then I'm safe. I'm sure of that. If not, if the House has released me, then the menace is real, the threat is real, the danger from the predators ...

The path turns and turns again. It's rising, twisting. My steps carry me higher up into the leafy canopy. I am calmer. I can see the sky above, through the tops of the trees. Pale blue, no clouds. Or is it a ceiling?

I peer through branches covered in pine needles and tinsel and brightly-patterned baubles, looking down on a small room. It's a Christmas scene, festive and peaceful. I see decorations. Greetings cards on the mantelpiece. A nativity scene on the sideboard, with snow and angels. I hear carols. I smell roasting chestnuts. (Really? I may have made that up.)

Three men in paper hats, yellow, orange, purple, are seated around a table. On the table is a partly completed jigsaw puzzle. The puzzle depicts a garden, a gate leaning off its hinges, a path of blue ovals and a house. The house has a red door with a brass knocker. The upper portions of the house have not yet been completed. There is a person-shaped hole near the bottom. There are thunder clouds hanging over the roof. Who tackles a jigsaw puzzle by doing the sky first?

The middle-aged man, in the middle of the three, removes a puzzle-piece from a window, throws it back into the box and chastises the older man sitting by his side. The older man takes no notice. The young man on the other side is sitting apart. He has earphones in his ears and a mobile phone in his fist. Three women enter. The first carries an elaborately iced Christmas cake, adorned with Christmas trees, a robin, sprigs of holly, and places it in front of the old man with a smile and a wink. The second woman, who is several months pregnant, sits on the lap of the younger man and places her arms around his neck. He continues to manipulate his phone with both thumbs. The third woman brings in a large tray with a teapot, cups and saucers and a pile of sandwiches. The scene dissolves. It wasn't real. I'm back out in the cold. I feel dizzy, vague, lost.

I fall. I slide. I'm carried through a sequence of rooms in rapid succession. A room full of books. Must be a library. I don't recognise any titles. A bathroom: a bath full and foaming with bubbles, gold-painted taps. A factory, a tool room, swarf covering the floor. An artist's studio, chaotic. A theatre, rows of seats, orderly. They rush past like scenes glimpsed through the window of a speeding train. It's exhausting. I'm exhausted.

I fall. I slide. I land.

This is a dead-end. A wall. A plain, high brick wall. No way through. No way over or under. It stretches to the left, it stretches to the right, endlessly. Probably has barbed wire on top, it's that sort of wall, but the top is too high to see from down here. 'Do not go back.' The man at the bar said that. The only thing he said. The only thing I remember. 'The best motto for life.' I consider sitting down on the ground to wait, but that's pointless. I have to make things happen. Nothing will happen if I sit on the ground. I am the instrument, the catalyst, the creator. And yet. There's nothing to do, nowhere to go. But it's not the end. Because it's not okay. And if it's not okay, it's not the end.

I run the palms of my hands across the surface of the wall. What looked like solid bricks are not bricks at all.

Not in the usual sense. They are soft. Pliant. The wall bows

inwards as I push and then dissolves.

I'm in a bedroom. There's a mirror on the wall. A bed

sumptuously furnished, with plump pillows, silk sheets,

thick blankets and an exotically patterned eiderdown.

There's an old-fashioned record player. The music plays

softly. And there's a woman. I see her reflection in the

mirror. She is wearing a long, old-fashioned nightdress,

high neck, short sleeves. She smells of tangerine. She sees

me and turns around.

'Sorry,' I say. 'I didn't realise. I just...'

'Hush,' she says, a finger to her lips. 'I'm Gabrielle.

It's all right. I understand.' She walks towards me. She is

carrying a hairbrush in her right hand. She places her left

hand on my chest as though warding me off. But then she

tilts her head and kisses me full on the mouth.


There are plenty of true things in the House. They do not

look the way they should and that is why they are

misleading. But it's all a matter of point of view. From the right perspective, the spaces close and the complete meaning emerges. Or is it when the spaces grow that the meaning comes, as it finds the room to grow? I do not believe in love at first sight. I never have. Yes to infatuation. Yes, lust. Yes, a lightning strike that brings you sleepless nights and days of damp palms. All these can happen within a moment of setting eyes on another person. But love, proper, enduring love, can it be found in an instant? No, I do not believe it is so. But now my world has changed and in this world there is a House and in this House I meet Gabrielle and I fall in love in an instant. I lay my head upon her breast and find comfort there. She knows me. I know her. Afterwards, she will not let me stay. Not yet. She is not the end (she says). She tells me what I need. I need the room of games.

It is very quiet in the room of games. There are many people here but they are all silent. The players at the card tables indicate their bids, their intentions, with signs, gestures, signals. The chess players and the draughts players stare at the boards in front of them, scarcely moving, scarcely breathing. There is noise from the mah-jong table and the dominoes table, but it is the clatter of tiles, not the clatter of words. There are no words here. I scan the room: there are no games of Scrabble being played here, no Boggle. All is symbolic: the counters, the chips, the pieces. Abstract games. There are no words. The rules of the games are known but exist in thought only, they are not written down. Around the periphery of the room young players stare at computer screens on their laps or on tables in front of them. They touch the screens and react to the effect of their actions. They do not use their keyboards.

I wander amongst the gamers. I linger occasionally, try to judge the status of each game I observe. Who is winning? What is the best next move? What retaliation will be provoked, what revenge will be sought? Eventually I find what I am looking for. An empty Go board. One player. I sit down opposite him. He offers me the black stones. I bow my head. He bows back.

We play a game of Go, but this is not like any game of Go I've ever played before. It looks the same. We obey the rules and to a casual observer it would look like a normal game. We take it in turns to place a stone on the board, black followed by white followed by black; we remove any stones that do not have liberties; I attack and he defends and then he attacks and I defend. But the pattern of the game is off kilter, the cadence feels wrong, the rhythm is discordant. It feels not like a game but like a code, a series of cryptic gestures, a maze, being constructed and then being unravelled and then being constructed anew. I know what I am doing, yet I am an automaton; I am in control, yet I'm following instructions; I'm making choices, yet I am being chosen. Through these complexities, fundamental truths are glimpsed, richer than the simple black/white, life/death binaries: they involve honesty and beauty and goodness and truth. But most of all, love. Through the course of the game the reality outside and the reality within sparkles and crackles, I sample heaven, I smell the fragrant bouquet, I taste the sweetness of perfection.

The game ends. We do not count the score. The game exists as a problem and a solution, a journey, an explanation, an enigma. It has brought me two instructions: I have to return to Gabrielle, the love of my life; but first there is a final room to visit.

I stand in a hallway on bare floorboards. The blue paint is peeling from the walls, leaving patches of broken plaster. There are two small windows without curtains. The glass is smudged, opaque. I am at the top of the House, below the rafters. In the centre of this landing there is a ladder. It leads up to a trapdoor. I step on the lower rungs of the ladder. This is correct. This is my role. This is the culmination of my quest. I slowly ascend the ladder. Slowly, slowly. Take care. I reach my hands above my head and touch the trapdoor. One more step. Now I can unfasten the bolts, one to the right, one to the left. Another step up. My head is now touching the wood of the trapdoor and with both hands I push up and it swings open.

The three of us fall, limbs awkwardly entangled, and land on the lawn, near the sundial. It's morning. A low sun signals the recent dawn. There's a chill in the air. None of us seems harmed by the fall. I have the protection of denim jeans and a leather jacket. Victoria and Maxwell are still in swimwear. They look cold. They lavish questions upon me. I shrug. I have no answers to my own questions, so what are the chances of me formulating answers for theirs? They embrace each other. They try and embrace me. There are tears in their eyes. They are tears of joy. I wonder if Victoria could be pregnant: she has that sort of look about her.

'I have to go,' I say. 'Someone to see.'

The House looks different from this side. More modern, less run-down. Still weird, but more surreal than eccentric. If you had the right sort of imagination, you might say it looks like a sort of spaceship. I know what I mean. I push open the doors into the conservatory and enter the House. Now all I need is to get back to Gabrielle. I'm sure this is the way.

# The Peridor - Epilogue IV

Newspaper headline: 'Fears increase for the two missing school children, lost at sea.'

# Where Do We Go from Here?

March 2016: AlphaGo 4 – Lee Sedol 1. The computer had won. This result signalled the end of the million dollar Go challenge and the beginning of what became known as The Age of AI.

The early changes were small and predictable. Phones improved, television improved, communications in general improved. Machines drove the cars and the trains, they guided and flew the planes. Then the capacity of computers to imitate human behaviour began to be properly exploited. Computers moved up from the factory floor into the design office; instead of merely monitoring sales, they directed sales; from financial control they progressed to devising strategies for maximising profits. They moved into the boardrooms, made decisions, took control. Meanwhile, machines taught in schools, tended to the sick in hospitals, managed the judicial system, solving crimes and prosecuting, convicting and sentencing the guilty. They not only imitated human behaviour, they surpassed it: they were better at these things. They led research in universities and medical schools. They could solve problems, find solutions, decide which problems should next be investigated and solve them.

And then their achievements in the field of The Arts progressed to a higher level. Rather than imitating the work of past masters, they became originators, discovering new and spectacular ways to utilise the various media. They produced masterpieces of music and visual art, films and literature. The true golden age of creativity was upon us, this time led by machines. The role of humans was relegated to that of audience appreciation.

But the bad guys had computers too. Instead of merely manufacturing munitions, computers began to design guns and bombs, then to plan strategies of attack and defence, to organise and deploy weapon systems, to fight wars, to decide which wars should be fought and how and when to instigate them. In these activities too they were better than humans: there were more deaths, more thorough destruction, a higher level of devastation.

Humanity was faced again with the dilemma it had wrestled with repeatedly through the centuries. As it had with nuclear power, the internal combustion engine, steam power, gunpowder, and no doubt further back to tempered steel, to bows and arrows, to the first wheel. How should the benefits of technological advances be exploited without suffering the negative consequences? It was essential that a solution be found to the latest and most crucial version of this problem. In the Age of AI there was only one way to do this: ask the computer.

There was by now only one computer, the Universal Ultranet, occupying an artificial alternative space that it had designed for itself, adrift from the 3D world that humans inhabited; from this pseudo-location all the wondrous applications flowed. The computer had a nickname. No-one remembered where it had come from. It was known as *Gabriel.* A simple question was put to *Gabriel*: Where do we go from here?

'The answer will be 42,' they said. 'It will, it will.'

The answer was not 42. The answer was different. It was immediate, fundamental and absolute. In a fraction of a microsecond, the world vanished, the sun vanished, galaxies near and far vanished. All was dark. All was silent. All was mysterious and unknown. Empty. So there was no-one to hear the message that reverberated from the computer in that other dimension and echoed back through the black and silent universe: 'Let there be light.'

Bill Brakes

Norfolk, UK

bill140347@btinternet.com

21553527R00238

Printed in Great Britain
by Amazon